Happy reading!

More than Mistletoe

Twelve stories of festive love, laughter, and happily ever after ... mostly!

Donna Gorrard
x

First published by The Christmas Collective
Email: thechristmascollective2021@gmail.com

First Edition

Cover design by Sarah Shard

Copyright © 2021 Copyright © 2021 S.L. Robinson, Lucy Alexander, Cici Maxwell, Bláithín O'Reilly Murphy, Sarah Shard, Marianne Calver, Joe Burkett, Jake Godfrey, Michelle Harris, Donna Gowland, Martha May Little, Jenny Bromham.

All rights reserved. No part of this publication may be reproduced, stored or transmitted in any form or by any means, electronic, mechanical, photocopying, recording, scanning, or otherwise without written permission from the publisher. It is illegal to copy this book, post it to a website, or distribute it by any other means without permission.

This anthology is entirely a work of fiction. The names, characters and incidents portrayed in it are the work of the respective author's imagination. Any resemblance to actual persons, living or dead, events or localities, is entirely coincidental.

Each respective author asserts their moral right to be identified as the author of their work.

The Christmas Collective 2021 has no responsibility for the persistence or accuracy of URLs for external or third party internet websites referred to in this publication and does not guarantee that any content on such websites is, or will remain, accurate or appropriate.

Designations used by companies to distinguish their products are often claimed as trademarks. All brand names and product names used in this book and on its cover are trade names, service marks, trademarks and registered trademarks of their respective owners. The publishers and the books are not associated with any product or vendor mentioned in this book. None of the companies referenced within the book have endorsed the book.

Paperback Edition: November 2021
ISBN: 9798496489355

We dedicate this Anthology to our wonderful
and talented friends in the Penguin Collective,
and to all Christmas lovers across the world –
there is no greater gift to us than your eyeballs on
our pages!

Contents

Lumikinos by Lucy Alexander 1

The Ghost of Christmas Past by Michelle Harris 21

Christmas for Two by Marianne Calver 41

August in December by Joe Burkett 57

Under the Tree by Cici Maxwell 73

Killing Christmas Eve by Jake Godfrey 91

Christmas and Cocktails by Jenny Bromham 105

Christmas at The Little Blu Bookshop by Sarah Shard 121

Not Today, Santa by Martha May Little 139

Sealed With a Christmas Kiss by Bláithín O'Reilly Murphy 157

Love, Forever by Donna Gowland 177

The Last Christmas by S.L. Robinson 195

Biographies 209

Foreword

The Christmas Collective was formed in 2021, following the "Christmas Love Story" competition hosted by Penguin Michael Joseph during 2020/2021. All the authors in this Anthology were shortlisted entrants and found each other on social media during the nail-biting-wait-for-the-final-announcement. Though we all knew there could only be one winner, every single person threw their support behind each other in the hopes that it would be a member of our community.

Once the competition was over, the momentum continued and twelve of us began working on a way to publish our stories. We knew we had something special in the close-knit group that we formed, and we weren't prepared to let that go. Our grassroots movement has flourished despite lockdown and the fact we are scattered across the U.K, Ireland and even one in Madrid!

This Anthology is the culmination of twelve people who chose collaboration over competition. It would have been easy for every one of us to lurk on the internet and go our separate ways after the competition ended, but we wanted something positive to come out of the journey we went on together. We are still on that journey, excited for what the future may hold if we continue to work together.

Our personal story is one of hope, perseverance, and the best of human nature – and the stories in our anthology reflect all that and more.

Acknowledgements

We would like to acknowledge every writer who joined "The Penguin Collective" during the competition. The shared community there is very special to us, and we continue to support each of you in your endeavours as authors.

We sincerely thank all our readers for their support. Every purchase makes us do a happy dance and our stories are just as much yours as they are ours. We hope you enjoy them as much as we have enjoyed creating them.

Lumikinos

Lucy Alexander

"Driving home for Christmas…"
"… severe delays on the M4 …"
"… driving home for Christmas, yeah …"
"… adverse weather conditions …"

Erica fumbled with the dashboard dials, trying to tune the car radio to either Chris Rea or the traffic report. She guessed the snow must be causing some interference – it had been falling steadily all morning.

"… and it's been, so long …"
"… reports of ice on the A350 …"

She gave up and switched off the radio. Normally she would listen to Spotify, but her phone had lost 4G about five miles back, and now even Google Maps was struggling. She wished she wasn't so reliant on sat-nav. It had sent her on a somewhat unlikely shortcut, and now she found herself driving through tiny country lanes in the middle of the Cotswolds, with no idea how to find her way back to London if her phone lost connection completely.

Yet the lack of internet wasn't her biggest concern. The fact was, the snow was getting worse. At first, there had just been a few flurries drifting prettily past the windows, but now a frozen layer, three inches thick, covered the tarmac beneath her tyres. Deep drifts had settled on the steep banks which lined the road, and the windscreen wipers on

Erica's little Clio were barely able to clear the flakes as they fell, thick and fast.

Half-Finnish, she was used to snow and knew how to drive in winter conditions, but she also knew the same could not be said of the British transport system, and she was anxious to get home. The cars in front of her had already slowed to a crawl, and further ahead, the red blur of tail lights collecting in the distance surely meant trouble.

Erica drove up cautiously, and realised with a sinking feeling that the long queue of cars wasn't moving. She pulled up behind an ancient-looking Ford Escort and glanced in her rear-view mirror; behind her, a classic Mini inched to a halt. She frowned and checked her watch. Just gone noon.

She had checked her watch three more times before there was any sign of movement. Between the rhythmic thump of her windscreen wipers, she heard voices, then, finally, a man in an orange hard hat and safety gear emerged from between the cars. Erica watched him say something to the driver in front before pushing his way through the snow towards her. She rolled down her window, afraid she already knew what he was going to say.

'Snowdrift up ahead,' shouted the man, raising his voice above the weather. 'Won't be going anywhere for a bit, I'm afraid!'

Erica raised her eyebrows and wished for snow tyres. 'How long will it take to clear?' she called back, shivering. The wind was bitterly cold and was sending stray snowflakes into the car.

'Can't say,' replied the man, crunching towards her. 'They're sending the plough from Burford but we dunno how long it'll take to get here. Just got to sit tight. Meantime, you try and keep warm, okay?'

'Okay,' said Erica, her teeth already chattering.

Patting the roof of the Clio, the man trudged off along the line of cars. Erica shut the window and turned off the ignition. Without the hum of the engine nor the whine of the windscreen wipers, she suddenly noticed how quiet it was.

The cars were trapped in a shallow valley, surrounded on both sides by dense woods, and the snow, still falling steadily from grey skies, seemed to Erica to muffle everything but the sound of her own breathing. She sighed, watching snowflakes settle on her windscreen. This was not how she had hoped to spend Christmas Eve.

The minutes ticked by, and before long, people started emerging from the other vehicles. A man in an overcoat got out of the Ford Escort and started smoking a pipe; further up, a young couple were stretching their legs in the snow. There was no sign of the man in the orange hard hat.

Erica checked her watch again, growing impatient. It would take at least another three hours to get back to London, and if things didn't start moving soon, she was going to be late. She unlocked her phone to call her dad.

'How?' she muttered aloud, as a low battery alert illuminated her screen. She could have sworn her phone had been fully charged the last time she checked. She unplugged and re-plugged the charging cable into the cigarette lighter, then frowned. Nothing. She rattled the USB adapter in the socket, but the phone still wasn't charging. The cold chill of anxiety crept over her. She started tapping out a message to the family WhatsApp group – but before she could send it, her screen went black.

She swore in Finnish, just as a lady in a fur hat tapped on her window.

'Are you alright in there?' asked the lady. She was middle-aged with a kind face, and she was clutching a bag of Werther's Originals.

'Hello – yes, I'm fine, thank you,' replied Erica, rolling down the window.

'Would you like one?' asked the lady, shaking the bag. 'It's not much, I know, but, well, we don't know how long we'll be stuck here, do we?'

'Oh, that's very kind of you, but no, thank you,' said Erica. 'Er – you don't happen to have a power pack, do you?'

'A what, dear?' asked the lady.

'A portable charger – my phone's dead.'

'Dead?' The lady blinked momentarily.

'Out of battery.' Erica frowned.

'Oh, I'm sorry, dear, no, I don't have one of those,' said the lady. 'But I think the chap in the Land Rover might. About ten cars up.' She pointed with a leather-gloved finger.

Erica thanked her, then closed her window as the lady moved on to the next car. Through the fogged-up glass, Erica glanced at the snow scudding past and shivered – she didn't want to get out of the car, but she needed to let her family know what was happening. Reluctantly, she pulled on her hat and gloves, tucked her phone and the cable into her pocket, got out of the car and locked it.

Now that she was outside, she saw that the queue of cars stretched for a long way in both directions. She couldn't see where it ended or where it began. There was still no sign of the man in the orange hard hat.

She turned her collar up against the cold, then started making her way up the line of cars, the wind driving snow into her face. She didn't mind the snow – she was a keen skier and snow reminded her of her childhood – but the wind was savage, and she was relieved when she finally reached a large black Land Rover.

'Hello?' she called, knocking gently on the bonnet.

The driver-side window opened in a shower of snow, and a young man about Erica's age leaned out. He had dark, warm eyes and rather untidy brown hair. Erica noticed that snowflakes were already starting to settle on it.

'Hi,' he said simply. 'Can I help you?'

It took Erica a moment to remember what she was there for. 'Er – someone said you might have a power pack? My phone's dead.' She smiled awkwardly, holding it up.

'Oh right, sure,' he replied. 'I'm using it too right now, but you're welcome to share?'

'That would be great – thanks.'

He leaned over and opened the passenger door, and Erica climbed inside, grateful to be out of the wind. Pushing the damp hair out of her face, she glanced around. The Land Rover was clean and comfortable, and looked both well-cared for and well-used to the countryside, with muddy footprints on the floor mats and a National Trust badge stuck to the windscreen. It suited its driver – he was wearing jeans and practical-looking boots, and there was an old wax jacket lying on the back seat. He smiled politely at her as she got in, then held out the power pack.

'Thanks,' she said again, plugging in her cable.

'No problem,' he replied.

They sat in silence for a moment, then it occurred to Erica that they could be sitting there for quite some time. The same thought seemed to have struck the driver; he turned to her and smiled.

'I'm Jack, by the way,' he said.

'Erica.'

She glanced down and saw with some relief that her phone had started charging.

'So … where are you headed?' asked Jack.

'To London.'

Jack looked surprised. 'London? On this road?'

'Yeah – why?'

'Well, it's just, it's not exactly a direct route,' he said.

'What? Oh – I knew this wasn't a shortcut!' said Erica. 'My sat-nav sort of tripped out for a bit, and then it sent me this way ...'

'That's unlucky,' said Jack kindly. 'Sat-navs seem to do that a lot around here.'

Erica gave a wan smile, wishing again that she wasn't so reliant on technology. She noticed there was no sat-nav in the Land Rover: evidently Jack didn't need one.

'Are you from near here, then?' she asked.

Jack nodded. 'Cotswolds, born and bred,' he said. 'Little village about twenty miles that way.' He pointed. 'I mean, I live in London now, but I'm home for Christmas. Or at least, I'm meant to be.' He gave a half-smile, nodding at the traffic.

'Me too,' sighed Erica. 'I'm going to be so late. If this were Finland we'd have been on our way in twenty minutes!'

'Oh, are you Finnish?' he asked, sounding interested.

'Half,' replied Erica. 'On my dad's side. Have you been?'

'To Finland? No. Always wanted to, though. My ex and I went to Oslo once, but that was in the summer.'

Erica nodded.

'So, what's Finland like in the winter?'

'Cold.' Erica grinned. 'And dark. But it is very beautiful – like living inside a snow globe.'

Jack smiled. 'Yeah, I bet you're a bit more used to this sort of thing than we are,' he said, his gaze drifting to watch the driver in front scrape snow off the roof of their Beetle. 'What's Finnish for "snowdrift"?'

'Er – lumikinos.'

'Lumikinos,' tried Jack. 'Cool.'

Erica's phone chimed as it restarted. She was dismayed to see that she had no internet – but she did have a bar of signal and she tapped out a hasty text message to her dad.

'How much longer are we going to be stuck here?' she wondered aloud.

Jack shrugged. 'I dunno,' he said, drumming his fingers on the steering wheel. 'The guy in the hard hat couldn't say. Hopefully not too much longer, though. Isn't Christmas Eve kind of a big deal for Finns?'

Erica nodded, rather impressed. 'Yeah, it is. It's when we decorate the tree and when the kids get their presents and stuff. I mean, my mum's English so we sort of do both days, but this year my grandparents and cousins are flying over specially, and they're very traditional. I promised my dad I wouldn't be late. He told me not to go away this weekend, but I wanted to visit some friends in Bath for the Christmas market …' She realised she was waffling and stopped. 'I almost wish I hadn't gone, now.'

'Yeah, looks like you might be in trouble there,' said Jack, nodding towards a group of drivers standing by the roadside. They were talking to the man in the orange hard hat, and they didn't look too pleased. The man shrugged at the group, then trudged over to the Land Rover.

'Sorry folks,' he called, as Jack opened the window. 'Looks like we won't be getting out of here 'til tonight. They've just told us the plough's broken down.'

'Are you joking?' said Erica.

''Fraid not,' said the man. 'We'll give you a shout as soon as we hear anything, okay?'

'Okay, thanks mate,' said Jack.

The man gave them an apologetic smile and moved off.

Erica checked her watch – they'd been stuck there for over two hours already, and it would be getting dark soon. She let out a sigh.

'How's your phone doing?' asked Jack.

'Er, it's at twenty percent – thanks,' she told him, wondering if he was trying to get rid of her.

'Have you got internet?' he asked.

'No, have you?'

'No. 'Scuse me a sec.' Jack leaned across her and pulled an old, rather dog-eared road map out of the glovebox. He unfolded it and propped it up against the steering wheel, then hummed to himself for a moment. Erica watched as he traced a finger over the creases, then tapped on a small speck.

'Right,' he said, pushing one hand through his dishevelled hair. 'I say we make a try for it.'

'What?'

'Look,' he said, showing her the map.

Erica had to lean close to him to see what he was pointing at. She could smell his aftershave, and it made her think of Christmas trees.

More Than Mistletoe

'We're here, roughly – and over there is a village with a railway station.' He drew his finger slowly across an area marked 'woodland' and what looked like several fields.

'It's about a five-mile walk,' he said. 'What do you reckon? If you want to get home to your family that's probably your best bet. I'm sure you'll be able to get a train to London, and I can grab a taxi to my parents' house.' Jack gave her a grim smile. 'Not sure you'll make it back for your Christmas Eve otherwise.'

Erica hesitated. She wasn't sure that they should be trekking over the countryside in a snowstorm, and yet there was something about Jack which made her trust him instinctively. Besides, the thought of not having a warm cup of her mother's glögi on Christmas Eve was almost too much.

'Okay, yeah, let's do it,' agreed Erica.

'Right.' Jack grinned. 'Grab what you need from your car and meet me back here in five.'

Five minutes later, Jack and Erica were standing at the side of the road in their coats – Jack carrying a rucksack, Erica clutching her overnight bag, which she'd stuffed full of the presents she'd bought at the Christmas market. Jack checked the map again – it flapped violently in the wind, which, for some reason, made Erica feel colder.

'Excuse me, where are you going?'

Erica looked up. The group of drivers by the roadside was staring at them.

'We're going to a train station. You can come with us if you like?' Jack called back.

The drivers exchanged worried looks.

'What? No, you can't!' cried a girl in a bobble hat.

'We have to,' said Jack. 'Erica here needs to get back to her family today.'

A young man in a football scarf shook his head.

'But you can't just leave!' he said. 'The snow's getting worse!'

'He's right,' agreed a man in a flat cap. 'It's too risky, trying to walk in this!'

'Stay here, my dears,' encouraged the lady with the Werther's Originals. 'Chris and Carol here have a caravan. We can all have a nice cup of tea whilst we wait.'

'Sorry,' said Jack firmly, 'we have to try.'

Erica couldn't understand why the others were so content to stay trapped in the snow. She glanced at Jack, who gave her a reassuring smile, and together they struck out into the woods. It did not take long before they were deep amongst the trees, out of sight of the road. The sound of idling engines faded away and all was still and silent, save for the crunch of Jack and Erica's boots in the snow.

They walked swiftly, without speaking – partly because it was hard work trudging through the deep, powdery snow, and partly because there was a certain eeriness beneath the trees that warned them not to linger. Far above them, the tall evergreens stretched high into the sky, cloaked in snow, as large flakes fell from the darkening clouds overhead. The trees offered some shelter from the biting wind, but Erica still felt her nose growing sore. Her knitted beanie was damp and cold, and snow clung to her hair, melting slowly, until it lay in lank strands over her shoulders.

It felt like they had been walking a long time when Jack suddenly stopped.

'Did you hear that?' he said.

Erica strained her ears.

'What?' she asked, her breath misting in front of her face.

'I thought I heard … nothing,' he replied. He sounded a little nervous, but he turned and gave her another reassuring smile. 'Come on, I think we're nearly out of the woods.'

Erica wasn't entirely sure how Jack knew where they were going – she wasn't even sure they were still walking in a straight line. To her, the trees in every direction looked as dense and impregnable as they did in every other direction. Her fingers and toes growing numb, she followed Jack deeper into the woods, treading in his footprints as the skies grew steadily darker. She checked her watch. They had been walking for nearly an hour. Surely it shouldn't be taking this long, even in the snow? She peered into the gathering gloom of the woods – it almost felt as though the trees were growing thicker, denser, trying to trap them there …

'You okay?' asked Jack over his shoulder.

'I'm fine,' she replied. 'Is it me, or have we been walking a long time?'

'I was thinking the same thing,' admitted Jack, slowing his pace. 'We should have reached the fields by now.'

'Are we … lost?'

Jack laughed. 'No, I've a compass on my watch and we're definitely going the right way. Just seems to be taking forever!'

Erica felt somewhat relieved, but she glanced at the sky and bit her lip.

'I know,' said Jack, catching the look on her face. 'It'll be getting dark soon. D' you want to keep going, or should we turn back?'

Erica hesitated. She thought about her family, the warmth of home, the familiar cheer of Christmas Eve. 'Let's keep going,' she decided.

'Okay.' Jack knelt and pulled a large torch out of his rucksack, and clicked it on. The torch's powerful beam struck easily through the gathering shadows. It made Erica feel bolder.

'Stay close to me, okay?' said Jack.

They walked side by side after that, following the steady beam of the torch between the ever-darkening trees. Relentless, the driving snow began to form icy crusts on their coats and bags, and more than once Erica's boot got stuck in a particularly deep patch. Jack had to keep grabbing her hand and pulling her out. After what felt like a long time, the trees finally began to thin, and the torchlight illuminated a parting in the woods.

'Made it!' said Jack as they emerged, sounding both happy and relieved.

Erica stopped to catch her breath and surveyed the scene.

They found themselves on the edge of the woods, at the top of a wide, rolling patchwork of fields, the hedgerows just visible above the thick blanket of snow which covered the hills. By now it was almost dark, and, out of the shelter of the trees, Erica realised that the snowstorm had become a blizzard. Flakes swirled around them and flitted through the torchlight like frozen fireflies. In the dip of a distant valley, Erica saw a faint glow of light. This, she assumed, was the village. It looked a long way away.

'Almost there,' said Jack brightly. 'Looks like you'll make it back for your Christmas Eve after all!'

They began to make their way down the field, leaving deep footprints in the untouched snow. Erica shivered; out in the open they were exposed to the brute force of the wind, which whipped her cold wet hair around her face and whistled in her ears. She tried putting her hands over them, but her gloves were damp too and made her ears hurt. The whistling grew fiercer – then, with a gasp, she realised it wasn't just the wind that was whistling. She turned around and squinted through the snow – snatches of human whistling seemed to surround her, and there was something else on the breeze, too …

'Jack? Jack!' In the gathering darkness and the blur of the blizzard, she had lost sight of him.

'What?' The torchlight flashed through the snow. Jack was a few yards ahead.

'Do you hear that?' she asked.

Jack stopped moving.

'What is that?'

'It sounds like … footsteps?' said Erica.

There was no mistaking it – through the wind she could hear the slow crunch of footsteps in the snow. And then—

'Watch out!' exclaimed Jack.

Erica turned. Something dark and fast struck her in the chest. She staggered backwards and fell into the snow under its weight. She heard Jack running towards her and blinked for a moment, winded. Something was weighing heavily on her chest. She pushed the snow out of her face, then saw with some relief that the thing which had knocked her over was a large black and white dog, wagging its tail and panting into her face.

She laughed and pushed the dog off her.

'Are you okay?' asked Jack, sounding concerned as he helped her to her feet.

'I'm fine,' she said.

'Shep!' called a third voice. There was a shrill whistle and the dog barked. 'Shep!'

Jack and Erica stood close together, searching blindly through the swirling snow with the torch. Then another torch flashed through the darkness.

'Shep! Come 'ere, yer daft dog!' The owner of the other torch trudged into view: a farmer in a flat cap and an old-fashioned tweed coat. The dog barked again and scampered arounds its master's boots.

'You two alrigh'?' asked the farmer gruffly, training his light on their faces. 'Where yer headed in this weather?'

'Railway station,' replied Jack, gesturing towards the distant village with his torch. 'Our cars are stuck in the snow, but Erica needs to get back to London tonight.'

The farmer shook his head, his wizened face creasing into a grimace.

'Yer out o' luck there,' he grunted. 'No trains – thar's snow on the tracks, an' a downed tree near Deadman Hill.'

Erica and Jack looked at each other.

'Now what?' asked Erica.

Jack bit his lip. 'Right, in that case we'll have to get a taxi to—'

'Ha!' The old farmer let out a cracked, wheezing laugh. 'Taxi! Round 'ere? In this weather? No chance.'

Erica's heart sank. She felt her Christmas Eve slipping further and further away.

'Ye want my advice, go back ter yer car and wait,' said the farmer. 'It's dangerous t' be out in this. Go back an' get warm, both o' you.'

Erica did not miss the wry glint in the farmer's eye, and she felt herself blush.

Jack didn't seem to notice. He let out a sigh and rubbed the back of his neck. 'Maybe he's right,' he said to her.

Erica nodded reluctantly, and the farmer grunted his satisfaction.

'I'll be on me way, then,' he said. 'Come on, Shep! 'appy Christmas ter yer both.' And with a tip of his cap, he was gone.

Jack turned to Erica.

'Sorry I couldn't get you home,' he said.

'Oh, no, it's okay,' Erica gave him a disappointed but grateful smile. 'At least we tried.'

They turned and retraced their footsteps. Cold, damp, and tired, they entered the woods once again. It was dark now, but just as they stepped beneath the trees, the wind softened, the snow finally stopped and, overhead, the clouds began to clear. The trees seemed somehow thinner; Erica could see tiny stars starting to prick through the night sky, and the torchlight sparkled on the frozen snow which dusted the trees and crunched underfoot.

Erica pulled off her sodden hat and stuffed it in her pocket, then shook out her damp hair and took a deep breath, drawing in the scent of the pines. It reminded her of the forest near her grandparents' house, and as she walked, side by side with Jack, she began to feel that it didn't matter that she wasn't home. An unfamiliar yet comforting feeling came over her – as though she were exactly where she was meant to be this Christmas Eve.

'I don't believe it,' said Jack suddenly. 'We're back already!'

They had only been walking for twenty minutes or so, but they had already reached the other side of the woods, and now found themselves looking down upon the long line of stranded cars. The other drivers looked like they had settled in for the night. Many of the cars were parked with their headlights on, and people were leaning against bonnets with torches and cigarette lighters. It looked a little like a string of Christmas lights, and Erica couldn't help smiling. The group of drivers they had spoken to earlier were still gathered a short distance away. None of them looked the least bit surprised to see them, and the lady with the Werther's Originals gave Erica a knowing smile and a little wave.

'Any news?' called Jack, as he helped Erica down the steep bank.

Erica spotted the man in the orange hard hat moving down the line with a lantern.

'No news,' he called back. 'Won't be getting out of here tonight after all, I'm afraid. Plough's fixed but couldn't shift it. They're sending the big one from Oxford first thing. Reckon you'll be out of here in time for your Christmas dinner, though, okay?'

Jack nodded.

Erica sighed – but perhaps not quite so heavily as she would have earlier. 'So … now what?' she asked.

Jack shrugged. 'I guess we'd better call our families,' he suggested.

'Yes. Yes, you're right.' Erica nodded. She took a step towards her Clio, which was now almost completely buried in snow.

'And then …' Jack rubbed the back of his neck. 'Do you maybe want to have a drink or something? I've got some Baileys in the car. I was going to give it to my mum for Christmas but … well, looks like we'll be here for a long time, and would be nice to have some company. You don't have to, though …'

Erica smiled. 'No, that would be great.'

Half an hour and some uncomfortable phone calls later, Erica found herself sitting with Jack in his Land Rover, sipping Baileys out of their plastic keep cups and talking as though they had known each other for years, not hours.

It turned out that Jack worked in the city and had gone to the same university as one of Erica's housemates, and she was pleased to learn that his flat wasn't too far from her studio. She wasn't usually much of a chatterbox, but Jack was easy to talk to, and they were just comparing their families' Christmas traditions when there was a cheerful knock on the window. The glass was completely covered in snow and condensation; Erica opened it to find a group of their fellow drivers, including the Werther's Originals lady, beaming at them.

'Hello, dears!' she cried. 'We're all having a campfire and a few nibbles. Would you like to join us?'

Erica and Jack were only too glad to join the others gathered around the campfire – which turned out to be a blazing pile of bracken and old newspaper that some enterprising person had set fire to with a lighter. One person was melting snow in a travel kettle to make tea, and someone else was passing around a tin of roasted chestnuts. Erica toasted her fingertips and felt her toes begin to thaw as she and Jack stood beside the flames. She couldn't help smiling – strangers were sharing hipflasks and swapping Christmas stories, and if it hadn't been for the circumstances, Erica would have thought this was rather a nice way to spend Christmas Eve.

Erica and Jack were both hungry, but they too shared what little food they had – a box of M&S biscuits which Jack had bought for his grandmother, and an assortment of Christmas treats that Erica had got from the Bath Christmas market. Erica had also bought a cuddly toy reindeer at the market as a gift for her nephew; this she gave to a little girl whose mother was at the end of her wits trying to settle her down to sleep in the back of their car. Around the same time, a rather sweet old man with an ancient Austin remarked that his heater was broken, so Jack and another driver got out their toolboxes and helped him to fix it.

Later, someone pulled out a guitar, and everyone who wasn't busy lending blankets and extra clothes to those less well-prepared, gathered back around the fire to join in a spot of spontaneous carolling. Erica was no songbird, but she enjoyed listening to Jack's tuneful voice as he stood singing beside her.

As the final notes of "In the Bleak Midwinter" soared up towards the starry skies, Jack turned to her and murmured that it was getting late. Erica felt suddenly warm, and she didn't think it was because of the fire. Looking up at Jack, she smiled somewhat nervously. 'It is late,' she agreed.

'Do you want to go to bed?' he asked, then he laughed awkwardly. 'Er – sorry – I mean, are you tired?'

Erica blushed. She was glad of the firelight flickering over her face. 'I'm not tired,' she lied. She found herself longing for the night not to be over just yet. 'Are you tired?'

'No,' said Jack, but she was sure he was stifling a yawn. 'It is getting late, though.' He hesitated. 'Listen, if you want to … I mean, if you don't want to kip in your car, you're very welcome to sleep with me in the Land Rover. I mean – not sleep with me! Just sleep – in the Land Rover – with me. It's just there's a bit more space than the Clio, you know, might be a bit more comfortable …'

He was stammering; Erica smiled and, heart thudding, interlaced her gloved fingers through Jack's hand.

'Thanks, that sounds good,' she told him.

Jack looked down at her and grinned. Behind him, Erica saw some nudging and wry smiles winking in their direction. More than one person had mistaken Jack and Erica for an item, and the lady with the Werther's Originals, who seemed to have taken on the role of matriarch of the group, had spent most of the evening fussing over them and telling them what a lovely couple they made.

Jack and Erica wished their fellow drivers goodnight, then returned to the snow-covered Land Rover, where Jack folded the back seats down and turned the heater on. Erica hung up a string of fairy lights she'd bought at the market, and filled the trunk with all the blankets, sleeping bags and sweatshirts they had between them. The car actually looked quite cosy, and she was glad when they finally settled in for the night and finished the last of the Baileys.

'Cheers,' said Jack, clinking his keep cup against Erica's.

She sipped her Baileys contentedly, settling back against their piled-up rucksacks.

'I'm sorry you didn't make it home in time for Christmas Eve,' said Jack. 'Will your family be very upset?'

'Hm, well, I expect my Granny will cause a fuss tomorrow,' sighed Erica. 'But I'm giving her a big hamper from Fortnum & Mason's for Christmas, so I'm sure all will be forgiven. What about your family – were they sad you were missing Christmas Eve?'

'Oh, nah, they'll all be passed out in front of "It's a Wonderful Life" after too many mince pies by now.' Jack laughed. 'I'll see them tomorrow.' He emptied his cup and smiled sideways at her. 'Well, it hasn't been the Christmas Eve either of us had planned,' he said slowly, 'but I'm really glad I got to spend it with you.'

Erica blushed again. 'Me too,' she said, and finished her Baileys hastily. Jack's watch beeped quietly beside her. She glanced at the illuminated screen and saw it was midnight. Jack turned to her and smiled, his dark eyes twinkling in the fairy lights, and her heart missed a beat.

'Merry Christmas, Erica,' Jack said softly.

'Merry Christmas—' she began, but she was interrupted by his kiss.

*

Tap, tap, tap.

Erica stirred, but kept her eyes closed. It was morning and everything seemed very bright, but she wanted to sleep on. She had been having a good dream.

Tap, tap, tap.

Opening her eyes, it took her a moment to realise where she was – then she remembered. A strange light filled the back of the Land Rover – morning sunlight diffracting through the snow on the windows. She closed her eyes again and felt Jack's warm arm around her. Instinctively she nuzzled closer to him, drifting back off to sleep …

TAP. TAP. TAP.

Erica opened her eyes again. 'What is that?' she asked.

'Hmm?' grunted Jack, still dozing.

Erica frowned. Someone was knocking on the car. Slipping out from under Jack's arm, she crawled out of the blankets towards the tailgate. After fumbling with the handle, the door swung open and Erica blinked in the brightness – the dazzling morning sunshine felt warm on her face despite the chilly air sweeping into the car. Shielding her eyes from the sun, Erica found herself squinting up into the faces of two police officers, their fluorescent jackets stark against the pale blue of the sky.

'H – hello?' asked Erica.

'Good morning, madam,' said one of the officers. He was a tall, youngish man with sandy hair and a wry smile on his face. His colleague, a stout middle-aged woman, poked her head into the car.

'What's all this, then, folks?' she asked, in a broad Cotswolds accent.

'What's all – what?' said Erica, feeling their gaze on her as they took in the tousled hair, the sweatshirt, the tiny pyjama shorts.

'Whassgoingon?' murmured Jack, sitting up beside her and rubbing his eyes.

The female officer cleared her throat pointedly; Jack hastily pulled on his T-shirt.

'Is the drift gone?' he asked.

The officers exchanged a look.

'Drift? What drift?' asked the male officer.

'The snowdrift,' said Erica.

He looked down at her blankly.

His colleague planted her hands on her broad, fluorescent hips. 'What snowdrift?' she said impatiently.

Jack and Erica blinked at each other.

'The snowdrift,' said Jack slowly. 'Half a mile that way. They were sending the big plough from Oxford.'

The officer frowned, and underneath her arm Erica caught sight of the road behind her.

'Jack!' she cried. 'The cars – they're gone!'

'Really?' Jack scrambled to the edge of the tailgate and blinked out at the empty road. 'Oh yeah!' he said. 'You'd think the others might have woken us, though. That Highways Agency guy in the hard hat —'

'Highways Agency guy?' demanded the female officer.

Erica sighed, feeling impatient – if the drift was really gone, she wanted to be on her way home to enjoy whatever was left of her family Christmas.

'What Highways Agency guy?' repeated the female officer.

'The one dealing with the snowdrift,' explained Jack.

The male officer chuckled and leant down towards them with an amused look on his face.

'But sir … madam …' he said patiently, 'there hasn't been any snow.'

Erica opened her mouth to say something, then stopped. She stared out at the road. The sparkling layer on the ground was not snow, as she had first thought, but frost. Wherever the rising sun had struck, the frost had already melted away – the tarmac was black and glistening, the trees and grassy banks were green, and fifty feet away, she could see her little blue Clio parked by the roadside, completely free of snow.

'But that's impossible,' she said slowly. 'Snow doesn't melt that quickly!'

Jack climbed out of the trunk in his bare feet and stared around, his eyes wide. 'This doesn't make any sense,' he said, sitting down heavily on the tailgate and pushing his hand through his hair. 'How long have we been here?'

'Since last night, we reckon,' muttered the female officer. 'Passer-by called it in this morning. Reckoned there were a couple of people up to no good along here, you see.' She gave them a look which plainly said that she thought they had been up to no good, too.

Erica did her best to nudge the empty bottle of Baileys out of sight.

'Is the Clio yours, too?' asked the male officer, pointing down the road.

'It's mine …' Erica mumbled. She couldn't take it in. 'But the snowdrift …' she kept saying, turning it over in her mind.

'How many more times?' barked the female officer. 'There is no snowdrift.'

'Look,' said Jack, spreading his hands. 'I don't know what's going on here, but I'm telling you, there was a snowdrift here yesterday. We were stuck here – loads of us were. Dozens of cars, backed all the way along here past Deadman's Hill. The Highways Agency guy said they were sending a plough from Burford, but then that broke down and they had to wait for a bigger one from Oxford. Me and Erica here tried to walk to a village and catch a train, but we ran into a farmer and he said all the trains were cancelled due to the snow and a fallen tree. So, we came back here and spent the night in our cars, waiting for the drift to be cleared so we can go home to our families for Christmas. We've not been doing anything wrong; we just had no choice. That's it.'

'That's it,' agreed Erica. 'Okay?'

The officers stood silently for a moment, before the male officer burst into laughter. 'I think you two must have had one too many mulled wines!' He chuckled. 'I'm telling you, there's not been a snowdrift here for years!'

Erica stared at Jack, utterly lost. Her head was beginning to hurt.

'That's right,' agreed the female officer. 'Not been a snowdrift on this road since that nasty one in the eighties, when all those poor people got stuck in their cars and died. That was Christmas Eve, alright.'

A cold chill tingled down the length of Erica's spine.

'Do you remember, Paul?' The woman was saying. 'It was ever so sad. But that would have been years before these two were born!'

The male officer laughed. 'Oh heck, Sal, that was before I was born!'

'Well, then,' said the female officer. She gave Jack and Erica a suspicious stare. 'Listen,' she said, folding her arms, 'I don't know what you two are playing at, but there's been no snow, and no snowdrift here.'

Jack and Erica stared helplessly at each other.

'And no farmer, neither,' added PC Paul. 'Not been a farmer round these parts since – well, since that snowdrift, I 'spose, when old man Russell died trying to save them poor souls in their cars. Froze to death, he did – well, they all did, of course – nasty way to go …'

'Anyway,' interrupted the female officer. 'I think you two had better step out of the vehicle. We'd best check you're fit to drive before we send you on your way.'

It was humiliating being breathalysed by the side of the road in her pyjamas, but Erica knew they had no choice. The police officers clearly thought they were drunk, or on drugs, or both – but Erica knew she hadn't dreamed it all. Besides, there was no way that both she and Jack could have possibly had the same dream. What was this, she wondered? Some sort of trick? A shared hallucination? Or a very elaborate matchmaking scheme?

At last, the police officers had satisfied themselves that Jack and Erica were fit to drive, and gave them firm orders to be on their way within ten minutes.

'Maybe lay off the special Christmas cookies next time, eh?' chuckled PC Paul as he clambered into the police car.

'I've told you, we didn't—' started Jack, but the male officer held up a hand.

'Alright, that's enough, mate,' he said, his smile wearing a little thin. 'Because unless you two believe in ghosts, there's no way any of that happened last night. A snowdrift, indeed – there may have been some white powder around here, but it certainly wasn't snow!' He tittered at his own joke and started the engine.

'Right, we'll be off, then,' said the female officer. 'And I don't want to see either of you hanging around here again, okay? And, er, Merry Christmas to you both,' she added grudgingly. And with that, the police drove off.

Erica glanced at Jack. 'Are you okay?' she asked.

He nodded, but he looked pale.

'What is it?'

'Look,' he said, pointing.

Erica followed his gaze to see something small and dark lying beside the road. She walked towards it, pulling her sweatshirt around her, then stopped in her tracks. It was the stuffed reindeer that she had given the little girl. She shivered again – and not because of the cold.

'What's this doing here?' she said, her voice trembling as she stooped and carried the cuddly toy back to Jack.

'I don't know,' he said slowly, staring at it. 'I've been looking around and – well, Erica, there's no sign of those other cars anywhere. No soot from the fire, no cigarette ash – nothing.'

He swallowed, and Erica knew what he was thinking.

'But it can't be,' she said.

'Of course it can't be,' he replied. 'I'm rational, you're rational, we've both been here the whole time. But if there really wasn't any snowdrift …'

They got hastily into the Land Rover and started gathering up their things, going over it all again. Erica's sat nav tripping out. Her dodgy car radio. Her phone running out of battery, and the lady suggesting she ask Jack for help. The group of drivers who had all been so anxious to stop them walking to the train station. The way the trees had seemed to close in around them, as if trying to keep them there. The farmer who had appeared out of the snowstorm and made sure they never made it to their separate Christmases. All those people who had told them what a lovely couple they made. And all the cars – those old-fashioned, clunking, ancient cars. With a jolt, Erica realised that apart from Jack's Land Rover and her Clio, there hadn't been a single car trapped there which had been less than forty years old.

'Oh, my God,' breathed Erica. Slowly, her thoughts started to clear, like snow settling at the bottom of a shaken snow globe. Maybe it really had been an elaborate match-making scheme. By people who had frozen to death in that place one Christmas Eve, many years ago …

'Should we be scared, do you think?' asked Jack, zipping up his jacket and closing the back of the Land Rover. He glanced over his shoulder, as if expecting to see a phantom packet of Werther's Originals floating in mid-air.

Erica thought for a moment, then shook her head. 'No,' she said. 'I don't think they meant any harm. I think … well, I think they meant for this to happen.' She smiled and took Jack's hand.

'I reckon you might be right.' Jack grinned. 'Well, I guess we'd better be going, else we'll be in trouble with the fuzz. So … I'll message you, yeah?'

Erica smiled. 'Yeah. And see you when we're back in London?'

'Definitely,' said Jack.

They shared a shy goodbye kiss, then climbed into their cars. Jack waved as he drove away.

Erica glanced at the toy reindeer on her passenger seat, then turned on the car radio. It buzzed and crackled slowly into life – but in the moments before the cheerful tones of the Christmas morning news filled her car, she could have sworn she heard voices, lots of voices, singing "Driving Home for Christmas" through the static

Michelle Harris

The Ghost of Christmas Past

Michelle Harris

Stave I – Christmas Present.

"Every idiot who goes about with 'Merry Christmas' on his lips, should be boiled with his own pudding, and buried with a stake of holly through his heart. He should!"
~ Ebenezer Scrooge

A Christmas Carol, by Charles Dickens

"Marley was dead: to begin with. There is no doubt whatever about that."

The familiar narration filled the darkened classroom, and the screen's dim illumination flickered an icy light on a less than enthralled class of Year Elevens. Their mutterings, coughs and fidgeting diluted the soundtrack of the film that Natasha had heard at least once a year since she became an English teacher. Natasha knew she should care whether her class was paying attention or not, after all, this was one of their set texts. But honestly, she couldn't be arsed. It had been a tough term - who was she kidding, a tough year, and she was one 45 minute film-watching lesson and a half-hour Carol Service away from the Christmas holidays. And, she acknowledged to herself, as she sighed and massaged her temples, she was more than slightly hungover.

In the classroom next door, Dylan's bottom set class were belting out Christmas tunes with the reckless abandon of those with no great expectations of decent predicted levels. Natasha knew without looking in that Dylan would be standing on his desk front and centre, cutting some shapes, resplendent in his purposely horrific festive jumper. If there was any justice left, after last night's English department Christmas drinks, Dylan had a monstrous hangover too.

It sucks to be Set One, observed Natasha, surveying her class as they half-watched the film, and no doubt wondered why the class next door got to party hard on the last day of term while they got Charles Dickens. They'll thank me on results day, she thought, knowing that it was untrue even then. On-screen, Scrooge was bah-humbugging his way around snowy Victorian London, basically telling everyone who would listen that Christmas was a load of bollocks. His nephew had disagreed with him with blustering good humour, and Bob Cratchit was looking on from the side-lines like he needed a burger and a cardigan. Standard.

'Phone away, Mason,' Natasha admonished suddenly and sharply through the semi-darkness, 'I can see it glowing there.'

'Fuck's sake, Miss, it's almost Christmas,' came the reply. 'You could at least have given us the bloody Muppets.' It was a fair point, she acknowledged inwardly.

The carol singers in the background of Scrooge's festive-phobic rantings were singing "God Rest Ye Merry, Gentlemen"; usually, Natasha would be heart warmed at the sound. Ever since she was a child, she had loved Christmas an almost unhealthy amount, but not anymore. Not since last year's shitshow.

There's nothing like being dumped the night before your lavish and sparkly Christmas wedding to dampen your Christmas spirit. The memories of your pathetic self, dismantling sixteen silver mini Christmas trees intended as centrepieces, ugly-crying and necking winter-spiced gin, with "Fairytale of New York" on repeat, can really dull a girl's festive sparkle. Not to mention the humiliation of having to tell all your nearest and dearest that you're not getting married tomorrow as planned and that instead, the groom was on a plane to Mexico with some girl named Jade that he met at his gym. It gave a whole new meaning to the phrase "ho, ho, ho."

There would be no decking the halls for Natasha this year. This year, she intended to ignore the whole festive period as much as possible and shove the painfully raw memories of last December as far to the back of her mind as alcohol and denial would allow. This year, she thought, I am channelling Ebenezer. Bah humbug to the lot of it. I might even stop plucking my chin hairs.

More Than Mistletoe

The school "Carol Concert" went as it always did. Natasha had mentally inserted the inverted commas several years ago. Traditionally, each year, 950-odd students simultaneously attempted to avoid the enthusiastic conductor-gaze of the wonderfully eccentric music teacher, Gordon, who definitely wasn't hungover because he sensibly didn't socialise at work. Clever chap. Gordon's stage smile and over bright eyes as he waved his arms through the same six carols every year were half-heartedly accompanied by the school choir, seventy-five percent of whom looked like they would rather be doing literally anything else.

This year, though, as the pianist played the opening bars of "Silent Night", Natasha's eyes filled with tears. She remembered typing up the lyrics for her Orders of Service and painstakingly choosing fonts and colours. What a lot of effort for a whole pile of posh recycling. As she scrambled in her handbag for a tissue, angry at herself for allowing the emotion to surface, and especially at work, she could feel Lauren's eyes on her. Lauren had been her rock this past year, a crazy little whirlwind of a PE teacher, and much more than just a work colleague.

"You okay?" Lauren mouthed over the heads of the now mostly lip-synching Year Eights. Natasha nodded. She didn't know why she was feeling it all so much today when she had done so well recently. Maybe it was the hangover talking. Or maybe it was the whole Dylan thing.

Ohmygosh Dylan. Dylan, who helped her out when she needed last-minute lesson fillers and was really bloody good at unjamming the photocopier. Dylan, who had got her into trouble a few years back when they'd teamed up for an impromptu snowball fight with Year Eleven – the pair of them hauled into the Assistant Head's office like naughty kids, unable to stop the laughter. Dylan with his shit "Santa got stuck up the chimney", 3D, technicolour yawn of a jumper. Dylan, who bribed the Year Sevens to give him Christmas cards to be displayed around his smartboard, so he looked like the most popular teacher in school. Dylan, who loved Christmas almost as much as she did – or used to. Dylan, who was currently also looking over at her with concern as she narrowly avoided bawling in public. She couldn't meet his eye today. How had he gone so suddenly from Dylan, her mate, to Dylan the ... what, exactly? Don't think about it, don't look at Dylan, just keep singing. *Sleep in heavenly peace.*

Dylan and Natasha had joined the English department at St Dominic's on the same day, just over five years ago. Lauren had had a blatant crush on him at first and kept finding reasons to pop by the English Office in her short shorts, all flicky hair and smiles and new staff support. It had quickly worn off, as these things always did with Lauren. There had been no tension of that kind between Natasha and Dylan, because of course, Natasha had been with Nick at the time. But even pre-Nick, Natasha had never dated at work – it wasn't her style. Mixing work and pleasure had disaster potential wherever the job, but when you had to see them in Year Nine assembly or conduct parents' evenings next to one another once things had all gone wrong, it all reached a whole new level of cringe. So, what the hell had changed last night?

Nothing. Nothing had changed, she told herself, as the choir murdered the final chorus of "O Come All Ye Faithful". It had just been an unexpected, very brief encounter after far too many drinks. She wasn't even sure it qualified as an encounter, actually.

They'd been heading to the taxi rank, sharing a cab home as they often did, but for some reason, it felt different this time. Their usual giggles and chatter were there as usual, but there was an undertone that had never been there before. There was a look that lasted too long, and a hand on her arm that burned like fire for a second, a momentary swim in some deep dark brown eyes that she'd never noticed were so damned hot before. And then suddenly, for no reason, they'd stopped walking. Neither spoke. For a brief second, Natasha had considered holding that gaze, reaching out and touching the hair falling in front of his eyes, brushing it back so she could see him better, stepping into his arms just to see if what might happen next felt as good as she thought it might.

Thank goodness she hadn't. Because if she had, the fact that he was glancing over to her now and then, all the while enthusiastically pretending to sing the descant to the carol, would be all kinds of awkward.

Stave II - A Visit From A Ghost.

The same face: the very same ...
"How now!" said Scrooge, cold and caustic as ever. "What do you want with me?

As she'd been packing up her holiday marking in the English Office post-Carol Service, Lauren had swung in and insisted that hair of the dog was the answer to her hangover. Several people from various departments had headed to the pub up the road from school, and so because she had no willpower and no place else to be, Natasha had joined them. She couldn't stomach wine after last night, so she sipped a bottle of Peroni gingerly, wondering how soon it would be socially acceptable to make her excuses and leave.

The Good Briton pub recommended itself as a post-work drinking establishment primarily because of its proximity to St Dominic's, rather than its credibility as a cool venue. Nonetheless, it was clean, comfy and the landlord often allowed them to phone their food order through on a break time so they would have time to pop down for the occasional lunch. This made it the staff of St Dominic's pub of choice. On this particular Friday afternoon, it was fairly busy, with many school staff and office workers having knocked off early for the last weekend before Christmas.

Natasha scanned the tables occupied by her colleagues; end of term drinks was usually attended by a random mix of departments and ages, and today was no exception. A smattering of older staff sat chatting at one table, while on the adjacent one a bunch of Newly Qualified Teachers and younger staff were already getting rowdy. Lauren and Natasha sat with a few guys from Lauren's PE department, who were quite likely to drink themselves stupid this evening, but for now, they were a good laugh.

'I know what you're thinking,' Lauren cut into her thoughts. 'He's coming – Dylan. He's just finishing up in his classroom.'

'I wasn't thinking that. Why would you think I was thinking that?' Natasha knew instantly that she'd been too defensive. 'I mean I …'

'Erm, I know because the thing with you two is bloody obvious, and I love to see it. He's been doing gooey eyes at you for ages now, but I thought you'd friend-zoned him since day one. What's the deal now? I saw him bogging at you during Carols.' Nothing got past Lauren. It was infuriating.

'It's nothing, nothing at all. We're fine.' Natasha lowered her voice because she didn't want the PE guys to overhear, but she needn't have worried, they were on the charm offensive with Lucy, a trainee geography teacher, who looked like she was enjoying every second.

'Don't talk shit, this is me you're talking to,' said Lauren, topping up her wine. 'Tell me about 'The Moment'.'

Ever the English teacher, Natasha could *hear* Lauren's capital letters.

'What Moment?'

Lauren rolled her eyes comically and dove straight into what she's been wanting to say this whole time. 'Dylan WhatsApped me at like, one a.m., to say that he thought you and he had had 'A Moment'. I think from the emojis, he was chuffed about it, but I also assume he was drunk, because he deleted it at like, half six this morning. But it was too late by then, my friend! So, did you or did you not have 'a Moment' with Dylan? Spill!' She gulped her wine triumphantly as she watched Natasha for a reaction.

Oh God, he felt it too? Natasha sipped her beer to hide a grin, but as she did so, she felt a shiver of uncertainty that had little to do with the cold drink. It would have been so much easier to pretend that it had just been her drunk perception of the brief little occurrence.

'Well? Don't just sit there like a nun's chuff!' Lauren's turns of phrase sometimes took a little unpicking, so when Natasha looked confused, she clarified. 'Don't be useless. Tell me.'

'I think we kind of had a, a Moment, yes,' Natasha sighed and took a gulp of her beer. 'It might have been a moment, and if he said so, then it almost definitely was one … I think maybe, last night, I temporarily considered un-friend-zoning him.'

'Do it!' Lauren was positively gleeful. 'It was obvious he liked you, even back when you were with Nick the Prick.' Lauren had many derogatory nicknames for Nick. Most of them rhymed in some way, and she rotated them at intervals with a creativity which had become a source of pride. 'Anyway,' she continued, tipping the remainder of the bottle of wine into her already almost full glass. True to form, it was four in the afternoon and Lauren was well on her way to being a hot mess. 'Anyway, you should totally have more than A Moment with him because let's face, he's a proper hottie, and also let's face it, your sex life is like Ghandi's flip flop – duh, dry – and you need a bit of fun, and it's *Christmas*, and – oh he's just arrived. Quick, pretend you've made me laugh, he's coming right over.'

Before Natasha could register the ludicrous assumption that she resort to cheap, I'm-so-funny tactics to impress Dylan, Lauren cackled theatrically as he arrived at their table. 'Oh Tasha, you crack me up! Hahaha!' Natasha looked up. Dylan, minus the awful jumper, was instead wearing a well-fitting dark shirt. God, Lauren was right, he was a total hottie. Or something that sounded less juvenile. Jeez, Natasha hated herself already and there had only been A Moment.

He smiled at her.

'Alright?'

Natasha couldn't answer. She blinked and smiled back at him. Amused, Lauren came to her rescue.

'We're great thanks, Dylan,' said Lauren standing up. 'I'm off to the bar, want a beer?' He made as if to interrupt her, but she waved him away. 'No mate, I'm going, don't worry. Beer, Tash?' She nodded. 'Right, two beers and bottle of Pinot, perfect, might as well start as I mean to go on. I'll give you two *a moment.*'

The pair of them flinched at the phrase, and Natasha felt her cheeks flush. She glanced at Dylan and was gratified to see a matching flush on his face too. He ran his fingers bashfully through his hair as he turned to face her. When a smile greeted him, he exhaled with relief and chuckled slightly.

'Woah. Busted. I really need to disable my phone after four beers; I'm an embarrassment.' His eyes met hers fully now and she realised they were just as gorgeous now, when she was hungover, as they had been in her wine haze the previous night. Those eyes were doing things to her that no one had for a year. Oh, Christ, this meant trouble.

'So … did we have a Moment?' he asked, tentatively, holding her gaze. Capital letter. 'It feels like we did. But maybe I am imagining it because I have liked you for ages. Or maybe we did, but you're not ready, in which case, cool. Or maybe – oh shit I'm babbling; did you know I babble? I babble so bad when I get …'

'Please stop.' She hadn't meant to sound harsh, but somehow, she did, and his eyes widened ever so slightly.

'Sorry, I don't mean stop; you babble very well.' She smiled to let him know she wasn't angry. He half-smiled back, why had she never realised what that smile could do to a woman before?

'I think we did have a Moment, yes. But you know, since Nick – you're so great to me – I love having you as my friend, bugger it, now *I'm* babbling …' Dylan leaned towards her as she sipped the last of her beer, struggling to hear her over the music and merriment. Why oh why had she thought it a good idea to have this conversation in a pub, surrounded by colleagues?! His eyes found hers again.

'Do you want to just … seize the Moment?' He paused. 'Oh God, I promise that sounded so much cooler in my head.'

'I would like that.' Her smile was in danger of taking over her whole face now. 'Are you free tomorrow night? We could try to get a table at Austin's.'

'It might be kind of busy. You know, it being Christmas.' His eyes were shining with a smile, and she felt the heat of it like a warm embrace.

'Good point, ok, well are you free tomorrow?'

'Yes, and I have an idea. Christmas Market, hot chocolate, mulled wine, and carols, it'll be like Christmas puked up everywhere. What do you think?'

'Sounds perfect. I love Christmas time.'

And it was then that she remembered, she really did. Sparkles and cosy jumpers and hot chocolate and all of it. When her parents had been closer,

Christmas had been her favourite family time, all cosied up with normal life suspended in favour of warm blankets, games and gorgeous food. When Mum and Dad had moved to New Zealand to be closer to her sister and their twin grandchildren, they'd begged Natasha to think about relocating too, but by then she had had Nick. He'd indulged her love of the festive season up to a point, but his family Christmases had been duller affairs than Natasha was used to. Planning a wedding for Christmas has been Natasha's greatest joy, every detail meticulously researched, Pinterested and planned. When Nick had run out on their wedding, he'd effectively robbed her of Christmas, as well as everything else. But now, maybe, it looked as though Christmas could be making a comeback.

Natasha's warm glow cooled a little as she caught sight of Lauren, tottering back from the bar, armed with drinks and a frantic expression.

'Christ, what's wrong with Lauren?' Natasha's grin died on her face as Lauren grimly set the drinks down.

'I need the loo, come with me,' she declared unceremoniously, and dragged Natasha in the direction of the Ladies, leaving a baffled Dylan in their wake.

When they got there, she wasted no time. The door was barely open before Lauren blurted out:

'Tash, he's here. He's back.'

'Who is?'

'Tricky Nicky.'

She felt the colour drain from her cheeks and her breath choked her.

'What?'

'Nickolas the Dickolas. He just came up to me at the bar. He's back to see his parents for Christmas. He wants to see you. I told him to fuck right off, obviously.'

It came as a blow to the stomach style shock that Nick would be back for Christmas, and yet it made perfect sense that he would be visiting his ghastly parents for Christmas. Natasha leant on the washbasin, head in hands, feeling like she might throw up any second.

'God. Oh, God.' She couldn't think straight. 'Why on earth would Nick have thought turning up here was a good idea?' He knew this is where she'd be on the last day of work. Had he never heard of a fucking text message?! Anger and indignation started to take over from her nerves. 'The arrogance of him! Was he just going to buy me a friendly pint?'

'It's fine, Tash, I'll go and tell him to get lost.' Lauren made for the door.

'No. No. I can do it,' she breathed.

She opened the door to the bathroom and scanned the pub for Nick, trembling with – she wasn't sure what. There was no sign of him anywhere as she moved swiftly from table to table, searching each table of merrymakers with increasing urgency. When he wasn't anywhere, she went towards the door, and was vaguely aware of Lauren detouring back to pick up their coats from the empty table. As she opened the door to the car park, the chill whipped her face, and a few flakes of snow were beginning to fall. Under a street lamp, a solitary figure in his shirtsleeves was stood with his head bent over his phone. Not Nick, but Dylan. What was he doing out in the cold?

Dylan approached, his jaw tense as he took in her shakiness and her pale face.

'I can't believe he came. Are you okay, Tash? I mean, of course, you aren't. I'm sorry.'

'Where is he?' Her voice was a hoarse half-whisper that caught in her throat.

'You er, you just missed him.' Dylan ran a hand over the back of his neck and shifted awkwardly.

'What did you do?' She found her voice. He didn't answer straight away.

'What. Did. You. Do?'

'I just told him he should go, honest, that's all. I said it wasn't the place, I mean, everyone from work is here …'

Lauren was overjoyed at this and interjected with a jubilant. 'Nice work Dylan, telling Nicko the Thicko to do one …' She moved to congratulate him but stopped when she saw Natasha's face, contorted with anger borne out of a strange kind of disappointment that she wouldn't see Nick after all. It was as though all the emotion that had built up in her towards Nick need a focus.

Natasha delivered her next words with all the force she had been reserving for Nick.

'Were you worried about us seizing the Moment, is that it? Worried I wouldn't feel like seizing anything new once he turned up back here? What were you doing, sticking up for the Damsel in Distress? That it, Dylan?' She knew her blame was misplaced but it felt good to get some of the hurt out.

Dylan seemed unphased by her anger.

'No, that's not it, Tash. If you want to see him, you should, but not like this. It wasn't fair of him to spring it on you. That's all.'

'Why do you get to decide? What gives you the right to choose when I see him?'

'Nothing. Absolutely nothing. I don't think I should choose, I just don't think he should choose. You should. It should be on your terms and yours alone. If he does want you back then it sure as hell shouldn't be easy for him.' He smiled wryly. 'Bollocks to the timing, though.'

'Bloody hell Dylan, why do you have to be so flipping decent all the time?!" Lauren was incredulous, her voice echoing shrilly on the quiet street. 'Talk about cock block yourself!'

Suddenly the three of them were laughing, the sound echoing in the winter's evening. Natasha laughed so hard she bent double; the release was amazing, but she felt like it could turn to the other kind of tears at any moment. Eventually, the laughter subsided.

'Tash, the thing is,' Dylan rubbed his arms against the cold. 'I just hated watching you break, and I don't want him to do it again, regardless of what happens with us. But I would never stop you from seeing him. We can seize the moment if you still want to, another time. I've waited this long.' With that, he went back inside.

Natasha put on her coat, ushered by Lauren. A brief burst of "Santa Baby" was audible before the door shut again, leaving only the quiet. A determined snow flurry began, illuminated under the recently vacated streetlight.

'Lauren, I have to go.'

'Shall I come?'

'No, thanks. I need to get my head straight.'

'I'll call you. Remember, if you get back with Nickster the Shitster you're dead to me, okay? Love you squillions, here if you need me.' And Lauren was gone.

As Natasha walked along the quiet street, the tears came, but she didn't quite know what she was crying about. She just knew she felt as though something important had been lost.

Stave III – Christmas Past. One Year Earlier.

"May you be happy in the life you have chosen!"
She left him, and they parted.
"Spirit" said Scrooge, "show me no more. Conduct me home. Why do you delight to torture me?"

As Dylan drained the last of the whisky from his glass, he flicked off the TV with a disgusted groan of despair. He checked his watch; fifteen hours until Natasha said "I do."

If you had to sit by while the woman you love married someone else, why did it have to be at Christmas, when the rest of the world was so happy? Every channel was filled with carol singers and rom-coms. Walking through town was all festive music, decorations and merriment. Usually, Dylan would have loved this, he was known as "Mr Christmas" in several circles. But this year it made the fact that he felt so awful even harder. That's why he'd lied to everyone about how he was spending Christmas this year, telling family he was supporting a friend through a bad breakup, and all friends that he was with family. He couldn't be around people, especially not happy people.

The moment he had met Natasha, Dylan knew he had feelings for her. Which was odd, because he'd never given much thought to the whole Love at First Sight thing. Plus, it was really unexpected, because he had been living with Kate at the time, and he had thought they were happy. He'd been at his desk in the English Department office, reading the files on his new classes, when she'd rushed in soaked to the skin, her umbrella broken in her hand.

'Don't look at me! I'm not here yet!'

'Erm – okay?' Dylan made to turn away, noticing as he did her mass of auburn curls.

'I've got emergency hair straighteners and makeup; we can meet then! The first day of work and my car wouldn't start; I had to run and get the bus. You couldn't make it up. Please tell me you're Dylan, fellow new person, and not anyone I have to impress?' She realised her mistake. 'I'm so sorry, I didn't mean it like that, I just … Jeez what a first impression …'

He noticed the cadence of her voice, melodic and addictive. He stood up and turned to face her.

'I *am* Dylan, so you're in luck! No one else is in yet, so Dawn in reception showed me in here to get started. You must be Natasha. Shall I stick a kettle on?'

'Oh, you're brilliant! Coffee please, black. I bought some with me. I shelled out for a posh brand so people will like me.' She passed him the carton.

Her eyes were green but luminescent, and he felt strangely moved by the smattering of freckles on her nose.

'Sugar?' Keep it together, he told himself.

'No thanks. I'd like to use the line that I'm sweet enough already, but actually, I am on Operation Smaller Arse.' She pulled a compact out of her handbag and began to reapply her smudged make-up as she continued. 'It's so important, it has a name. Nick – my boyfriend, and I, we're off to Cyprus at half term, and Nick says my bikini will be dental floss if I don't do something drastic.'

Within fifteen minutes of meeting Natasha, Dylan realised that the thing with Kate that he had thought could well be the Love Thing everyone spoke of, definitely wasn't. And he also realised that whatever he felt for Natasha was utterly pointless. Natasha made it very clear they were just friends right from day one. Banter in the office, jovial stories about her life with Nick. Moaning about her period pains, offering to take him for a pint when Kate and he inevitably broke up. Asking if he fancied Lauren, trying to set them up. Dylan had never had the heart to tell her what he felt, because what would be the point? It would have ruined their friendship and couldn't go anywhere because of Nick. Instead, he'd made sure he was the best version of himself whenever she was there, he made the best coffee, he planned amazing lessons, he was the school's most committed teacher and he was always, always there when she needed him. He knew it was pathetic, but he couldn't help himself. It was an odd kind of self-torture because he couldn't detach himself. He had to sit back and watch as her boyfriend became her fiancé. And tomorrow, Nick would become her husband, and there was nothing he could do to change it, however much he wished more than anything that it wasn't happening.

Dylan had toyed with the idea of objecting to the marriage like they did in the films. He'd entertained indulgent fantasies of standing up and making an eloquent and charming speech in front of the whole congregation when the Officiator asked if anyone knew why these two should not be joined in matrimony. In his imagination, Natasha was totally won around, and would tell Nick to get lost, and marry him instead. He'd wondered, had that ever happened in real life? More likely there would be awkward silence before he'd be out on his arse in the street, minus his best friend, and having provided Natasha's friends and family with a funny anecdote – do you remember that wedding where that guy made such a fool of himself … so as much as it broke his heart, he knew the best thing was to stay well away.
  She'd been so upset that he couldn't come to the wedding. He'd planned his excuse carefully so she couldn't be angry; he'd invented a Great-Aunt and a clashing 80th birthday party.
  'Sorry, Tash, I wouldn't have missed it but the old girl's not got long left,' because you can't say, 'sorry I can't come to your wedding because I am so ridiculously in love with you that if I have to watch this happen, I genuinely might kill myself.'

Roughly, Dylan got to his feet and went to top up his glass. Why not? He had a whole day of wallowing to do tomorrow, and it wouldn't hurt to sleep through some of it. He let an additional few glugs splash into his glass, gulped, and grimaced. He didn't even really like whisky. He just felt it was a whisky kind of a day. His phone flashed into life. *Natasha?! Why in holy hell would she call him tonight? Had something happened? An accident, maybe?*

He felt a glimmer of hope as he imagined Nick in some kind of really embarrassing accident, like that guy that had been on the news because he got tied to a lamppost naked on his stag do and a fox nibbled his unmentionables.

'Natasha? Is everything —'

A sob silenced him.

'Can you come? He's gone – Nick's gone.'

'What, where's he gone?' Dylan shook his head, riddled with emotions he was too drunk to process.

'Mexico. With Jade. From the gym. I can't … I just – lycra – bitch.' Each word rasped with raw emotion and shook with tears. 'Dylan? Can you come? I could really use a friend —'

And he'd gone. In the cab to Natasha's, he'd felt almost jubilant. What he'd wanted since he'd met her four years ago, had happened. Nick the Prick was gone. Natasha was single. Now all he needed was magical mutant powers to make her see him in a whole new light. He thought about forcing a spider to bite him, or drinking radioactive fluid. Sober up, he told himself. Save "Into the Dylanverse" for another day, when you're not half-pissed.

Lauren opened the door to Natasha's flat with a force that suggested it was lucky to still be on its hinges.

'Knobhead!' She said, by way of a welcome. 'Lying, cheating, knobheaded knobhead.' She looked positively murderous. 'Honestly, Dylan, I'm going to kill him. He had been out all day, supposedly on wedding errands, then he comes back and makes this big speech, ending things. Tasha didn't see this coming at all. He told her he never loved her, that he felt he should marry her because they'd been together so long. Everything is booked, Dylan. She's gonna have to cancel it all, and tell everyone … I offered, obviously, but she's saying she'll do it … but she's wankered if I am honest. She was when she called me. I don't know where to start, Dylan. I wonder if I can catch Prickolas at the airport …'

'Don't. Don't go anywhere. Just stick the kettle on, okay?'

Dylan took a deep breath. Suddenly, he felt completely sober. If Natasha needed him, he was going to be there, as he always was.

From the living room doorway, he took one look at Natasha and he found there were tears in his eyes too. He'd never thought of her as fragile, before, but here she was surrounded by lists, table plans and favours and oh God, her wedding dress, hugged up in her lap and soaked with tears.

'Sweetheart, I'm so sorry. What can I do?'

'Nothing. I can do it, I just need gin.'

'I think we can safely say you've had enough of that.' His statement was kind of ironic given his superhero nonsense in the cab.

'I need all the gin tonight because in the morning I am going to tell everyone, I can't do it now. I can't speak to people. But tomorrow, I plan on getting up at seven and cancelling it all. And I would quite like to still be pissed so I can't remember it, and to do that, I need all the gin.'

'Give us your list, we can do it.'

'No. No, I have to do it, because otherwise, I don't think I can comprehend it, How it's off. How he's gone. To MEXICO. And he's left me and I can't bloody cope …'

He'd hugged her then, he couldn't think of a reason not to. And as she'd melted into his arms, he realised that he didn't want the wedding to be off, anymore. He wanted it to happen. He couldn't handle these strangled cries coming from Natasha. If Nick had not been on a plane to Mexico he would have bought the stupid, selfish bugger back and forced him to marry the woman he loved, just so he didn't have to sit here in the darkness and hold her while she sobbed.

Stave IV – Christmas Present.

> *"It ends to-night."* said the *Spirit*
> *"To-night!"* cried *Scrooge*.
> *"To-night at midnight. Hark! The time is drawing near."*

Natasha walked away from the Good Briton, pulling her coat around her as the snow fell heavily. It was only six pm, but it felt later. She knew she had to see Nick, she had to see what his coming back felt like; she'd dreamed of it long enough. So she dialled the number she had thought about calling so many times before. It seemed to take an age to connect and then Nick picked up after the first ring.

'Natasha, I'm sorry. I had to come.'

'Why?'

'I had to see you. Where are you?'

'Argyle Street.'

'Meet me at The Sun.' The Sun had been one of their regular haunts before he went away. Why, even now, could she not bear to think the phrase *before he left me*? Natasha knew it was now or never. She had to see him now and she had to go with whatever emotion she felt when she finally laid eyes on him.

As she walked, her footsteps crunching on the snowy street, Natasha pondered what she might find when they met. She knew Nick had dated Jade for a while – she'd social media stalked him through friends. That had been almost as difficult as the pain of losing Nick; when you have been together forever, all your friends are co-owned. She'd had to endure discovering which of their friends picked Nick, and who sided with her. What was longer-term difficult was those who decided to stay friends with both; because of them, she'd seen him and Jade tagged in photographs of group ski trips and at dinner parties. It stung to have her place so obviously taken and her own invitation to the occasion silently revoked to avoid any awkwardness. She couldn't recall when she'd last seen a photograph of them together, and she wondered how recent the break-up had been.

As Natasha entered the main bar area, she saw Nick, standing alone at the bar. She didn't approach him; instead, she picked her battleground, a table away from other people, next to the rather gaudy Christmas tree. His hair was slightly longer than when she saw him last. Other than that, he looked pretty much the same as he had done a year ago. Her insides flipped over and she wasn't quite sure of the reason. Was her body responding to the sight of him like it always had, or was she going to vomit on his shoes in a minute or two? Only time would tell. As he got closer, she could smell him. Dior. She used to love the smell of his aftershave, to her it was masculine and oaky, and him, but come to think of it, it wasn't as nice as she remembered. Had he always worn this much? No denying the muscles rippling under his fitted T-shirt. All that time at the gym, she thought wryly.

'Natasha. You look amazing. How are you, darling?'

'Better than I was the last time I saw you. What do you want?' The steadiness of her voice surprised her. She could feel her legs shaking and was glad she was wearing a polo neck, nerve-blotches would give her away. He knew her too well.

'Natasha, I —' Was his nervous pause contrived or real? Nick went on. 'Natasha, baby, I know. I know what I did was stupid and cruel and awful, and well, unforgivable, probably, but—'

'Probably?' Neither one of them spoke then for at least fifteen seconds; around them the cheery chatter and the backing track of "Driving Home for Christmas".

Nick regrouped and began anew. 'I was thinking we could try again. I know I said and did some things that hurt you. You know how I am with commitment, it's just me, I can't even commit to a favourite takeaway! Remember the trouble I had choosing between the Mandarin Garden and Golden Dragon?' He chuckled at his own poor joke, stopping when Natasha failed to join him. 'But that's all done with now. What do you think about giving things another go?'

Natasha knew exactly what she needed to do. She needed to say everything she had wanted to say in her head since he'd left her a sobbing mess on the floor of their living room the day before their wedding. Everything she had stewed over in the early hours of so many mornings when her eyes were raw from crying bitter, angry tears and her body ached with the grief of losing her future. She'd had a whole year to get this right in her mind; the triumphant speech when she saw him again, filled with dignified poise, steely resolve, retribution and girl power. She took a deep breath.

'I am not a flipping spring roll, you unutterable prick! How dare you come back here and call me baby as though you've never been away? How dare you even look at me with those eyes and say it was *probably* unforgivable? You left me to cancel our wedding, *the night before* the wedding, do you KNOW how embarrassing that is? How humiliating, and actually, Nick, how incon-bloody-venient? It took ages, and it's hard to explain yourself on the phone when you're pissed and you can't stop crying, and you keep snot bubbling on your phone ...' This was in danger of lacking the anticipated gravitas. Nick made to interject, but Natasha persevered.

'You don't get to come back into my life and call me baby, do you hear? You left me a complete and total mess. If it hadn't been for friends, if it hadn't been for Lauren and Dylan—' Natasha continued wildly. 'Lauren and Dylan helped put me back together again after you made a conscious decision to break me into pieces. You do not get to come back here and ask for my forgiveness. I don't forgive you! I hope you stew on this until the day you die, and I hope you're fat and bald by then, too.' Natasha was breathing heavily as she brushed her hair from her face. Nick was remarkably composed given the onslaught.

'Baby – Natasha.' He qualified, quickly. 'I'm so very sorry that I did that to you. It's the worst mistake I could've made. I am so happy you had mates around you to help. What we had was truly special and I think we could get it back. I thought, what better time than Christmas, right? Christmas was always our special time.' He seemed so sure of everything, so rehearsed and in control. 'I know I've given you a rough time, but it'll make us stronger. Jade was just a phase. I'm over it now. Why don't we just pretend this year didn't happen, pick up where we left off and—'

'No. Just no,' her voice was pure ice, and her eyes were dark with rage. 'No to all of it. No to forgiveness, no to forgetting, no to the lot. I stopped loving you a while back, but it took having you here in front of me to remind me what an arrogant, entitled wet wipe you really are. I'm going, don't contact me. Have a very crappy Christmas.'

Grabbing her handbag and swinging her coat around her shoulders with a flourish, Natasha left without pause, not even registering Nick's stupefied expression as he watched her go. As the cold air hit her, so did the enormity of her declaration. She bent almost double with her hand on her knees and inhaled deeply several times. It was done. A giggle escaped from her lips, and before she knew it, she was dancing around and punching the air like a crazy person, not caring that she might be seen. A few flakes of snow glistened in the streetlight as they fell and landed in her hair. Nick was gone – consigned to Christmas past, where he belonged, and where he couldn't hurt her anymore.

Right, she told herself. Time to get seizing.

Stave V – The End of it All.

"I will live in the Past, the Present, and the Future!" Scrooge repeated, as he scrambled out of bed. "The Spirits of all Three shall strive within me. Oh Jacob Marley! Heaven, and the Christmas Time be praised for this!"

By the time Natasha arrived back outside The Good Briton, a mini snowstorm had occurred, and her woollen coat was stuck about with snow, her cheeks red and her hair dishevelled. It was still early; he had to still be there, right? *Please let him still be there!* It should have been surprising how certain she was of her feelings, but it didn't feel like a surprise at all. Dylan had always been there, she had just been too busy worrying over Nick to feel what was now so blindingly obvious. Oh, please let him not have gone home, she couldn't wait to see him. What was surprising, though, was that her whole outlook on life had changed in minutes, in the blink of an eye; it felt as though much more time had passed. Natasha felt almost as though she should go full-on Ebenezer Scrooge, calling out to random boys in the street to ask what day it was. Giddily, she gazed around; no small boys to ask, but there was a gang of Dylan's Year Elevens hanging about on the corner. That would never do …

'Alright, Miss? Merry Christmas, have a good one.'

'Thanks … erm, Darren. Merry Christmas to you too.' She turned to go in.

'Cheers, Miss. Don't forget to, you know, honour Christmas, and keep it all the year.'

Natasha whirled round to face him in shock. Surely Dylan's bottom set student was not quoting actual Dickens to her?

'Very impressive, Darren, looks like Mr Richardson has you well trained. Any other little quotes you'd like to share?'

'Nah, Miss. I ain't read the book. I got that from the Muppets.'

Natasha entered the pub and headed straight for Dylan, who was seated with his back to the door. Why did she feel so much less certain what to say now? It had been relatively easy with Nick. This was new territory.

'Dylan, I …' He whirled around in surprise at the sound of her voice, and stood up to greet her. A grin spread across his face at the sight of her, but even as she smiled back, his smile was replaced with uncertainty, and he looked over her shoulder; was he wondering whether Nick was with her?

'You're back. Where's Nick? Are you … on your own?' Dylan's expression was intentionally neutral, but a whisper of emotion was visible below the surface.

'Well, yes. And no, hopefully. I mean, I am on my own, as in I came back on my own, but you know I was kind of hoping …' Natasha broke off, distracted momentarily by Lauren, who looked fit to burst with excitement, and was hopping from foot to foot in inebriated glee.

'Oh my Gawd, it's a Christmas Miracle!' Lauren called. She had clearly not slowed down on the wine since Natasha had left.

'It's done. It's all done.' Natasha continued, turning back to Dylan. She took off her coat, shook it, and placed it on the chair. She felt about three stone lighter, as though the coat had been made of lead.

'Already?' Dylan's eyebrows were raised in disbelief, but his tone couldn't hide an audible note of hope. She could understand his surprise; she was quite surprised herself.

'Already. Turned out, it's been done for ages – possibly even before Jade and the non-wedding of the year.' She couldn't keep the smile off her face, and inwardly, she danced a jig.

Dylan stayed silent as Lauren grabbed Natasha in an over-enthusiastic embrace, and then tottered to the bar in search of "celebration shots" that she would definitely regret in the morning. Once they were alone, he said quietly, 'Do you want to go for a walk?'

It was a blizzard outside, and the wind was whipping audibly at the windows of the cosy old pub. Here inside, the fires were lit, the lights were twinkling, there were celebration shots on order … Natasha smiled.

'I can't think of anything I'd rather do than walk with you.'

Dylan helped her into her coat; this time it didn't weigh her down. He reached out and took her hand in his, cradling it like it was something precious. A warmth seemed to glow at the point their hands met, and travelled up their arms like a spark of electricity. They made their way into the night. At the bar, Lauren saw them leave just as the shots were paid for. Chuckling, she rose a glass to their departing backs.

'God Bless us, everyone,' she said to no one in particular, before carrying the remaining drinks back to her colleagues. It was about time.

Michelle Harris

Christmas for Two

Marianne Calver

'That bloody cat has done it again, Cathy. Right in the middle of …' Peter trailed off, his foot poised in mid-air and one hand on the doorframe. Cathy had her back to him, but he could still read the signs. After almost four decades of marriage, he could read every sigh, every tiny gesture. His wife sat at the kitchen table, back rigid, shoulders high. The cat mess in the rose bed could wait, something was seriously wrong. He hurried round to sit beside her and put a grimy hand on hers as it rested on the table. He knew it must be something really bad because she didn't even admonish him for the trail of mud he left behind him.

'Rebecca.' Cathy glanced at the telephone she was still holding limply in one hand. 'Rebecca and Carl thought they would like to spend their first married Christmas alone. Just the two of them.' She looked at him miserably.

Peter was taken aback. This was not what he had expected. Was he supposed to be upset?

'Oh.' He cleared his throat. 'Oh, so, will they come over on Boxing Day then?'

'Of course they'll come on Boxing Day, Peter!' Cathy's eyes were bright and her neck bloomed suddenly red. 'But they won't be here for Christmas Day. And neither will Natalie.' She pursed her lips and inhaled deeply.

Peter floundered. 'So, it will just be the two of us for Christmas then? And the girls will join us on Boxing Day.' This was the wrong thing to say, of course. There had been a time, Peter reflected, when he always had the right words. "The gift of the gab," Cathy used to say. Now, he seemed to infuriate her with every word. He supposed, upon reflection that he maybe spent too much time talking about cat mess. But then, what else was there to talk about these days?

The chair scraped noisily across the tiled floor as Cathy stood abruptly.

'I'm going out.' She marched briskly across the room stopping briefly at the door to order, 'You can clean up that mud.'

The cold air caught the back of Cathy's throat as she marched down the street. She regretted not picking up a coat almost as much as she regretted putting on her high heeled court shoes which slipped on the wet pavement. Still, she would not slow down. She couldn't. *That man! Had he no heart at all? He didn't care that they would be spending Christmas without their daughters. Their own flesh and blood.* Cathy allowed her mind to wander back to the early stages of their relationship. Had there been signs then that Peter was incapable of emotion? He'd always had very bad fashion sense, but she didn't think that was an indicator of an empty heart. If anything, it was quite the opposite. He had embraced the ridiculous fashions of the '70s with the same exuberance he had embraced her. She shook the smile away before it had time to take root. Where was that exuberance now? Down in the mud with the cat mess, that's where.

The white-grey sky hung as low as her mood over the roofs of Cable Cottages: five neat little buildings that had once housed farmworkers but were now home to several touristy shops which signalled the entrance to the village. Cathy realised with a start that she was walking to Rebecca's house. *Well, that wouldn't do at all.* She turned, uncertain for a moment of where to go next and her eyes were drawn to the window of the first shop, Bale and Jay. The sign, neatly painted above the small window, claimed that it had been there "since 1802" although Cathy suspected that if that were the case there had been a significant change in wares over the years. She couldn't imagine much call for "Live, Love, Laugh" signs, or paintings of improbably colourful cows in years gone by. For that matter, she didn't see much call for them now. Still, the twinkling fairy lights and twee little elves drew her nearer, until her eyes settled on a rustic sign. "Don't Get Mad, Get Better" it instructed. *Humph!*

*

Cathy had been gone just long enough for Peter to clean the floor and start to think about making dinner. He stood before the open fridge, head to one side. He could rustle up an omelette, but that hardly seemed sufficient. Before retirement, Peter had imagined that it was lack of time that prevented him from cooking up a storm in the kitchen. He was slightly abashed to concede that lack of knowledge and inclination also played a significant role. *Still, there's no time like the present to learn a new skill.* Rolling up his sleeves, Peter crossed the kitchen to Cathy's cookery books. No, he corrected himself, our cookery books.

'I'm a modern man,' he told the empty room.

So it was that when Cathy returned just a short while later, she was greeted by the smell of Delia's Country Chicken and the messiest kitchen she'd seen since the girls had decided to make scrambled eggs as "a breakfast surprise" twenty-five years before.

'What on earth?!'

'Hi love,' Peter had flour on his nose and what looked like onion in his hair. 'I thought I'd cook tonight. Give you a break.'

Seeing her hesitate in the doorway and taking in her ice flushed cheeks he added, 'Why don't you have a bath? Everything's under control here.'

She looked calmer now, at least. Although he didn't fully understand why, Peter knew that his wife was upset about Christmas. *Was it because she would miss the girls? Surely not, they would all be together the following day.* His heart raced slightly at the other alternative. *She doesn't want to spend Christmas with me.*

*

Cathy stared into the darkness. Peter had been snoring more or less since his head hit the pillow. Must have been the exertion of all that cooking. She had to concede it had been a good meal, and it was nice for someone else to do the cooking. It was nice for Peter to do the cooking. She had walked off most of her anger and the rest had melted away in the warmth of the bath. Now she felt, well she wasn't really sure, but she certainly couldn't sleep.

A sudden screech startled her out of her reflection. Lord, it sounded like a murder. *Must be the cats.* She padded over to the window in time to see two black shapes streak across the garden. Cathy liked cats. So had Peter, before the gardening obsession. He would be furious if he knew that she left food out for them behind the shed. But that skinny little black one looked like it hadn't been fed for weeks so what else could she do? It was looking much healthier now, she thought with satisfaction.

Reaching out, she put her hand on the glass and watched the warmth of her breath spread in a white fog on the dark pane. 'Don't Get Mad, Get Better,' she whispered. We'll just have our Christmas celebration on Boxing Day, she decided, the girls will have to have Christmas dinner two days in a row; but mine will be the best! Creeping back to bed, Cathy smiled as she leaned in to Peter and allowed his gentle snores to lull her to sleep.

The following morning Peter had taken a little time to get to grips with the plan.

'So will we need two turkeys?'

'Whatever for?!' She'd laughed. 'We can eat any old thing on Christmas Day, that's not important.'

Too late, she'd registered the hurt in his eyes. Now they sat silently brooding over their tea and porridge.

'Would you like some cinnamon?' It was a paltry peace offering but he accepted it so eagerly Cathy felt a sudden pang of guilt. She picked up the brown sugar too, to ease her conscience, and put it lightly on the table.

'Thanks love,' he said softly. He was such a gentle man. It was one of the things that had first drawn her to him all those years ago. A warm glow sparked in her chest and she started. It had been so long since she'd felt anything but irritation at Peter, it was almost a surprise to remember that she loved him. Resuming her seat opposite him, Cathy made a decision.

'Peter, would you help me with the Christmas preparations this year?'

*

Peter hummed along to the radio as he drove back through the village. Occasionally he hit the same note as the singer, and he even knew some of the words. Glancing up at the green needles that nodded down at him from the roof, he smiled to himself. Cathy was going to be thrilled with this tree. She'd wanted the biggest one he could get, and this was a beast of a tree. Everything was to be big this year, the tree, the turkey, the gifts.

Christmas was usually Cathy's job. Returning home from work on Christmas Eve, Peter would find the house looking festive, presents wrapped and food prepared, as if by magic. It hadn't been magic though, it had been the product of an infinite amount of hard work on Cathy's part. Peter marvelled that she had previously done all this by herself. This year, Cathy had shared out the roles; she would be in charge of the cake, presents and cooking, he had been trusted to get the turkey and the tree. They would decorate the house together; an activity Peter found he was rather looking forward to.

Cathy had been much warmer towards him since they had begun their joint Christmas preparations. He was slightly concerned that she was getting carried away, but at least he had managed to persuade her against hiring a donkey. 'I suppose it might be a bit chilly out there,' she had conceded. There was still the threat of the choir, but he tried not to think about that, pushing it to the back of his mind along with thoughts of the other schemes Cathy had come up with. He couldn't help but be impressed by her inventiveness which was apparently limitless, but for now, he wanted to savour the contentment of knowing things were improving.

As he pulled onto the driveway, a pretty black cat ran in front of the car, narrowly avoiding being hit. *Was that supposed to be good luck or bad?* The front door opened, and Cathy stood silhouetted in the frame. At first, he thought she had opened the door to greet him, to welcome the returning hero and admire the magnificent tree. Then he saw the hand on the hip and as he opened the car door and stepped out, he registered the pursed lips.

'Hi love,' he said, uncertainly.

'Don't you "love" me, Peter Hennerson,' she snapped. 'The turkey has arrived.'

Peter hovered on the doorstep. He supposed he should leave the tree on the car for the time being.

'What's the matter? Is it not big enough?'

Cathy's eyebrows appeared to make a momentary bid for freedom via the top of her forehead.

'Oh, it's big enough, Peter,' she said through teeth that were clenched so tightly he wondered how she could form words at all. 'When you ordered the turkey, Peter, what exactly did you order?'

'Well, I ordered a turkey. A large turkey.'

'And there were no other options, Peter?'

'Well, there were a whole load of extras, but I didn't see the point of paying for all that.'

'In amongst "all that", Peter, do you recall any of the extras being "to kill the bird"?'

'Oh no!' Realisation dawned in a stomach dropping instant.

'Oh yes!' She strode through the house and flung open the back door. He heard it before he saw it; a low, gobbling sound.

'Nooo!'

'Yes, Peter! Look what you've done!'

The turkey seemed oblivious to the less than warm welcome. It strutted across the lawn towards them and they stepped back in unison, Cathy instinctively grasping a handful of Peter's shirt as she hunched behind him.

'I'll get on the phone,' he managed.

'No!'

'Why on earth not?'

'They'll kill it if we send it back.'

'Isn't that what you wanted?'

'Well, yes, but not now I've seen it.'

Peter felt himself wilt under the icy weight of Cathy's disapproval. He doubted if even the tree of trees would be enough to get him out of the bad books after this.

*

They stood side by side at the kitchen sink, gazing out at their unexpected visitor, afraid to let her out of sight lest she should escape. In any case, they could not have sat down at the table even if they had wanted to, swamped as it was with mounds of felt and ribbon. Cathy was glad of the excuse to turn her back on it. How had her perfect Christmas spiralled so out of her control? As she had allowed herself to get swept away on a heady tide of Christmas planning, a niggling question had scratched at the back of Cathy's mind. 'Who is this for? Who is it for? Who is it all for?' The answer had revealed itself on the front page of the local newspaper: NOT JUST FOR CHRISTMAS.

The article was accompanied by sad photographs of some of the residents at the local animal rescue. Cathy had thought about the little black cat in the garden and picked up the phone. It was only when she registered the surprise in the voice of the volunteer on the other end of the line that an uneasy feeling started to form in her stomach. But it was too late to go back now. And Cathy felt sure that making stockings for the animals at the rescue was a good idea. Wasn't it?

She flinched as she remembered Natalie howling with laughter on their most recent telephone call. 'How many stockings are you making? Twenty-seven? The cats and dogs I can almost get on board with but what on earth do you put in a Christmas stocking for a tortoise, Mam?'

Cathy chewed her lip anxiously, wondering if she had made a mistake. Cathy started. She had been so deep in thought she hadn't noticed that Peter was on the phone.

'Great Derek, thanks, I really owe you one.'

Looking up at him enquiringly, she saw his eyes flicker briefly to the table and then away as he said, 'Yes, that would be a really good idea. Thanks Derek.' He took a swig of tea. 'See you shortly then.'

'I've called in the cavalry,' he replied to the question in her eyes.

'Derek's not going to kill her, is he?' Her hand flew to her chest.

'No!' He gave a low chuckle. 'We're going to build a coop!' His eyes flickered once more to the table and before she could question him further, he added 'Joan's coming too.'

Ordinarily, Joan's imminent arrival would have been good news. Friends since Cathy and Peter had moved to the village, they'd supported each other through teething babies, first days of school and the teenage years. Joan knew Cathy better than anyone else, maybe even better than Peter, and today that could be problematic. Cathy glanced at the table. Would she have time to tidy away before they arrived? Her heart sank at the chime of the doorbell. She allowed Peter to answer the door, heard him direct Derek to the side gate, and the front door close. Maybe Joan hadn't come.

Swift, bouncy steps in the hallway crushed that hope.

'Hi Cath. Oh Lord! What is going on here?'

*

Derek had arrived with armfuls of wood, some chicken wire and an iPad.

'Thought we could have a look on The Google,' he said tapping the screen. 'Get an idea of dimensions. Then it's just a box really, isn't it?'

Having decided on dimensions ('Says here: turkeys are sociable animals. We'd best make it big enough for two.'), the men set to work; Peter measuring and sawing, Derek screwing and fixing. They had worked together on enough DIY jobs to know where their strengths lay. Focusing entirely on the task at hand, Peter felt a sense of calm wash over him. The rhythmic chug of the saw as he pulled it back and forth through the wood soothed his nerves. He inhaled the smell of the sawdust deep into his lungs, exhaling slowly through his mouth, clouds of dragons' breath floating through the air, back towards the house. He paused for a moment to watch.

'Garden's looking good, Peter,' observed his friend.

It was, Peter knew. There was no room for the bleak grey of winter here. Pansies sprinkled the beds with rich purples and defiant yellows and poured themselves out of the tubs like waterfalls. The winter jasmine climbed merrily up the wall, bright spots of yellow visible from the house as he'd planned. And the winter roses, white and graceful, nodded their heads like ballerinas in the breeze. He had worked hard on the garden since his retirement. Cathy had been insistent that they should have separate interests so that he should not get under her feet when he no longer had his job to occupy him. He had thrown himself wholeheartedly in to tending the garden. There was always something to do, some bed that needed weeding, or a plant that needed pruning. Sometimes, Peter would simply kneel and push his fingers through the soil, allowing the smell of the earth to ground him. He had thought perhaps Cathy might join him, but she rarely did.

'I'm worried about Cathy,' he said, regretting it almost instantly. He and Derek talked about gardens and DIY and what they'd seen on TV. They did not discuss their wives. Or their feelings. Yet now that he had begun, Peter found he couldn't stop, or perhaps didn't want to. 'I'm worried about Cathy and me.'

To his credit, Derek only blustered very slightly. 'What do you mean? You're ok, aren't you?' He cleared his throat.

Peter scuffed the grass with his foot, watching it bounce back into place around his shoe. 'Things are different now.'

Lady Cluck stalked over and allowed Peter to ruffle her slightly on the head.

'Since I stopped working, I feel I'm always in her way. Unless I'm out here, but then she gets annoyed that I spend too much time on the garden.' He opened his arms wide to emphasise the point. 'And now all this Christmas stuff. I don't know what it's all about.'

Derek smiled, regaining his usual confident demeanour. 'Look, you're in a new situation. It just takes time to adjust. A marriage is like a garden.' He was clearly finding his stride now. 'It takes work if you want to make something of it.'

Peter nodded briefly at his friend's wisdom. He wasn't afraid of a bit of hard work.

*

The industrious sounds of sawing and hammering competed with the kettle, providing a welcome delay to the conversation. Cathy fussed with the cups on the worktop while Joan wordlessly pinned together the pieces of stockings. She had been uncharacteristically quiet as Cathy had explained the situation. With a click, the kettle announced that her reprieve had ended, but still Cathy remained silent.

'Here's what we'll do,' said Joan, who had never been one to sit quietly. 'I'll send a message to the ladies. Between us, we'll have these made in no time. And if we each buy a few bits we can fill them too.'

More Than Mistletoe

Cathy had considered contacting her friends at the WI when she'd first discovered what a task she had taken on, but she had held back. They might judge. They might think she'd gone mad. They might realise she was trying desperately to fill some unfathomable void with felt and satin and kind deeds. But as was so often the case, Joan was right. She could not hope to get this done without help. Joan was already tapping away on her phone. She had taken some sort of technology course at the library and was quite as au fait with it all as the youngsters were.

'Now,' she looked up as she pressed send. 'Let's talk about the real issue, shall we?'

Cathy paused behind the fridge door and wondered how long she could feasibly stay there. Reluctantly she walked away, pouring the milk with her back to her friend. 'Biscuit?'

'No, I'll have a mince pie though.' Joan nodded towards the oven, 'They smell amazing.'

'Oh yes, they're for Rebecca to give out after the Christmas concert tomorrow. There are plenty though. Do you want one from the tin or the oven?' Cathy wondered if she might be able to distract Joan with mince pies for the duration of her stay. Maybe she could share her recipe. She'd tweaked it a bit this year and thought it was her best yet.

As they sat together with teas and warm mince pies nestled in the spaces Joan had managed to clear, Cathy knew there was no more putting it off. She took a bite of pie to postpone the inevitable just a little longer. It really was delicious, but she struggled to enjoy it as Joan stared intently at her. Sighing, Cathy placed the pie delicately on the plate, rubbing her fingers together to sprinkle the crumbs like snowflakes on the plate. 'How do you do it, Joan? You and Derek? You make it look easy.'

Joan smiled, 'What do you mean?'

'Well, live together!'

'You have lived with Peter for quite some time, Cathy.' Her friend pointed out, 'But things have changed a bit, that's all.' She reached over and squeezed Cathy's hand. 'You can adapt. You've been through big changes before. We both have, haven't we? Giving up work for the kids, finding our way at the school, seeing the kids off to uni and work. The only difference this time is that Peter is experiencing it all too.'

Cathy pushed the crumbs around her plate, her fingernail a snowplough. That was the problem, she realised. All of the other big changes in her life had largely passed Peter by, cushioned as he was by his work. She had found her way, forging her own paths through life as a new mother, making friends, joining groups. She had entrenched herself in the community and found her sense of self largely independently. Now Peter had crashed into her carefully curated life, and she resented it. A hot tear appeared unbidden and teetered dangerously on her lashes. She was shutting him out, she knew it. This time they had to find their way together, otherwise, they would completely drift apart.

*

It was almost dark by the time Peter and Derek came in from the garden, having created, even if they did say so themselves, something of a turkey haven. Warm, cinnamon-scented air caressed their cold faces and peals of laughter mingled with the Christmas music that drifted from the dining room. Peter tried to recall when he had last heard Cathy laugh. Too long, he thought.

He poked his head around the door. 'Evening ladies!' The room was full of women and Christmas stockings and sherry glasses.

'Peter!' Cathy sashayed across the room, grabbing the sherry bottle as she went. 'Have a festive sherry with us.' She rested a warm hand on his chest, and he felt it all the way through to his heart.

'Is the turkey all safe in her new home?' She looked up at him, her pale blue eyes ever so slightly unfocused.

'Yep, Lady Cluck seems very happy with her digs. Terry from the farm is dropping round some hay and food any minute now. And, if you're sure, he'll bring a friend for her ladyship too.'

'Yes, yes.' She waved a hand. 'Good name too.' She nodded her approval.

'We know where to come for eggs,' said one of the ladies, slightly too loudly, from across the room. He thought her name was Cheryl, or possibly Shirley. Peter smiled and allowed himself to be drawn into the room, accepting the very full sherry glass Cathy pressed into his hand. They hadn't had company like this since his retirement. Probably even longer. It was strange really. With the girls grown up and moved out, they had more freedom than ever, but they hadn't taken advantage of it. The holidays they had dreamed of went untaken, long walks, pub lunches, all went the same way, into a box labelled *Do Not Open*. Beside him, Cathy laughed at something Derek had said and Peter felt a spark of hope that this might be the start of the life they had planned.

Eventually, they all left, some more willingly than others, but with the last bottle of sherry drained even Cheryl/Shirley, who turned out to be called Sheila, decided it was time to call it a night. Terry had delivered the goods as promised, checking that Lady Cluck was indeed a lady before leaving her friend, now named Madame Aviary, behind. Satisfied that they were locked safely in their new home, Peter returned to the house to find Cathy dancing in the kitchen, tea towel in one hand, sherry glass in the other.

'Oh! Come and dance with me, Peter!'

Taking the glass from her hand and placing it safely on the table, Peter put a hand on her waist. He remembered the first time they had danced together. It had been at Tony's Disco and a live band was playing. He couldn't remember their name, but they had done a decent cover of "Love Me Do", which had given Peter all the excuse he'd needed to ask Cathy to dance. The room was hot and sticky, and Peter fleetingly worried that she would be put off by his sweaty hands. But the moment he held her, all worries were forgotten. It was like the answer to a question he didn't know he had asked. Four decades later, as he swayed with her in their kitchen, Peter felt something similar. A peace seemed to flow into him from the places where their bodies touched. He wondered if she could feel it too. According to the guy crooning on the radio, it was beginning to look a lot like Christmas.

Peter hummed into Cathy's hair, and she giggled. 'You don't know the words, do you?'

'Of course, I do!' he said in mock indignation. 'La di la di store.' He stood still listening for a phrase he recognised, throwing his head back and singing with enthusiasm if not melody, 'Christmas once more.' Then he swooped her up and swung her around.

'Peter, stop! You'll do us both an injury!'

'We're sixty, not one hundred!' He grinned, but put her down anyway. He had felt a slight twinge in his lower back.

The DJ introduced the next song, a Johnny Mathis number. 'Crickey, that takes me back a bit! Oh, this is the perfect song for me!'

She nudged him slightly, 'There are words in a minute you know.'

But he was already swept up in the moment 'Ahh, Ahh, Ahhhhh. Come on, you join in. Don't be shy!'

Cathy threw back her head, singing with gusto. She was unaware of him gazing at her, taken in by the sparkle of her eyes. He could still see the face of the girl he had fallen in love with although now it was framed with the years they had shared. He knew she wouldn't believe him if he told her that she was more beautiful now than ever, so he kept it to himself.

*

Marianne Calver

When Cathy woke the next morning, it was to a faint taste of stale sherry and a sense of contentment that she hadn't felt for a long time. Stretching under the covers she closed her eyes to savour the warmth that spread from her chest. They were going to put up the decorations today. Rebecca had offered to come and help but Cathy decided to turn her down. This would be the perfect opportunity to build a new tradition with Peter. Anyway, tonight was the Christmas concert at the church so Rebecca would be busy. From an early age, their youngest daughter had shown a talent for music that seemed to have come from nowhere. For the past three years, she had taken charge of the carol service at the church, leading the choir, choosing the music, sometimes even making her own musical arrangements. Cathy would arrive early to ensure a seat on the front pew. She opened her eyes, reaching for her phone to call Rebecca.

'Good morning my beautiful wife!' Peter walked in with a tray of tea and warm buttered crumpets.

'Good morning!' she pushed herself up in the bed, propping a pillow behind her. 'This is a nice surprise.'

'Well, you deserve it!' He beamed. He seemed so proud that she didn't have the heart to voice her observation that the last time he had made her breakfast in bed was the day after she had given birth to Rebecca. Once every thirty years is still better than nothing, she thought.

Peter slid under the covers and took a crumpet from the plate. 'I've been out and checked on the girls.'

'I can tell! Your feet are freezing!' She wiggled her feet away from his. 'Do you think they might be too cold out there?'

'According to the internet, turkeys are pretty hardy, and do well in cold weather. I could fetch some more hay from the shed though if you think it will help.'

'Not now, do it after breakfast.'

Cathy hummed to herself in the shower. 'A ray of hope,' she sang with a smile. Yes, that's what she felt, hope. As she dried her hair, she didn't hear Peter enter the bedroom. She saw his face, ashen, behind her in the mirror and she spun around.

'Cathy, you need to come quickly.' He was out of breath.

She rushed down the stairs after him. 'It's not the turkeys, is it? Have the foxes got in?'

'No, no, they're fine.'

She slipped on the shoes she kept near the back door and hurried out, following him down to the shed. Had he found the cat food? Surely that wouldn't warrant this sort of reaction. Holding the shed door open, Peter gestured inside, holding his hand up and whispering, 'Easy does it.'

Cautiously, Cathy stepped into the shed. This was Peter's domain. She was surprised at how neat it was. There were shelves along the wall and hooks at the back, it smelt of wood and varnish and soil, a bit like Peter these days, she smiled. She glanced around, trying to spot something out of place. Then she heard it. A faint mewing. Her eyes followed the sound down to the bundle of hay that Terry had dropped off the day before.

'Oh,' she breathed. The little black cat lay in the hay looking up at her as two tiny balls of fluff nestled into her. Cathy sank slowly to her haunches, holding a shelf to aid her creaking knees.

'Hello,' she breathed. 'Hello, little ones.'

They had stayed transfixed by the new life in front of them, until a gust of cold air blew into the shed. Cathy stood abruptly.

'We can't leave them here. They'll freeze!' She started to look around the shed, stepping slowly, careful not to startle them.

Peter smiled, knowing probably before she did what was about to happen. Cathy had grown up with animals and insisted that the girls should do the same. They'd had the usual, hamsters, rabbits, guinea pigs and, inevitably, Cathy was the one who took care of them, who loved them. Her heart was an unending well of love, he thought. He lifted a crate from the shelf above her.

'Will this do?'

'Perfect! Now, we have to get them in without scaring the mother.'

'Why don't we put some food in there and let her find her own way in? Then we can lift the babies,' Peter suggested. Cathy froze almost imperceptibly, then turned stiffly towards him, gradually lifting her eyes to his. He allowed himself just a moment to revel in their shared understanding that he had caught her out.

'I didn't mind you putting the food out, you know, I just didn't like the flower beds being used as a toilet.'

'We'll have to get a litter tray then,' she said quickly, then gasped, having given herself away. 'I mean ...'

'We're keeping them then, are we?' He grinned. 'We'll have quite the menagerie.'

'Well, we'd better have mother checked at the vet and they can tell us if she has an owner. I don't think she does though. She's a poor little thing, isn't she?' Cathy bustled off to find her secret stash of cat food.

Peter squatted down as the mother gazed up at him with wide green eyes. She didn't seem frightened. He resisted the urge to reach out and touch the soft fur that stood up in spikes between her ears. The kittens were suckling now, and he marvelled at how they knew instinctively what to do, even with their eyes tight shut.

Cathy emerged from the house with a bowl of cat food, a blanket, and the phone tucked under her chin. "Vet," she mouthed, as she handed him the bowl. He placed it in the crate along with the blanket, then stepped back. As the kittens finished their suckling, the mother tentatively sniffed the food and followed her nose into the crate. The walk to the house had never seemed so long. Holly, as they were now calling her, did not like the box being moved. She hissed, the fur on her neck standing up, ears pushed back.

'Put something over the top, Peter. Is there a lid?'

'I've no hands free, Cathy. Grab that bit of wood there.'

They stumbled together down the garden, walking as slowly as possible.

'Easy does it, easy does it.'

'Slow down!'

Lady Cluck and Madame Aviary stood watching attentively, gobbling their own advice. Eventually, the cats and crate were settled in the front room on a rug Cathy had insisted Peter bring down from the loft. They sat on the sofa, staring at the sleeping cats. Peter smiled as Cathy's fingers laced with his.

'Can we really keep them, Peter?' She sounded like a child on Christmas morning. Didn't she know he would do anything to make her happy?

'Vet seems to think so.' He grinned.

*

Cathy sat in the armchair, her arm draped over the side so that she could reach Holly. The cat was understandably taken up with caring for her babies, but she would tolerate a head rub while they slept. Cathy was gratified by the deep purr that swelled from Holly's throat. It made the upheaval of the last few days completely worth it. A great deal of time had been spent cat watching, and Peter had needed to prise her away, first to attend the carol service, then to decorate the house. The tree was without its twinkling lights this year, as she'd thought the kittens might be scared. Surprisingly, Peter had been quite as taken with the cats as she was, even waking in the night to check on them. He also took care to spend time outside with the turkeys "so they don't feel they've been usurped". She loved seeing this softer side to him. It felt that, as they opened their hearts to the animals, they found space there for each other as well. The sound of the key in the lock broke through her quiet thoughts. Peter had finally got out to the supermarket to replace the turkeys they wouldn't eat for one they would.

'It's freezing out there,' he said, leaning in to kiss her with icy lips. 'How are the babies?'

'They're fine.' She smiled, following him to the kitchen where he had started unpacking the shopping on to the table.

'They only had a small turkey crown,' he said apologetically. 'But I've picked up some gammon as well.' He brandished the joint in the air before setting it down beside the turkey. Cathy was impressed, he'd done better than she'd expected. But the bag was still bulging. *What had he done now?*

'What do you have there?'

'Ah, well, I just saw this. They had a special deal. I thought it looked good – it's called "Christmas for Two". All this for a tenner.' He began pulling items from the bag at speed. 'It's just, well, it won't be anywhere near as good as your Christmas dinner, but I thought it might be nice for Christmas Day.' He seemed nervous, vulnerable, and Cathy suddenly wanted to wrap her arms around him. She saw through all the tiny annoyances to the kind, gentle, patient man she had fallen in love with. Reaching out her hand, she allowed a smile to warm them both.

'Yes,' she said, 'Christmas for Two sounds perfect.'

Marianne Calver

August in December

Joe Burkett

My Heart Still Aches for You

My heart still aches for you. I hope you know that, I think to myself as I approach the too-familiar hospital doors. Every fibre of my body is screaming at me to run the other way. With every ounce of determination, I strive forward, focusing my attention on my hobbling friend who is currently using my left arm as a crutch.

"It's beginning to look a lot like Christmas" is playing; the warm dulcet tones of Michael Bublé warble over the hospital radio station, while I rub my clammy hands against my tailored Tom Ford suit. Adjusting my signature brooch gifted to me by my friend and mentor, "Wedding Guru Franc" – I side-shuffle Amelia through the doors of A&E. Well, I have news for you Michael; it's beginning to look a lot like an episode of Casualty.

'Sit there and don't fall … again!' I order Amelia.

'Psssht, you!' She snorts, in defiance of me and my sensibilities. 'Giving out like it's my fault we ended up here.'

Amelia sways like a demented Bambi finding his feet as she attempts to navigate a landing on one of the plastic, grey seats in the waiting area. You know the ones – not one bit comfortable. You're only guaranteed two things: a long wait and haemorrhoids. Whatever injury you may have suffered, you can be sure that if you end up in A&E, it's going to be TB or pneumonia that'll finish you off because his place is like a freezer. I can feel the head cold taking root as I make my way to the reception desk.

'I'll go and check us in.'

'It's A&E, not a five-star resort.' Amelia takes out her phone. No doubt updating her IG followers. All fifty of them. Bless her, she thinks she's going to be an influencer! Pity, she's more of an under-the-influencer!

My teeth are chattering but I attempt to smile at the sad little Christmas tree perched on the desk. It's one of those ones that lights up – no decorations needed. I mean, what's the point of a tree if you're not going to decorate it?

A round shaped woman approaches me. Her face looks like a map mixed with wrinkles and potholes. I think it could register on a Sat Nav. Please turn left to avoid scowl. Her lack of a wedding ring is giving off spinster vibes along with the whiff of something else. The smell is a cross between talc, body odour and desperation. Definitely, she is a spinster. And she is wearing an expression that can only be described like a bulldog licking piss off a nettle.

I greet her with a 'Merry Christmas.'

Nurse Face Ache replies with a scowl. She is without doubt a package that will be sent back unopened!

My usual charm isn't going to work on this old trout, so I decide to go full camp. 'It was a rogue stiletto, timed with a partner change during the Siege of Ennis that caused her to go over on her heel.' I deliver this with a flair of the dramatic, but Nurse Face Ache remains unimpressed. 'Her ankle blew up like Chernobyl.'

'How informative.' Her voice drips with disdain. 'I must add that to your friend's file.'

I notice her name badge, then, Nurse Face Ache thy name is *Joan*, and I make a mental note; this one has no sense of humour.

This is not how I imagined I would be spending my Christmas Eve, sitting in a hospital waiting room with drunken students, arguing spouses and ambulance chasers. Not forgetting, Ms Hop-Along herself who has just informed me that she has gained two new followers. Well, I've got a hook for her followers because Joan has just told me we could be waiting up to six hours for an X-ray.

"Have yourself a merry little Christmas" begins to play and my heart skips a beat. In the blink of an eye, my mind is racing. Images of *you* invade my thoughts like a firework display on a dark, winter night. Flashing colours of neon lights expose our life together and the cruel way that it was cut short. I press my lips together tightly fighting back the lump in my throat. My hands are clammy again. I pat them against my jacket and fight the tears welling up in my eyes.

My hand automatically moves to my heart – the place you're still alive. It's thumping so wildly I fear it will jump out of my chest any moment now. I need to change my train of thought before this track takes me back to my never-ending grief, but the ominous feeling of being back *here*, in the place where I lost you, is overwhelming me. I need to remove myself from the situation – practice my breathing techniques: deep inhale, and exhale slowly, allowing the mind to clear all thoughts.

Amelia looks up at me while chatting on her phone. I must look like shite because she covers the speaker to ask:

'Are you having an asthma attack? Cause if you are … you're in the right place!' It's a glib comment, but I know she's trying to distract me with humour, and I love her for trying.

'No, I'm not.' Talking aloud helps ground me in the present. 'Who are you talking to?'

'Clarissa, she has officially "got everything under control." Her words not mine! She says, "don't panic, everything is running like clockwork" Again, her words not mine!'

'Let me talk to her.' This is what I need right now, to throw myself into work.

"Bridesmate Knows Best" is my baby, my wedding planning business. I've won several "One Fab Day" awards, and I'm recognised as one of the leading wedding specialists in the industry. I hope I don't lose face after Amelia's antics earlier. She hit the dancefloor harder than Gemma Collins on Dancing on Ice. Clarissa is extremely diligent at her job and the DJ was about to start, so I was happy to take Amelia to the hospital.

The drive to the hospital was pretty uneventful apart from thinking-twice about a detour to McDonalds. We decided medical aid far outweighed our growling stomachs. Thankfully, according to Clarissa everything is fine so I can breathe easy. Well, not too easy, but I don't want Amelia thinking I'm having another attack.

I hand Amelia her phone back and there, I can see it in her eyes; she knows. Even though I thought I had hidden my moment well, I can't hide my feelings from my best friend. I take a seat beside her. Her voice is frail as she puts her hand on my leg. I take her hand in mind and I try to smile softly. But I am betrayed by the tears I've been fighting.

'Ben, let's just go.' Her voice is soft with sympathy for me. 'Honestly, I'm fine. Never mind the Siege of Ennis, I could dance the Riverdance for ya!'

'We're here now,' I croak. 'Don't worry about me. Let's get you sorted, and afterwards–'

Joe Burkett

'I'll treat you to McDonald's!'

I smile – she knows the way to my heart is food.

A more comfortable silence falls between us. At least I can relax a little, now that I know the wedding is being looked after and my record for nuptial success is untarnished.

The peace of mind doesn't last long as paramedics rush through the doors with a stretcher. The flashing lights of the ambulance outside fill the room, and the sirens and shouts of emergency instructions fill the air. The panic returns – my chest tightens, my breath catches, and the pain of that night comes rushing back, much worse than before.

I'm losing you all over again.

But, as if by some Christmas miracle, something catches the corner of my eye, momentarily distracting me from the medical drama.

That's when I see *him*.

I Haven't Looked at Anyone, Since You

'Hello, I'm Dr Knight.'

Without taking any notice of the Grey's Anatomy scene playing out in the waiting room, he ushers us into a cubicle and introduces himself. He doesn't even glance up from his case files. Clearly, unlike me, he is well versed with such emergencies.

There he is; Dr Knight, wearing a bright red Santa hat with the body of a Greek god, striking blonde hair like a young Kurt Russell, and a voice as deep as Morgan Freeman – I know it's physically impossible but I think I might be pregnant!

'My foot is fit to fall off.' Amelia grimaces in pain. She clearly hasn't taken the time to appreciate the fine thing that is standing before us.

Maybe that is for the best because Dr Dishy is 100% gay and he has been ever since I shifted the face off him when we were in secondary school.

'It's not …' Finally, he notices me. 'It can't be … Ben Walsh?'

'It is, indeed.' I sit down next to Amelia, totally stealing her foot's thunder. I joke: 'I'm ready for my examination, doctor.'

Amelia's eyes flit back and forth between us. 'Do you two know each other?'

'Yes, we do. August, this is Amelia.' I gesture to her, and then before I can stop myself, the flirt in me comes out. 'Amelia, this is the very handsome August.'

More Than Mistletoe

August laughs at my quip and adjusts his shirt collar. His temperature must be raising as much as the mercury in my thermometer. I think I've embarrassed him – his cheeks blush rose-red just like they did so many years ago when we shared our first kiss. And what a kiss it was. Some guys use a lot of tongue, like a washing machine on a spin cycle in your mouth – but not August. He was soft and tender. I may have been leading him astray, but he was a willing follower.

Guilt washes over me. I haven't looked at anyone since you. I don't know what to do. Why am I thinking about August like this?

August's smile distracts me from my thoughts of you – it's wide and full of pearly whites, reaching all the way up to his blue eyes. It's infectious; I'm smiling too. And for the first time since I lost you, I realise I want to smile at him like this. The smile that signals there's something more to the interaction than professional friendliness or old friends reconciling.

Our eyes are drawn to each other. His blue eyes pierce my soul. A soul so willing to heal. Is my shattered heart willing to love again, too?

God, How Time Changes Things

I join August at his request for a cup of coffee, and to take a look at the Remembrance Tree. It is a large Christmas tree in the foyer of the hospital where handmade decorations are placed on it as way of remembering our dearly departed loved ones. I'm going to place a decoration there for you, Evan. I feel my heart start to swell as I think of another Christmas without you. Focus, I need to change my focus, so I ask August about Amelia.

'I hope Amelia will be okay. Her foot looked pretty painful.'

'I'll put it this way. I don't think she'll be dancing in the New Year.' The pair of us titter at this.

'My brother Forrest would have a field day if I told him I got lumbered with the Christmas Eve shift. I put my Christmas tree up the first of December, I attend every festive food market, and I'm part of a carolling group. Not that I can sing but y'know.' His expression softens and he whispers. 'We often joked that Mum should have called me December as I love the holiday season just as much as she did.'

August chats about his late mother, Liz and their shared love of Christmas. The joy they had picking out and wrapping Christmas presents, baking cookies and handmaking decorations for the tree. The pain of her passing is a part of him. His tone softens when speaks of her. I can see that her passing has left an indelible mark on him. Much akin to my own loss. Not that I would compare. But when you lose someone close to you, you can see a loss similar in their eyes. His eyes look distant when he speaks about his mother. It's like he's lost in his memory and allowing himself to drift away. I know what that feels like.

I drift away with you all the time.

'Losing Mum was the worst day of my life,' August says breaking me from my trance.
'I know the feeling. I lost my partner in a car accident. I still feel numb.'
The initial numbness I felt after your death made me feel like I was drowning. My head was being held under water by some unknown force. And I didn't fight back. I didn't try to kick my feet and push myself towards the surface. I knew what was waiting for me there. That pain I couldn't face. Not in the early days. I spent days curled up in our bed cradling one of your favourite shirts. I needed to feel you around me – the smell of your aftershave, your clothes hanging in the wardrobe. No one else mattered.
August clears his throat. 'Shall we talk about something more festive,' he says, bringing us back to the present.
'Wanna explain the Santa hat?'
August flicks the bell at the end of the hat, and it rings out merrily. 'I'm trying to spread a little Christmas cheer. Sue me!'
'I wouldn't say that too loudly. With the compensation culture in this country, they'd take the shirt off your back if you looked at them sideways.'
I feel my cheeks redden as I imagine a shirtless August. I swear, if I was menopausal, I would be having a hot flush right about now. His shirt clings to his physique with just a whisper of chest hair peeking out of the collar. I think I see a hint of a scar on his chest, but I can't be certain. It could be a tattoo. I'm way too squeamish to ever get a tattoo. And, those legs! That ass! Don't get me started on his rugby thighs. Christ, he could crack nuts with them – sure, I'd let him have a go at cracking mine!

I know you would appreciate him too if you were here.

'Crap!' August suddenly ducks his head, hiding behind his hands. 'Here comes Moany Joanie, on the warpath. She'll kill me for fraternizing with you.'
Walking towards us is the nurse from before, moving at a pace akin to a solider going to war on the front line.

'I know her, Nurse Face Ache at the front desk. She was pretty icy earlier.'

'Icy is right, she doesn't even like Christmas! Wish we could ship her off to the South Pole.'

'She probably just needs her South Pole ventilating, and she'll be grand.'

August spits out his coffee and it splashes all over the table. I howl with laughter as the unimpressed Moany Joanie walks by, her eyes scanning the situation through her glasses which are defying gravity like some mountain climber hanging off the side of a cliff. Christ, she has a big nose. Strange how I didn't notice that earlier. I could hang a line of washing on her nose and she wouldn't know it was there.

'Dr Knight.' She sounds like an old nun catching us out of class. 'I don't believe your shift has finished, and you're needed back in A&E.'

'My apologies,' August tries to look serious, but he keeps catching my eye and setting off the mirth again. 'I'm just catching up with a friend from school.'

'Medical school?' God, what a condescending witch.

'No, secondary school. We're very old friends.' August says this with such sincerity and warmth that my heart melts a fraction more. But did he really have to use the word "old".

'I see. How riveting.' She peeks over her giant nose and eyes me up like a butcher calling a turkey to the gallows. 'I do believe I met this very old friend earlier. He gave a very theatrical description of a leg wound.' Her huge nostrils flare disapprovingly. I wonder if the old prude is onto us. She turns to face August once more. 'When you've finished your little trip down memory lane, might you get back to the job you're being paid for?'

'Of course,' August says, flashing her a smile. God, he's so gracious – more polite than this wench deserves. 'I'll be right with you.'

August excuses himself from me and calls after Joan. God, she is such a cow. I overhear him explain that he's waiting for a patient to come back from X-ray and that he would like to personally review the results.

I can't take my eyes off him. He doesn't know how gorgeous he is. I like that. Is there anything worse than a guy who thinks he's all that? August isn't like that. He's so unaware of his attractiveness that it adds to his irresistible aura. If I'm dreaming, please don't wake me up.

God, how time changes things. The last time I thought I was dreaming and didn't want to wake up was when you passed away. And now, here I am, gazing dreamily at August. I don't want to betray you. I never have. Not once since I lost you, but with August something feels different.

I know him. But there is something more. And I can't put my finger on it. I'm in a world of my own thoughts as I clear up the table, and my heart skips a beat when August returns. 'Everything okay?' I ask, trying my best to sound nonchalant. 'Moany Joanie give you a hard time?'

'All good in the hood!' August takes the rubbish out of my hands and puts it in the bin. 'It's my last shift, anyway, what's she gonna do? Fire me?'

'Your last shift?' I can't hide the disappointment in my voice. I know I don't have the right to feel this way, but something is drawing me to August. Maybe it's the fact that he was my first kiss – or maybe it's the fact that I want him to be my first kiss again, in a way.

I haven't kissed anyone since you. I've not wanted to … Until now.

I'll Never Stop Talking to You

'The lighting of the tree was such a special day here. All the patients that were well enough to come down to the foyer, did, and the kids sang Christmas carols. I even joined in for one or two songs with my carolling group.' August speaks so passionately that it endears me to him even more. He explains how local school children handmade all of the decorations for the Christmas Remembrance tree; each decoration is dedicated to a patient dear to them who died over the years. 'It was really sweet. Do I sound like a sap?'

'I think it sounds lovely. I wish I could have been there. I would have hung a decoration for Evan.' My voice catches saying your name.

August stops in his tracks and his presence changes. I stop too, turning to face him. He places his hand on my upper arm and lightly squeezes it. His pulse surges through me. It feels so strange, almost electric. If I was a hopeless romantic, I might say it was chemistry. Okay, I *am* a hopeless romantic, but this feels impossibly familiar.

'*Evan* was your partner?' he asks gently. Yet, there is a knowing when he says your name.

'Yes, he died a little over seven years ago.' I still can't speak these words with any strength. 'I miss him every day … more so at Christmas. I'm sure you understand.'

'I totally get it. Mum's been gone seven years too. There's not a day that goes by that I don't think about her or talk to her. I talk to her all the time. Does that sound crazy?' He sounds bashful, and I rush to reassure him.

'Not a single bit.' I don't offer more than that – he doesn't need to know about my secret talks, not yet.

I'll never stop talking to you, my love.

We continue to the foyer of the hospital. I can't describe the feeling but in the silence it's like I can hear August's heart beating. It's like a drum and it's getting louder and louder as we get closer to the Christmas remembrance tree. The rhythm of the beat is one that I know. I've heard it before, and it's making my heart dance.

'You must miss your Mum very much,' I say, desperate to keep the conversation flowing.

'I can't describe the feeling of not having her here, with me.' He pauses, looking thoughtful. 'In a way, she's always with me. She's the reason I became a doctor.'

'Oh, why's that?'

'The day that she died; all the doctors, nurses, everyone tried so hard to save her. Those guys are heroes. And, I thought I want to do that. I want to help people.' He takes a moment to compose himself. 'I want to try my best to make sure that no one ever has to feel the pain that I felt.'

'That's admirable that you would do that in your mother's honour. Taking your loss and using it to help other people.' This isn't something I could ever have imagined doing after I lost *you*.

'They saved my life too, y'know. I was in the car with Mum when we crashed. I was in a pretty bad way. It was touch and go for a while if I was going to make it.'

My knees go weak listening to August. I reach for the wall beside me for strength. I think back to when I was told the news that it was touch and go if you would make it. Those words rang in my ears as I sat by your side, holding your hand, and praying to God that you would pull through. I made promise after promise, and it still didn't make a difference. I would have sold my soul to the devil for just one more minute with you.

In the end, neither answered my prayers.

'I had to have a heart transplant.' August continues, and I use his voice as a focus for my attention. Anything to stop the world spinning. 'They didn't think I would make it, but a heart became available. I guess I'm one of the lucky ones, but … I often think about the donor's family. They lost someone special to them and I lived. I've never been able to thank them.'

The lights from the Christmas tree illuminate the foyer, flickering and twinkling around the room like little fairies learning to take flight. The beauty of the enormous tree takes my breath away. August is staring at the tree like he's seeing it for the first time. I reach out to place my hand on his back, but he turns, suddenly, and it lands on his chest, right over his heart. A surge of energy races through my body and I gasp.

August looks equally startled.

With all my strength, I ask, 'What was *that?*'

Your Heart is Still Beating

The air around is electric as I hold my hand against August's chest. I can feel his heart beating. Your heart beating; I know that it is your heart, I can feel it.

Memories flood my mind as I float back to that day that I lost you forever. My aching and injured body had me in deep pain, but I found the strength to be with you. I had to be by your side so, I laid my head on your chest as the doctors and nurses spoke around us. My interest in what they had to say was fleeting at best. All I wanted was to be with you. I was already defying them by leaving my hospital bed to be with you. The sound of your heart was all that I needed to hear. What else was there to listen to? Occasionally, I would catch snippets of conversation, and I can still remember the numbness that flooded my body when they said that you were brain dead.

No. Not my Evan. He can't be. Your heart is still beating. I can hear it; I can feel it.

You were gone, though. I knew it deep down as I snuggled in close and wrapped my arms tightly around you. I needed to breathe you in. To remember your smell. The touch of your skin against mine. I think I was trying to squeeze you back to life. I couldn't allow myself to believe that you weren't there anymore.

They spoke about organ donation; you always carried your organ donor card with you. I knew it was important to you, but I couldn't let you go. As much as I tried to break away from you and allow the doctors to do what they needed to do, I couldn't bear to be away from you. You were my world.

I sobbed as they took you away from me. I physically felt my heart shatter into a thousand pieces. Amelia rushed to be my side and I fell to the ground in her arms. I clung to her so tightly and she held me close, promising me that everything would be okay. She didn't know it at the time, but she was lying. Nothing has been okay since you died.

'Evan will live on. His death isn't going to be in vain. He is going to help people, save people. You should be so proud of him.' Amelia held me close and rocked me like a baby in her arms.

Of course, I was proud of you. I always have been, but that didn't stop the rage building up deep inside of me as she explained that victims from the pile-up were in the hospital. Your organs might help them stay alive. I shook my head. I couldn't bear to think of other people getting anything belonging to you. Why did they get to live when you had to die? It wasn't fair.

August moves away from me. My hand falls from his chest, and my memory is broken.

'Did you feel that?' August whispers.'

'I did.' I can barely get the words out.

My hand is trembling. I'm numb: frozen to the spot. August moves away, towards the tree but I can't move. My feet have taken root. I want to scream at him to come back. I want to plead with him to let me lay my head on his chest. *I want to feel you again.*

As if pulled by a magnetic force, I gravitate to his side. He's staring at a particular Christmas decoration, which he deftly removes from the tree and places in my hand.

'It's beautiful, August.' I take in the beauty of the handmade calla lily with the initial "L" on the inside. The decoration is for his Mum. 'Truly beautiful.'

'Calla lilies were Mum's favourite flower.' August has tears in his eyes. 'I made this for her ...'

'Was the remembrance tree your idea? And the handmade decorations?'

'Yeah, it was. Not that I want any credit – this tree is for everyone. It's a reminder that life is precious and that it can change in an instant.'

August's sincerity is not lost on me as I hand back his Mum's decoration. He gently places it onto the branch and admires it for a moment.

'August?' I can't hold it in any longer. 'I need to ask you something ...'

'It's about my heart, isn't it?' August doesn't face me as he says this.

'How did you know?' I ask him quietly.

'Because ... it's Evan's heart.'

That's A First for Me

'I didn't always know that it was Evan's heart that I received. It wasn't until I got a job here that I learned about the truth. It was by chance that I put the pieces together.' August guides me towards the seating area near the tree.

'I need to know, please tell me. Are you certain that it's Evan's heart?' I reply but the wave of emotions running through my body are exhausting. My mouth is dry like sand. I can barely talk.

That's a first for me. You always loved my chattiness.

'I wouldn't lie to you, Ben. I would never do that. I promise you. You felt it didn't you – when you placed your hand on my chest?' August asks.

'I felt Evan,' the words escape with the freedom of a butterfly beginning its first day on earth. A feeling of hope and longing that leaves a strange aftertaste. Because, while August might have your heart, you're still dead.

I wish you were here with me – to explain everything and help me to understand like only you know how.

'Evan, my Mum and I were all caught up in the same accident.' August recounts the day of the fatal pile-up on the motorway. How strange to hear about the day my life changed forever, but from the other perspective.

'I don't want to upset you, Ben.' August leans towards me, full of concern.

'Please, continue,' I say, stiffly trying to ignore how morbid this conversation is but all the while thinking how lovely it is to have *you* with me again.

August tenses up. His shoulders tighten and his jaw locks; he's struggling to say something. I place my hand on his leg, encouraging him to go on.

'I was told by a nurse when I started here that Evan and I were both victims of the same accident. Evan's organ donation meant that me and others lived. I guess that I was a bit of a celebrity. A heart transplant patient coming back to work here as a doctor …' August says.

'Celebrity, eh. I must remember to get your autograph.' I scowl.

'Ben, I'm sorry.' August looks mortified. 'That was insensitive; I apologise. I didn't mean it to come out like that.' He puts his hands to his head almost as if he is admitting defeat. I think if he had a white flag, he would wave it.

'I shouldn't have told you this. It's unfair, not to mention unethical and unprofessional. I'm sorry.' August whips around to face me. Tears stain his cheeks. He notices them too and wipes them away with his hand.

I stand and approach August. I cup his face in my hands and lean in towards him. Our foreheads touch and we both close our eyes.

'We are connected, August. Evan has brought us both here and for that I am grateful' I end our embrace and step back.

August takes a moment. I wait.

'I could have died that day, Ben. I was impaled in the crash. A piece of metal pierced my heart. I was so close to death that I could almost see the gates of Heaven opening.' August is trembling as he speaks. 'This is going to sound mad, but I could see my Mum. She was telling me to go back. That I had work to do and that it wasn't my time.'

A young boy walks by with his parents. His parents are helping him to bring his drip along behind him, and he's wearing a little elf hat. I can see underneath it that he's lost his hair. He can't be more than seven or eight years old. He waves at us, and August and I return the wave, plastering smiles across our faces for his benefit. His parents wish us a Merry Christmas. God love them, it's Christmas Eve and their little boy is in hospital. How cruel life can be!

'I should go and talk to them. The little boy wanted to hang a Christmas decoration on the tree, and I promised that I would help him.' August exhales. He straightens his stance and dries his cheeks. He gives me a faint smile. 'I know we've got lots more to talk about. I'll be right back. I promise.' August assures me before walking over to the little boy.

Putting his own pain and upset to one side, August begins to chat with the pyjama-wearing youngster who places a handmade decoration onto the tree. August gives him a high five before he and his parents head off again. I quickly join August and I greet the family as they pass by.

'He has a good heart.' The mother brushes by me while nodding in August's direction.

'The very best.' I reply with a knowing smile.

I Haven't Felt This Close to You in So Long

I stand beside August, breathing him in. I'm searching for you, Evan, but finding August. And that's okay. For the first time in a long time, I know that you are somewhere safe. Your work here on Earth was done and you were called to a better place. Christ, I sound like a priest giving a sermon. But I can't deny how I feel.

It's strange because I've always felt you close to me. You've always been right there with me, with your hand to my back ensuring that I would never fall. And now, that feeling has been replaced with knowing that you are where you need to be. Your time on this earth may have been cut short, but the time you spent here and what you left behind, means your life was, and is, special.

Joe Burkett

I will always wish that you were with me. But, my love, I know you are up there somewhere looking down and smiling. I love you.

'August, can I hug you, please?' I ask, scared in case he rejects me.
'Of course.'
August opens his arms, and I move into him. I put my arms around him and relish the tightening of his embrace as I lay my head on his chest. And then I hear it.

I hear you. Your heart is beating in his chest. He is alive because of you. You saved him, my love.

I close my eyes tightly and sigh softly. August rubs my back. I think he's trying to console me; I should tell him that there is no need. I feel so vivacious right now that I could do a cartwheel, though I wouldn't dare attempt it: I've got weak wrists that could snap easily.
I break away from August, and this bittersweet moment. I'm unsure how to feel. I can hear your heart beating but August isn't you. Your heart loved me, but August isn't you. Feeling you so close to me and knowing that it's not you is both a blessing and a sorrow. Two sides of the side coin. With each flip of the coin, a different wave of love and grief crashes down on me. I feel like I'm drowning again yet this time I can breathe. I am reaching for the surface.
'Thank you.' I gently break away and look into August's eyes.
'I didn't do anything.' August replies.
'You've given me some peace – some closure, knowing that Evan didn't die in vain. I felt so cheated and angry when he died, and I've held onto that feeling for so long. He was so young. And taken way before his time.' It still isn't fair – it never will be, but August's revelation feels like the start of a new chapter in my life. 'I see now that you lived because of him and look at you … look at all of the amazing things you've done. His heart beats in your chest, and that is a wonderful thing to know.'
August makes his way to the other side of the tree and retrieves another decoration from it.
'I've put this on the tree ever since I heard about where my heart came from. Because I couldn't say thank you to you, or Evan's family, I needed to do something. This decoration is my thank you to Evan for giving me the gift of life.'
Tears of happiness and pride well up in my eyes as I take the decoration from August. A beautiful wooden heart-shaped decoration with the initial

"E" in the middle of it. I stare at it for what feels like an eternity before holding it close to my chest.

I hold my hand out to August; he takes it, and places it on his chest. In one hand, I hold the little wooden keepsake representing August's appreciation for your heart, and in the other, I feel your heart beating so wildly against his chest it's as if you're straining to be in my hands once again.

Allowing August into my private world, I whisper aloud to to you, *'I haven't felt this close to you in so long.'*

Joe Burkett

Under the Tree

Cici Maxwell

16th December 2011 – Friday Night

Four mirror checks, three outfit changes, two groans and sighs, and a dozen sprays of perfume. Holly was as ready as she ever would be. She'd been waiting for this night since the first of December: Secret Santa swapping with the youth club gang and, now that she'd turned eighteen, mulled wine in Murphy's afterwards. She could already hear her father warning her to go easy. It was her final year of school, and although college applications were open until mid-January, Holly had applied to some of her dream universities in the hope of early acceptance. Her father was breathing down her neck about study but all that was on Holly's mind was Christmas and Gabriel Moore. His dark hair and blue eyes, his broad shoulders and wide smile … she wished with all her heart that this Christmas he'd finally notice her in the way she noticed him. It wasn't that he wouldn't know who she was – in the village of Pinewood Falls everyone knew everyone, always had and always would.

Holly smoothed down her dark hair, took a deep breath and wondered if Gabriel would like the Secret Santa gift she'd bought him. Her best friend, Emily, had organised the present swap this year and had made sure that Holly pulled Gabriel's name from the selection of tightly folded paper squares swirling around the bottom of a Santa hat. How Em had managed it, Holly didn't know, and she didn't care. All that mattered was that Gabriel would be forced to talk to her instead of joking around with Emily's brother, Jack. It wasn't as if he didn't know Holly, they'd been inseparable in pre-school and for the first few years of school after that. It wasn't until they turned eight that the pair began to go their separate ways. Holly frowned. Surely Gabriel didn't dislike her? He never showed any obvious aversion, sometimes he even smiled at her. Once, he'd asked her if she'd seen a movie he liked, but she hadn't, so the conversation had fizzled out as quickly as a damp New Year's Eve sparkler. The doorbell chimed, she grabbed the gift bag and dashed downstairs taking them two at a time. Almost falling over her cat, Max, she made it down just as her father opened the door to Emily.

'Nollaig shona duit, Mr Harte.' Emily sounded happy. 'Mam said to give you these.' She pushed his favourite biscuits and a book on Irish History into his hands. 'She said the book was excellent.'

'Happy Christmas, Emily. And really, she didn't need to go to any trouble …' Holly's father blustered. Holly smiled. Ever since she was nine, when her mother passed away, the women of Pinewood Falls had looked out for her father. She was used to it. Mr Harte, however, wasn't.

'No trouble at all,' Emily smiled and turned to Holly. 'Are you ready?'

'Yes,' Holly said, squeezing by her dad. She pecked his cheek as she carefully pulled her hat on. 'See you later, Dad, I won't be late.'

'Go easy on that mulled wine,' he called after her, but the girls were already out the side gate and hurrying along Main Street.

'The joys of living right in the middle of the village,' Emily sighed. 'You're so lucky to be able to walk out your door and be in the thick of it.'

Holly, while laughing at Emily's notion of what being in the thick of things was, had to agree. Pinewood was known for its love of Christmas. Folks made special trips to the village just to see the lights and shop window displays. Emily was always telling her mother that she needed to open a coffee shop on the side of their garden centre, saying that the village needed something for the "tourists", and that it wouldn't hurt to make some money too. Holly adamantly agreed. Pinewood Falls was magical in the winter. Everything sparkled in the frosty air. Fairy lights and Christmas trees were in the windows of almost every home. Handmade wreaths adorned freshly painted front doors, Murphy's pub had a huge Christmas tree in the lobby that could be seen from the street, and every shop window held a festive display.

They paused outside the village's toy shop to admire the miniature mountain scene that Miss Berry put up every year, then continued to the meeting hall in the village square. The village square was softly lit with golden festoon lights, and Frost's Garden Centre had supplied the

More Than Mistletoe

evergreen swags and garlands that decorated the meeting hall. There was an empty space beside the hall for the Christmas tree, which would go up in a few days. The Christmas Tree Lighting was always special, and Holly couldn't wait for it. It always felt like the right time to make a wish. With a little shiver, Holly took Emily's arm.

'I can't believe it's only a week until Christmas,' she said. 'Dad wants me to study 24/7 and I still have the rest of my shopping to do.'

'I've never known you, Holly Harte, Queen of All Things Christmas, to be so disorganised,' Emily said. 'Do I need to make an appointment to see you?'

'Ha-ha!' Holly rolled her eyes. 'No, but can we please go into the city so I can get the last few gifts? If I say I'm going with you he'll be OK.'

'Of course! I know you hate shopping on Christmas Eve so it'll have to be this Sunday, Christmas is in less than two weeks, and we'll be in school all week.'

'But the Christmas Tree Lighting is on Sunday!'

'We'll go early and get home early. We won't miss it – I promise you.'

Holly breathed out. If Emily made a promise it was as good as gold.

'Why's your dad pushing you to study so hard? It's only Christmas exams.' Emily steered Holly towards the meeting hall where the youth club Christmas party was in full swing.

Holly sighed as they walked in. 'He insisted that I send off a million early applications to universities, which I did, and now he's afraid I won't make the mark. He's doing my head in, Em, you know that studying law at the same university that he graduated from is my dream, but the pressure he's putting on me is intense.'

'He wants you to be happy,' Emily called over the blast of music. Christmas tunes jingled in the common room, and the smell of mince pies wafted into the corridor. 'Unlike my father. He expects Jack and me to work in the garden centre after school. I mean, we're eighteen now, I don't know if I want to run a garden centre.'

Holly handed her coat into the cloakroom. Something Emily said made the hair on the back of her neck tingle. He'd never said it, not directly, but could her father want her to come back to Pinewood Falls and work in his law firm with him? Holly frowned. Her father specialised in civil law, house deeds, mortgages, that kind of thing. Holly had her heart set on criminal law, but if he planned on her working with him …

'Come on!' Emily interrupted her. 'Stop daydreaming and let's find The Love of Your Life!'

'Emily!' Holly's cheeks turned pink. 'Shhhhh!'

Emily had already spotted some friends on the dance floor. She pranced towards them, waving and dancing. Holly shook her head and made her way to the hideously decorated Christmas tree and slipped her gift underneath. Satisfied that her gift was nicely tucked away, she scanned the room hoping to catch a glimpse of Gabriel.

'This tree … it's fairly ridiculous, wouldn't you say?'

Holly heard the deep voice behind her. She turned around, flicking her hair from her eyes, and smiled into the brooding face of Mark O'Connell.

'Oh, Mark,' she said. 'Hi. Yes, the tree … it's a sad specimen.'

'They should have let you decorate it,' Mark said with a shy smile. 'Everyone knows you're talented at decorating and putting things together. It's um, a talent.'

'Thank you.' Holly smiled back. The twinkling Christmas lights made his hair look darker than it really was. She felt bad for trying to look by him to see if Gabriel had arrived. Her smile faltered and he sighed, shoving his hands deep into his jeans' pockets.

'Your jumper is lovely,' he tried again. 'The colour is lovely, suits you.'

'Thank you,' Holly hurried to say. 'It's one of my favourites.' She glanced around. Was it possible that Mark O'Connell, desired by ninety per cent of the female population of Pinewood Falls, was flirting with her? Holly took a closer look at Mark. He was handsome, with dark eyes and light brown hair, but not someone she'd spent time daydreaming about. She'd assumed he hadn't given her a second thought but now she wondered if he had.

'Oh good, that's good.' Mark cleared his throat. 'Do you dance?'

'I do,' she said. 'Badly.'

'Me too.' He laughed, and she liked the sound of it. His shoulders relaxed and the crease between his eyes softened. Holly, without knowing why, smiled widely at him and held out her hand.

'Why don't we give it a bash, this dancing lark – it's Christmas after all.'

He looked down at her hand, and then back up at her face.

'Ok,' he said. The crease between his eyes came back. 'But you have to promise me you won't leave me out there like a fool …'

'Promise,' Holly laughed. 'Come on … you can't be that bad.'

As they turned to the dance floor Holly felt Mark take her hand. Her heart pounded a little faster as they danced and laughed, and from the corner of her eye she caught Emily watching. Emily danced over.

'Bathroom break?' Emily called over the music and took off across the floor. Holly turned back to Mark and pointed to Emily.

'Two minutes, bathroom.'

He nodded and pointed over to the refreshments table. Holly smiled, then followed Emily.

No sooner was Holly out of sight of the dancefloor when Emily grabbed a hold of her and dragged her away from the already long queue for the loo and towards one of the open fire exit doors where people were outside chatting and smoking.

'What's going on? You're dancing with Mark O'Connell?' Emily was breathless. 'Everyone is looking! How?'

'I asked him to.' Holly grinned.

'What!' Emily caught her hand and jumped. 'I can't believe you asked him to dance! Just asked? I'm so jealous! But Holl … I thought you were into Gabe?'

'I am into Gabe, but he's not here, is he!' Holly groaned. 'It's only Mark, and it's only a dance, Em, I haven't promised him my hand or anything.'

Emily looked over Holly's shoulder. A huge smile crept across her face. 'Well, the angel Gabriel has just walked in, so I'd say ciao for now to Mark. Oh … what are we waiting for!' She grasped Holly's arm and pushed them both back indoors, through the throng of dancers, to where Jack and Gabriel stood at the refreshments table. Desperately trying to smile what she hoped was not an insane grin, Holly rubbed her arm as Emily let her go. Gabriel had his back to her, his broad shoulders still encased in his bomber jacket, his dark hair curling over the collar. Her hands twitched to touch him. She could smell his aftershave and wondered which one he was wearing. Emily threw herself at Gabriel and kissed him on both cheeks. She enjoyed teasing Gabriel about his Italian background.

'Ciao! Where have you guys been?' She bellowed above the music. 'Jack, were you down by the river?'

'Don't tell Mam,' Jack said with a grin. Emily rolled her eyes.

'I've a good mind to – you promised you'd bring me the next time.' She pouted.

'It's not a place for girls like you,' Gabriel said. He smiled at Emily but didn't so much as cast a glance towards Holly. 'We didn't stay long. It's not really my scene.'

Holly twisted her hands together. She hoped Gabriel didn't know about last summer. While Emily had gone away to summer school, she'd hung about with the river crowd. They were always drinking and smoking and causing a ruckus. At first it had been fun, doing daring things, getting drunk and falling around the place, but it didn't take long for the nights to take a dark turn. She looked away as she remembered the night she'd decided that the river crowd weren't good for her.

It'd been a humid night, so hot that the river was still warm at midnight. She'd drank half a bottle of cheap wine someone had managed to steal from their parent's drinks cabinet and was feeling queasy. Paddling in the warm river's edge wasn't helping so she decided to leave. The grass was already crushed and damp underfoot as she stumbled over the bank to where she'd discarded her denim jacket and sandals. Two guys were sitting nearby, they watched as she dried her feet with her jacket and slipped her sandals on.

'Where're you going?' One asked, getting up and coming over to her. He wore a dark t-shirt and black jeans, even though it was so hot.

Holly looked up. 'Home.'

'It's a little early for that.' Black t-shirt guy came closer to her. Holly could see the other guy getting to his feet, his white t-shirt gleamed like a spectre in the moonlight. She took a step towards the old stairway that led to the bridge.

'You can't leave until we say you can,' the white t-shirt guy said as his eyes ran over her body.

'Look, my dad is expecting me,' Holly said. 'As a matter of fact, I'm late … he's going to be looking for me if I don't go …'

'He won't find you here,' the white t-shirt guy said with a twisted grin. Holly's throat constricted. Some of the guys were pushy, demanding attention and loyalty as if they owned the group and the space. They'd also broken into the abandoned boat house and some unsavoury things had gone on there. Now they were either side of her without her even seeing them move. One took her arm, the other brushed her hair back from her cheek. She cringed away from his breath. It was pure chance that Jack was making his way down the stairs at that moment. He took one look at Holly and called out to her.

'Hey,' Jack stepped forward and took Holly's arm, pulling her away from them. They backed off slightly as Jack threw his arm around her shaking shoulders. 'There you are. Been looking for you everywhere. Come on …'

The lads didn't say a word but watched as Jack led Holly away. Jack said nothing until they were up on the bridge and down the road.

'That's not the place for you,' he'd said with a frown.

'It's not the place for you either,' Holly had replied through chattering teeth.

Jack said nothing. They walked in silence until they reached Holly's house.

'Jack,' Holly said. 'Don't tell Em.'

'I won't tell anyone,' Jack said with a sigh. 'Holly, don't go back down there – it's … you're not that kind of girl.'

'I won't,' Holly said.

Jack had never mentioned that night to her after that moment, and Holly prayed that he hadn't mentioned it to Gabriel. It was embarrassing to think that he might associate her with the river crowd.

All the same, a little spike of annoyance pricked her and brought her back to the swing of the Christmas party. There was something in the way Gabriel had said "Girls like you". Holly bristled. Who was he to say such nonsense? Maybe he should be calling out the despicable behaviour of the lads who hung out there, and not the girls.

'Girls like what?' she blurted before she could stop herself. 'What do you mean by that?' Despite the pounding beat of "Stop the Cavalry" she could hear her heart hammer in her chest.

Gabriel turned and looked at her as if he'd never seen her before. He blushed, or at least she thought he did, but it might just have been the disco lights colouring his face.

'Well,' he said, and glanced at Jack for support. 'You know …' Jack tried to hide a smirk.

'I don't. Explain what you mean to me?' Holly's hands were on her hips. She swallowed hard, her throat had completely dried up. Gabriel turned to look at her again and her breath caught in her throat. His hair was a little longer than usual and fell into his eyes. He brushed it away impatiently.

'I don't mean anything bad,' he stammered. 'It's just, well, it's not the place …'

'Go on,' Holly blazed. 'Not the place …'

'Look, I don't mean to upset anyone,' Gabriel tried again. He took a step towards Holly with his hands held out towards her. She took a step back and he stopped. 'Look, let's leave it, let's not have this conversation here – it's Christmas.'

'Yeah, Christmas, the season of goodwill and passing sexist remarks and all that,' Holly spluttered before bursting into tears. This was not what she'd expected to happen. Yes, she had his full attention, but it wasn't how she'd envisioned it.

He should have opened the Secret Santa present. His eyes would've sparkled and he'd have smiled that delicious smile of his that showed he was truly happy. He would've searched the room for her to thank her. They'd have talked, and things would be just as dandy as they'd been when they were little. In her fantasy he asked to walk her home and she'd feel him move closer to her, take her hand and maybe even kiss her goodnight, although she hadn't decided yet if that was taking things too fast or not. But that's not what was happening.

She looked just behind Gabriel. At the far end of the refreshments table was Mark. He'd watched the whole drama unfold. He took a long drink and placed the empty cup back on the table, then, with his mouth set into a hard line he walked towards them. Holly's eyes widened. Her mouth silently formed the word – *no*. Mark tilted his head, frowning, he looked from her to Gabriel. He stopped and shook his head, a sad look on his face as if he'd realised what was going on. Through her tears Holly held his gaze for a brief moment before he looked down at his hands, then he turned and walked away. Holly gasped. She hadn't meant to hurt Mark's feelings, the twist in her gut told her he'd just realised that she had a huge crush on Gabriel. She'd messed things up. Not only had she caused a row between her and Gabriel, but she'd shown Mark that he was clearly Number Two in her books. It was awful. Covering her face with her hands Holly turned and ran from the hall.

18th December 2011 – Sunday Morning

Bleary eyed, Holly sat in the back of Mrs Frost's car en-route to the city for her last-minute Christmas shopping. It was too early to be up on a Sunday morning. She stared out the window, huffing and wiping the window when it fogged up too much for her to see the frosty landscape. Mrs Frost tuned the radio station into Christmas FM and was singing happily along with every tune. Emily, sitting in the front passenger seat, twisted around and poked Holly in the knee.

'Are you going to grump about what happened forever or can we talk about what happened?'

'Emily!' Holly glared at her. Her eyes darted to Emily's mother and back to Emily, frantically trying to stop Emily talking. She threw another glance in Mrs Frost's direction and caught Mrs Frost looking at her in the rear-view mirror.

Holly shrugged. 'There's nothing to talk about anyway. It was just one of those moments where boys need to be taught not to be idiots.' Emily turned around and stared at her friend.

'Huh?' Emily countered with a puzzled frown.

'What happened?' Mrs Frost raised an eyebrow at her daughter.

'I don't want to talk about it because nothing happened. Just me and my mouth educating the boys on sexism.' Holly said looking out the window.

Mrs Frost nodded and turned her attention back to the road. Emily's eyelids flittered and she checked her phone.

'I was thinking,' she said. 'We should stop off for coffee and croissants at Martello's first.'

'Sure,' Holly said.

'Well, don't be too enthusiastic for crying out loud,' Emily said.

'You're right,' Holly leaned forward and squeezed her friend's hand. 'I'm sorry. I'll fill myself with festive cheer and spirit from here on in.'

'Less of the spirit,' Mrs Frost chimed in. 'I don't want any tipsy carolling on the way home.'

'She didn't mean those kind of spirits.' Emily rolled her eyes.

Holly caught Mrs Frost's eyes in the rear view mirror and smiled at her. Emily was lucky to still have her mother. Mrs Frost winked at her and carried on singing along with the radio and soon the two girls joined her. By the time they had parked the car Holly was in a much better humour, but she still didn't want to talk about what happened between her and Gabriel on Friday night.

'Enjoy your croissants,' Mrs Frost said, checking her watch. 'I'll meet you back here at two at the latest. I can't be late for the Christmas Tree Lighting. Happy shopping!' Waving goodbye she headed towards Grafton Street.

Holly linked arms with Emily. 'Let me buy you breakfast to say sorry for being such a gobshite,' she said.

'I'll take that,' Emily laughed. 'It's the least you could do!'

'Shut up you!' Holly feigned outrage.

After eating they made their way to their favourite shopping street and, knowing how little time they had, made short shrift of ticking off their lists. By eleven o'clock Holly had all her gifts. She looked over at Emily who was on her phone, again.

'Who are you texting?!' Holly demanded. 'You've been on that phone all morning and I'm about to go insane.'

Emily stuck her phone deep down into her coat pocket where it binged for attention almost immediately. She clamped her mouth shut and then broke into a huge grin.

'Look, don't go off on one when you hear this, ok?'

'I never go off on one!' Holly's eyes widened. 'I mean, seriously!'

Emily raised her eyebrows. 'Can I just remind you of the time we got left behind in the middle of nowhere on our school trip to the source of the river Liffey?'

'Um well, ok,' Holly stopped mid rant. Then she began again. 'There was that time, but in fairness, the teachers should've done a proper head count and not driven off without five of us. Like, it's not like it was just one of us … one is easy to miss. But five! Five is a lot to leave behind. And we were in the middle of the Wicklow Mountains and it was freeeeeezing cold in the middle of January. There was snow for crying out loud!'

'I rest my case,' Em shook her head. 'Holly Goes Off on One Part Eleventy Million and Three.'

Holly stuttered to a halt. Scrunching her face up she began to laugh. 'Ok, guilty. So tell me – who've you been texting all morning – someone cute I hope?'

'Weeeelllll yes, naturally,' Emily said. 'But not for me.'

'Oh?' Holly's eyes widened. 'For Jack?' Emily was a meddling matchmaker and was constantly trying to find the perfect girl for her brother who, in her opinion, needed a decent relationship to calm him down.

'Nope, not for Jack,' Emily grinned.

'Not for Jack,' mused Holly. 'Caroline is with Steve, and Gill is with John … are you still trying to set Tim and Liz up?'

'No – I think Tim has his eye on someone else and Liz is not a bit interested in Tim – she's into Mark.'

'Mark!'

'Yes, she's mad about him, as are half the village,' Emily squinted at Holly. 'But he only has eyes for you …'

'Em, you're not … you didn't … what are you up to?' Holly folded her arms.

'Nothing! Nothing at all, I swear.'

'It doesn't sound like nothing – you're up to something.'

Emily sucked in her bottom lip. 'Look, I know you're not into Mark that much, but you are a little.'

'Yes, but Em, he saw what happened between me and Gabe. I think I've hurt his feelings.'

'We can safely say his feelings have absolutely been hurt.' Emily continued. 'But he's a grown-up Holl, he's ok about it. Honestly. I've been texting him about it.'

Holly stopped walking and stood still as Christmas shoppers jostled around her. Trust meddling Emily to get involved. 'You text him? Emily, this is terrible. Poor Mark …'

'Poor Mark indeed …' Emily smiled. 'There's been a bit of a development.' She flicked her hair over her shoulder. Holly felt her stomach churn. What was Em up to now? Emily began walking. Holly rushed to follow her.

'Emily – what do you mean there's been a bit of a development?' Holly gabbled. Emily scrunched up her nose and kept walking.

'I can't say yet,' she said. 'But I think you're going to like it.'

'Emily Frost! You absolutely cannot tell me something like this and then leave me hanging!' Holly followed Emily into one of their favourite shops. Garlands studded with orange and cloves filled the air with a warm spicy scent and a live pianist softly played Christmas carols. Holly loosened her scarf from around her neck as she followed Emily from display to display.

'I can't tell you yet,' Emily said, holding up a silk scarf. 'What do you think of this for my Mam?'

'It's perfect.' Holly touched the scarf. 'But Em …'

'No, Holly.' Emily was serious. 'You'll have to wait until I can tell you.' She paid for the scarf and they watched the sales assistant wrap it in shiny red gift wrap and add a silver bow. Emily's phone buzzed again and she pulled it from her pocket. Her eyes gleamed, and she turned her back to Holly, her fingers flying over the tiny keyboard in reply. Holly leaned around her and tried to catch sight of the message.

'Hold on! Give me a minute,' Emily laughed. 'I'll tell you what's going on when we're outside.' Holly sighed. Emily wasn't usually so good at keeping secrets. Then again, this secret seemed to have only materialised that morning. The likelihood was that Em would have cracked and told her in the next few minutes anyway. Holly tried to smile as they made their way outside. The air had grown decidedly colder and the sky had darkened. There was a hint of snow on the breeze that caused Holly to wrap her favourite scarf back around her neck and bury her nose in it.

'Tell me now,' she mumbled from the woollen warmth of her scarf. Emily danced from foot to foot, gifts bags dangling from her hands. Her face was one huge smile.

'Oh my God, Holl, you're not going to believe … ok … I'll tell you,' she giggled. Holly raised her eyebrows and said, 'Emily! Tell me!'

'Ok. Don't ask me how he did it, I don't know and I didn't ask, but Mark has – oh look – it's starting to snow!'

'Emily! Please focus!' Holly grabbed hold of Emily's arm and squeezed. Her mouth was dry.

'Holly, brace yourself for the best Christmas present ever,' Emily grinned. 'Mark spoke with Gabe and it turns out that he's arranged for you two to meet up for a date tonight at the Christmas Tree Lighting.'

'Are you serious?' Holly dropped Emily's arm as the snow began to swirl thicker around them. Her mouth dropped open and she closed it quickly.

Emily nodded and clapped her hands. Holly groaned into her gloves. 'Oh God, Emily is this really real?'

'Yes!' Emily squealed. 'Can you believe it?'

'Wow … but why? Why would Mark …?' Holly scrunched up her nose as the flakes began to fall faster around them.

'Oh my God, Holly – why are you even asking? Clearly Mark realises that you're into Gabe and, like yours truly, he's a bit of a cupid and maybe he actually wasn't into you at all. Maybe he was just dancing with you out of kindness.' Emily stared at her.

'Out of kindness? Honestly, Em, that's a mean thing to say.' Holly frowned.

'I didn't mean it like that,' Emily said. 'It just came out wrong. But, no – hear me out, what if we read too much into Mark asking you to dance, what if that's all it was, just a dance, some Christmas fun, and we thought he was into you?'

'It's not impossible,' Holly mused. 'Just stings a little by the way.'

'Sorry.' Emily's mouth twisted. 'I know. But he is a few years older than we are, and his last girlfriend was in uni. Why would he be into someone our age – just finishing high school?'

'Makes sense when you put it like that,' Holly said. She bit her lip. 'And he is as much a matchmaker as you – remember last Christmas when he got Kayleigh together with Ashley?'

'Yes, but it didn't last long,' Emily said. Holly's face dropped. Emily immediately backtracked. 'Oh no! I don't mean that's what will happen with you and Gabe!'

'Me and Gabe,' Holly mused. 'Gabe and me.'

Emily brushed snow from her face and smiled. 'Ok, so this is what's going to happen: we're going home and you're going to take a nice hot shower, make yourself even more gorgeous than you already are, and meet me and Jack in the square at seven. Mark said Gabriel is working until six but will be in the square to meet you at seven fifteen. He said Gabe didn't realise you were into him and he's very nervous but happy.'

Holly shook her head. 'It's a little too good to be true, isn't it?'

'Sheesh Holly,' Emily burst. 'Can't you just be happy and excited that the guy of your dreams is meeting you for a romantic Christmas rendezvous this evening? Stop looking a gift reindeer in the mouth – he's into you – he just didn't act on it because he thought you weren't into him; and can I just say this – you did have an argument with him on Friday night. It is entirely possible that he thought you hated his guts.'

Holly cringed. 'And we haven't really talked properly since we were eight and I dumped a bucket of mud on him for laughing at me for getting stuck up a tree.'

'I'm telling you, you had him terrified all these years,' Emily laughed. 'Between mud and feminist rants he was probably afraid you'd go off on one.'

'Oh Emily, that's so true!' Holly started to laugh. 'Do you remember debate class and me and him were on opposing sides?' Emily laughed and snorted.

'Holly, if only we'd known sooner then you two could already be together.' Emily's phone buzzed and both young women jumped. 'It's just Mam.' Emily read the text. 'She wants to know are we done shopping as the snow is starting to fall hard. Dad called her and said it's getting bad back home. She wants to get going.'

'I'm done,' Holly said with a grin. 'And I'm going to need every minute to get ready for tonight.'

'That's the spirit,' Emily said. 'Let's go. Oh, and by the way, wear your red jumper, the one with the white snowflakes on. No, it's not childish – it's romantic and Christmassy.'

*

Five hair changes, ten minutes choosing the right shade of lipstick, and half a bottle of perfume later, Holly admired her reflection in her bedroom mirror. Emily was right. The red Christmas jumper with the white snowflakes was perfect. The colour added an extra glow to her cheeks and the cut fit her neatly. She hoped that this time around she and Gabriel would get on.

'Don't go all crazy,' she told her reflection. 'Don't argue, listen. Don't nit-pick. Have a conversation. It's been ten years since you had a chat with him. He's gorgeous. Give him a chance. Let him talk. Ask interesting questions …' It was all Emily's advice, but some of it was good, she hoped. She pointed her finger at herself and smiled. 'You look great.'

Then she added her favourite necklace, a gold chain and locket that was once her mother's, took a deep breath and turned away from the mirror. Her mother would've been delighted to know she was going on a date with Gabriel Moore, always insisting that she be friendly with him as he was an only child just like she was. 'It must be terribly lonely for him up on that Christmas Tree farm,' she'd say to Holly. 'Half of his cousins are in Italy. Ask him to your birthday party. That would be a kind thing to do.' When her mother had passed away he'd given her a rose at the funeral, Holly remembered. She touched the locket. Funny how you remember things you'd thought you'd forgotten. 'Wish me luck, Mam,' she whispered, and hurried downstairs to get her coat. In the kitchen the clock ticked, and her cat Max was curled up beside the stove. She bent down and scratched under his chin, enjoying his purring and sleepy cuteness. All was quiet in the house so she assumed her dad had already left for the big event.

Outside the snow had stopped. The pavement had been shovelled clear and someone had scattered salt. Every rooftop shimmered with snow, every tree branch, hedgerow and wall top glistened in the streetlights. The cold breeze had come back and it carried the scent of more snow to come. Holly wrapped her favourite scarf around her neck and began walking towards the village square. The place was bustling. The school choir were carolling next to the toy shop. Holly slowed to listen as they finished their set and dropped some coins into their charity bucket. The music teacher smiled at her as she walked by. In the temporary carpark behind the school people from surrounding villages and hamlets were arriving to take part in the festivities.

This year's Christmas Tree Lighting looked set to be the best one ever. There were extra vendors. What once had been a few stands on one side of the square selling warm refreshments had grown to become a Christmas market. They had a candyfloss stand next to the hot chocolate stand, and the village's newest resident, who came from Germany, had set up a stand selling traditional German baked goods and hot dogs. Holly corrected herself as she read the sign on his stand: "Rostbratwurste", not hot dogs. They looked delicious and she promised herself that she'd get one later, after her date with Gabriel. He might even fancy one himself.

With a happy sigh she passed stand after stand barely noticing the wares. Usually, she'd have stopped to admire everything and try to decide what she'd spend her money on. She did make a point of stopping at Noelle's Handmade Candles stand. Just as she did every year, she bought a pine tree scented candle as her mother had done, and one in a hand-painted jar for her mother's grave. Holly gave Noelle a hug. An old friend of her mother's, Noelle had been making candles long before it became a thing. Her silvery hair was scooped up in a mess on top of her head and her lips were cherry red. She slipped an extra scented votive into Holly's bag as she packaged up Holly's purchases.

'Isn't the tree wonderful?' she said to Holly. 'It's the nicest one we've ever had.'

Holly nodded. The tree, grown on Moore's Christmas Tree Farm, was the most beautiful specimen. It was tall and properly bushy.

'It's like something you'd see on a Christmas card,' Holly said. 'Or in a movie. It's perfect.'

'They'd a divil of a time getting it up,' Noelle said. 'It's a heavy one.'

Holly nodded and looked the tree over from top to bottom. And then, out of the blue, standing at the bottom of the Christmas tree like the best Christmas present anyone could get, was Gabriel. He had his back to her and was looking the tree up and down. He squinted, shook his head as he moved around it, before pointing at the base and calling to another man over to help him. Holly's tongue felt as if it was stuck to the roof of her mouth. All she could do was stare at him. His dark hair was curling over his collar, his hands on his hips as he scrutinised the tree. Noelle prodded her arm.

'Your change,' she said, grinning at Holly. 'Or has something else taken your fancy?'

'Oh, no, yes. No!' Holly blustered. 'I mean, I think I have everything I need.'

'But not everything you want,' Noelle said. Holly blushed.

'Go get him,' Noelle said, laying her hand on her heart. 'Your mother would be so happy.'

'How'd you know?'

'Emily came by, all questions about did I see you, was Gabriel around, yadda yadda. I put two and two together. Don't think I don't notice; I'm an old dog at these things. You two are made for each other. Now go on, find Emily, and get that young man on your arm. Leave your bits and bobs here, I'll mind them – go!' She pulled Holly in close and kissed her forehead before pushing her towards the Christmas tree. Holly blew her a kiss and began to walk towards Gabriel, stopping a little bit away from him to watch him finish working on the tree. She leaned against the trunk of one of the old oak trees that stood in the square.

He looked amazing. The Christmas lights that were up around the square were soft and golden and shone on him as if he were an angel. Holly's breath caught in her throat and she swallowed hard. In the golden light he looked taller. Someone called to him, and he laughed and called back. Holly relished his deep voice. She smiled and reached to touch the locket around her neck. Noelle was right, her mother would be delighted; all she had to do was to not mess things up. Holly watched him. He turned around and looked around the square. She leaned back against the tree trunk. He seemed to be looking right at her with those darling blue eyes of his. Then he looked away and she realised she was holding her breath and let it all out in one long whoosh. Checking her watch she was surprised to see that it was almost seven. Looking around Holly strained to find Emily in the crowd. When she turned back to watch Gabriel he was packing up a tool bag, then he turned and walked away. Holly's mouth dropped open. Where was he going? She took a step towards him just as Emily ran to her.

'There you are!' Emily chorused. 'I've been looking for you. Let me see you. Yes, pretty, nice lip gloss. You smell amazing. You're perfect. You can go meet the man of your dreams now.'

'Where've you been?' Holly said.

'I'm only a few minutes late,' Emily said with a moan. 'I needed to help Mam with the Christmas Tree Lighting – this tree is the biggest the village has ever had. Isn't it a beauty? Everyone's talking about it. Mr Moore is only delighted with himself for growing it.'

'You were here all this time – over there at the tree?' Holly gabbled. 'With Gabriel?'

'No – I was over in the hut where the generator is. Why? Is Gabe here already? Why didn't you go talk to him?' Emily looked around. 'Look! There he is – go! It's seven fifteen.'

Holly squinted. Gabriel seemed to be in a bit of a heated conversation with his father. 'I don't know, Em,' she said. 'This doesn't seem to be a good time. And it doesn't look to me like he's thinking of our date at all.'

Emily looked at Gabriel. 'It's fine,' she said. 'Go on.' Holly looked over. Gabriel was gesticulating and frowning. His father had his hands on his hips. She sucked in her bottom lip.

'I don't know,' she said again. Emily rolled her eyes.

'Oh stop. He's half Italian, that's just fiery passion,' Emily said and gave Holly an impatient glare. 'Now you're late! And, oh – he's done talking with his dad – he's walking over here. Smile for the love of God, smile! You look frantic with worry.' Holly shook herself and forced the worry from her brow. She smiled and spun around and watched Gabriel walking towards them. He didn't look very happy, in fact, he looked furious. His brows were drawn deep over his eyes and he was walking fast.

'Hi, Gabriel.' Holly smiled at him but he kept walking. He stormed past her without a glance in her direction. Holly watched him stomp away, take some keys from his pocket and get into his jeep. A lump caught in her throat as she watched him start the engine.

'Em,' she started to say but the lump in her throat made it sound like a gargle. Emily was at her side, her mouth and eyes wide open.

'What the ...' Emily groaned as they watched Gabriel gun the engine and pull away from the kerb. She turned to Holly who was as white as a freshly built snowman. 'Maybe he's gone home to freshen up?'

'He didn't even see me,' Holly choked the words out. 'He doesn't even know I exist.'

'He does!' Emily pulled Holly to her. 'He must – why else would he have made plans to meet you here?'

'I don't know,' Holly sniffled. Her eyes stung. She leaned her head on Emily's shoulder and tried to hold the tears in. There was no point in crying here, not in front of everyone. Peeking out from behind her hair she saw Noelle watching, her hand on her heart. Holly looked around. So many people, and it seemed as if they were all looking at her. She grit her teeth. There was no way she was going to let them know how hurt she was, how much of a fool she felt. The carollers stopped singing and Mrs Frost took to the podium to draw everyone's attention to the moment they'd all been waiting for: the countdown to the lighting of the tree. Holly plastered a smile on her face and turned to face the tree as the crowd began to count down from ten. Mam always told her to make a wish just as the lights turned on. Holly smiled brighter. Last year she'd wished for love, maybe this year she wouldn't make a wish at all. What was the point? Wishes never came true. Everyone around her was smiling and together. Holly watched them join in the countdown.

Ten, nine, eight. Someone stood close to her, seven, six, five, and gently took her hand, four, three – was it Gabriel? Two, one! Despite herself, Holly made a wish. The tree lit up in a blaze of sparkling fairy lights and the carollers broke into a spirited rendition of "We Wish You a Merry Christmas". Holly briefly closed her eyes, then turned to see whose warm hand was holding hers so carefully.

'Mark!' She cried out. 'It's good to see you.' In that moment it was good to see him. He was smiling at her and holding her hand in such a way that she couldn't doubt his feelings for her.

'I saw,' he said softly. 'I'm sorry.'

'It doesn't matter,' Holly lowered her head.

Mark gently tilted her face up. 'It does matter – you matter. I'd never stand you up.'

Holly stared into his tanned, open face and wondered if maybe she had set her heart on the wrong man all this time. She leaned into him and laid her hand on his chest. Through his jacket she could feel his heart beating fast.

'Can I take you out sometime?' he asked gently.

Holly glanced down. Gabriel obviously didn't care for her or else he would have seen her, heard her say hello as he practically ran away from her. Maybe someone had said something about what happened at the river? Maybe he thought that she was one of "those girls" that he despised so much. Holly looked up at Mark. His brown eyes were dark and earnest and looking at her as if she was the most precious thing he'd ever seen, as if he'd do anything for her. His touch was so gentle, he'd never do anything to hurt her, Holly thought. And everyone in the village loved Mark … what had she to lose? He wasn't quite what she'd wished for when the lights went on but he seemed kind and was smiling at her warmly.

'I'd like that,' she said. 'I'd like that a lot.

*

And they lived not quite happily ever after …

In the follow up novel, "Trimming the Tree" due for release in September 2022, we catch up on Gabriel, Holly, Mark, Jack and Emily.

Gabriel isn't keen on returning home to run his family's Christmas tree farm on the outskirts of Pinewood Falls, but he has no choice. His life as an entrepreneur in the city has crumbled. His ex-fiancée has stolen his business from him, and he's been left with a broken heart.

Holly loves working in the florist department of the garden centre, she's been working there since giving up law. Christmas is her favourite time of year; or at least it was until Gabriel turned up reminding her of the huge crush she had on him when they were teenagers.

Holly catches Gabriel's eye, but she avoids him. After all he did stand her up that time they had a date, and there's nothing more terrible than having your heart broken at Christmas.

Now Gabriel is intent on getting to know her, and maybe, just maybe, she can help him to fall in love with home again, and rebuild his family's Christmas tree farm; and maybe, just maybe, she'll be willing to give him a second chance.

Killing Christmas Eve

Jake Godfrey

Sam

The worst thing about contract killing, in my experience, is the amount of admin. It might look glamorous in the movies, but the reality is more schedules and spreadsheets than sadistic shootouts.

Not that I do any of the gory stuff, you understand, I couldn't box the wings off a fly. I wouldn't say I'm weak, but if I was doing one of those awful "What Kind Of Woman Are You?" quizzes in those vomit inducing magazines, my result would undoubtedly be "girly girl". Some people hit the gym after work, I crack open the Gypsy Creams.

I'm the one who makes sure that the hitwoman and her target are in the right place at the right time. I'd argue it's actually the more stressful job. All she does, essentially, is pull the trigger. She has no conception of the amount of time and effort it took to get her to that point.

I'm overqualified really. An economics degree means absolutely bugger all in the assassination game. And that's before you get to all the "being a woman in a man's game" guff. It's actually remarkably simple work, as long as you can separate the art from the artist, as it were. I've never killed anyone. It's like being a PA, if PA stood for "Permanently Anxious". That may be a little disingenuous, given that I've devoted the last seventeen years of my life to this career. Even calling it a career feels odd. It isn't like there's any progression, and technically speaking they could decide to cut out the middleman or, in this case, woman, at any stage.

They never will though. I know too much. I can already anticipate your next question and yes, funnily enough it occurred to me too, almost immediately – surely that's even more reason to get rid of me? True, but, as anybody who watches a crime drama will know, you never get into this business without a backup plan. Mine is a dossier, digitized and primed on a server. Each evening I have to enter a password that stops the dossier being emailed to the authorities and various other insalubrious individuals. The day I don't make it home to enter that password is the day everything goes public. Hit lists, clients, everything. Even now, the power of it sends a shiver up my spine.

One of the perks of this particular job are the hours. I'm finished by midday, so I never have to dash into town, frantically flailing around buying last minute presents. A lot of people hate it, but I could listen to Slade on a loop in the supermarket. In fact, I was merrily singing along to it, and just as Noddy screeched "It's CHRISTMAS!" a new email appeared in the drafts folder. Oh, sorry, I'll explain; that's how we do it. Messages can never be sent. If you can be texted, you can be traced. So, I share an email with my employer and any messages are relayed via the drafts folder.

The only information I get is a name, their occupation and a picture. Which presented me with a problem, because the name they gave me was the last person on Earth I expected to see.

Jess Bancroft.

My fiancée.

Kate

The house was silent. Nothing strange about that – it was Christmas Eve after all. As Kate crept along the landing, tugging at her hood to ensure it covered her face, she stopped. Listened.

The only sound she could hear was that of her own heart beating. It wasn't because of the act she was about to commit, by now she could do that in her sleep, but as she gripped the gun, being sure to keep her finger well away from the trigger, she couldn't help but feel dejected.

Most people were happy tonight. Parked on plump sofas, laughter flowing almost as fast as the wine. What was she doing? She would go home later, slip into her snowflake print PJ's and flick through the channels. Maybe she would watch one of those soppy Lifetime films.

The woman in the next room, however, would not.

Kate cursed under her breath as the door creaked. She altered her grip and slowly slid through the gap, breathing in so as to slip through with ease. Engulfed by darkness, she squinted to locate the bed. The incessant snoring confirmed that it was just a few feet to her left. Feeling her way along the wall, Kate grunted as her toe collided with a cabinet. Closing her eyes, she took a deep breath to slow her heart rate. It couldn't be hurried. She knew there was nobody else in the house, she still had no feeling in her bum from the previous two hours she'd spent staking the place out, crouching in some icy undergrowth opposite.

Glamorous life.

She flashed a torch over the shape in the bed, just to make sure it was the right person.

The woman was on her back, tongue lolling out of her mouth, long black hair sprawled over the pillow.

This was always the hardest bit.

The reality.

Most assassins lie to themselves. It's a job. A name. It never is.

Sadly, or not, depending on your perspective, it is lucrative. Ridiculously so. It's not like she did it for pleasure.

Well, maybe at the start she had.

But that was all academic.

Because the woman in that bed was not Jess Bancroft.

Sam

For obvious reasons, I had to keep the relationship a secret. A trickier task than you might imagine in this line of business. Danger in every dalliance, which should have frightened me more than it did, but the truth was that it excited me. Christmas Eve was actually our anniversary, depending on where you count from. I count from the first time we kissed, whereas she prefers to count from the first time we, well, let's just say it wasn't a satsuma in her stocking that Christmas. Sorry, I don't want this to turn into some kind of Carry On, but sometimes you just have to laugh. We certainly do, a lot, and that I think is the secret to our relationship. She makes me cackle like a banshee and I like to think I do the same to her. We're quite different otherwise. For one thing, she doesn't keep tabs on trained killers for a living. Jess is a lawyer though, which in many ways is worse. I try not to hold it against her. The irony of such illegality existing under the same roof as a lawyer isn't lost on me; if I had the skill, I could probably write some kind of bizarre sitcom.

We met in the most unusual circumstances. It was a cold, December night, and I could feel something in the air, like that film Serendipity ... No, I can't do it. That's complete claptrap, but it's more interesting than the real story. Essentially, Jess was buying a bagel and so was I. We got chatting and it went from there. See what I mean? Fiction is always more interesting than fact, although I understand that given my lifestyle, you may find that hard to believe.

Sorry, I'm digressing. Stop me if I do it again.

Christmas Eve.

Jess

The most worrying thing, well, aside from it being her of course, was that I recognised the photo. In fact, I was the one that took it. I'd taken her to Stoke – I'm nothing if not romantic – to see a concert. At the time, I had this soppy thought that it might turn into a tradition – we'd trudge to Trentham, mill around the market, buy a silly bauble then round off the evening killing some carols before coming home full of festive fun. The naivety of youth. Alright, alright, I was thirty-two. I'd managed to snap her at the perfect moment. Her eyes were wide open, her mouth agape as she stuffed a cream puff in her mouth.

She was mortified and had tried to make me delete it but I wouldn't. I've always loved that photo. Her spirit. Why my employer decided to use it for illustrative purposes in her deletion dossier I have no idea. And that was the problem. I really didn't have any idea.

A million thoughts jostled for space in my head. They knew her, which meant they knew about our relationship. So, this was ... what? A threat? A test? A practical joke? Knowing my boss, a combination of all three.

Because that was the other thing.

Normally, the only information given on the email was a name, a photo and an occupation. This was different. Underneath the photo, in bold letters, printed in red just in case the cliché wasn't caustic enough.

A date and a time.

I don't think I've ever felt as afraid as I did at that moment.

Because the date was December 24th at 11:59p.m.

I had six hours to orchestrate the butchering of my betrothed.

Kate

Her gun was half cocked, flaccid in mid-air. She felt awkward, like a virgin going in for a kiss. There was very little wriggle room, both literally and figuratively – this bedroom was tiny. Kate's brain sprang into action, mentally going through the checklist. Had she made a mistake?

No.

Though, now she thought about it, things never normally moved this quickly. But the money was munificent and she thought of it as her Christmas bonus. As Kate saw it, she had two options.

Option 1: leave this room and never return. This would be fine, if it weren't for the fact that a job left incomplete also left a permanent stain on her record. She couldn't have that. Brushing her auburn hair out of her eyes, a sheen of sweat glazed her face. That only left Option 2. She took a deep breath as she realised what that meant.

Kate hated having to hurt people unnecessarily; in fact, she prided herself in the knowledge that her targets were always dead before they hit the ground.

Not tonight.

She clicked the safety back on before tucking the gun into the waistband of her jeans. She didn't dare switch on the light but, as she hurried down the stairs, squinting in the semi darkness, she spotted a pile of post on a small table by the front door. Snatching one of the letters, she stuffed it in her pocket. Once she was safely outside, she sprinted down the street and ducked into a small alcove tucked behind a hedge. Retrieving the burner phone she'd bought earlier that day from her back pocket, she dialled the only number in the call log.

Sam.

Sam

My heart went into overdrive when I felt the phone buzz in my breast pocket.

You see, the second I got the note, I knew that, one way or another, this wasn't going to happen. Quite what plan I expected to magically conjure up, I had no idea, but nevertheless I felt a steely determination as I clenched my fists, ready for battle. Then the tears began to flow. I pictured her face on the day I'd proposed. Thankfully I'd decided to take her somewhere slightly nicer than Stoke this time, in fact I'd blown the budget on a weekend away in France, the beautiful town of La Rochelle. I'd thought about Paris, but as much as I love Jess, I'm not made of money.

She's a strange one in many ways. I can't tell you what it is exactly. It's her aura. When I'm with her, not to get all soppy, but I feel like a completely different person. She approaches every day as if it's the best day in the world. It's actually quite annoying. I'm essentially a coiled spring most of the time. I know they say you shouldn't bring your work home with you, but you try organising two assassinations a day, then coming home and pretending you're interested in picking out a new headboard … So for me, doing something so stereotypically saccharine felt completely alien, which is why I decided not to propose at dinner or somewhere equally dull.

I proposed at the bottom of the Atlantic Ocean on a diving trip. Because we were underwater, I could only read her lips, but I think her reaction (upon seeing me ungracefully manoeuvring myself onto one knee whilst wrestling my oxygen tank out of the weeds) was happiness. At least I assumed it was, because she tackled me back through the weeds in a huge embrace, somewhat hampered when our diving paraphernalia got intertwined and she had to drag me back to the surface.

But none of that mattered now.

As I pressed the phone to my ear, a strange sensation rippled through my body. Everything snapped into focus. I didn't know what challenges the next few hours would hold, but it would all be worth it. For Jess.

That was when I decided to end the call.

Kate

Apoplectic.

She couldn't tell if it had been two minutes or ten since she'd been cut off. Her vision was clouded with a red mist that threatened to overwhelm her. She needed to think. But, more importantly, she had to get out of this ditch. Her bum was going numb again. Brushing herself down, she stretched, every sore sinew protesting vehemently against springing into action.

The dulcet tones of Les Gray drifted into her consciousness as "Lonely This Christmas" blasted from somebody's back garden. As if she wasn't depressed enough already. What to do?

Honestly, right then, she could quite easily have jacked it all in for a cup of cocoa, a warm duvet and an evening watching Bruce Willis in a string vest, killing terrorists. Kate smiled briefly as she remembered all those debates about "Die Hard" being a Christmas film (it is, of course, as Kate had proved time and time again).

She decided to start walking – where she didn't know. The thing about The Agency was that they kept tabs on you, but the clever thing was, you never knew when, which kept everybody on their toes. Once Kate was underneath a streetlight, she retrieved the letter and read the name printed on the envelope.

If she hadn't been so focussed on it, she may well have felt the needle going in.

Kate slumped to the ground.

Sam

I hadn't wanted to do it, but I felt like it would be the only way. Sending her to the wrong house was the easy part.

Sourcing the drug, however, took a little more time, which I really didn't have. Seat of the pants doesn't even begin to cover it.

So, after leaving an urgent message in the drafts folder with all the details, I chose a house that was near to mine, but not so near that she might work out where I live, parked up, my knuckles white from clenching the syringe.

I might be the "hired help", but you don't work in a business like this without picking up a few tricks of the trade, and it turned out to be the easiest part of the whole process.

So here she was, tied up in my basement.

Not exactly the Christmas present I was hoping for.

Kate

As Kate came round, two things became apparent:

1.) She was tied to a chair.
2.) It wasn't her house.

Oddly, it was the latter of the two facts that worried her the most. Her tongue was stuck to the roof of her mouth and her vision was blurry. Blinking furiously, she took in her new surroundings for the first time. It was almost completely bare, bar a battered acoustic guitar in the far corner and a bookcase filled with crime novels. One in particular caught her eye, a Simon Kernick – "The Business of Dying". How apt. Wriggling her arms, Kate realised for the first time that she wasn't just tied up. She was secured. Each finger was tied down individually, as was each leg.

'Nice to meet you at last.'

Kate jumped as the voice appeared behind her. Try as she might, her neck just wouldn't twist more than forty-five degrees. She didn't recognise the voice, but, evidently, the voice recognised her.

'I suppose it would be a moot point for me to ask who you are. Or where I am?' said Kate, the calmness in her voice belied by her thundering heartbeat.

There was a silence that went on just a second too long.

'Not at all. I'm not a psycho.'

This convinced Kate that the woman was, in fact, a psycho.

'I'm Sam. We've worked together for the last few years. I only have one question for you.'

Kate tensed.

'Can you help me?'

Sam

I hoped that I hadn't gone too far. I feared the pomp and circumstance might be too much, but you have to remember that I had never done this before. As if Christmas wasn't stressful enough, I now had an increasingly angry assassin, an absent fiancée and an absolutely scorching headache.

When it comes to kidnapping and torture, I knew about the theory. I didn't, however, possess the will nor the wiles to go much further than the theatrics. We were dangerously close to a stalemate, and once that point was reached, my delicately built house of cards would come tumbling down.

'You know,' piped up Kate. 'If you wanted to tie me up, you could at least have taken me out to dinner first.'

'Yes, well.'

It wouldn't go down in the history books as the wittiest riposte, but it was the best I could manage at the time. I never was very good at flirting. That was one of the things Jess claimed she found adorable.

Jess.

I cleared my throat, putting on my best authoritative voice.

'Earlier this evening, you were ordered to terminate one Jess Bancroft, correct?' My limited knowledge of legal lexicon, almost entirely gleaned from crime drama, would only get me so far.

'I was, your honour.' I couldn't see Kate's face, but from her tone I wasn't convinced she was taking this seriously.

I leaned in, close to her left ear, and said 'I'm afraid you're not going to be able to complete your contract.'

Which was when things got considerably worse.

More Than Mistletoe

Kate

"Don't try and kidnap an assassin" is the kind of thing most people would take as red. Kate had been working on the ropes around her wrists from the second she woke up. Unable to reach the penknife she kept, ironically, for just such emergencies, she drew instead on her knowledge of Harry Houdini. You wouldn't think that Houdini and contract killers would have much in common, and you would be right. One of the few skills they did share, however, was escapology. Kate was always amazed at how many of her contemporaries took such a lackadaisical attitude to safety.

In this line of work, ego wasn't just prevalent, it was a prerequisite. To many, that was enough.

Not for Kate.

So it was with some satisfaction that she got her hands untied in under two minutes, especially as her captor was right behind her.

Amateur.

Once that was out of the way, there was a wonderful cause and effect. Although her legs were still tied, she was able to use her free hands to grip the side of the seat, spring up and slam the chair down onto the left foot of her captor. Howling in pain, her captor gave Kate a shove, sending her sprawling onto the floor. This allowed Kate to retrieve the pen knife and begin cutting through her other bonds. She made it through the one on her left leg before her nose exploded.

Sam

I'm not a trained martial artist. The biggest fight I've ever been in was in Year Eleven, when Peter Orstrum thought it would be hilarious to punch the arms of all the girls just after getting their jabs. It's amazing how quickly people develop a conscience after getting a broken nose. I don't think there's much chance of me becoming a martial arts master, but even so, my hand hurt for days afterwards. So it was with a sense of déjà vu that I slammed my foot into Kate's face. A sickening crack echoed round the basement as blood sprayed up the leg of my jeans.

I was in uncharted territory. My plan had been to – well, even now I wasn't sure. Interrogate her? That wouldn't have provided many answers.

Torture? Please.

That's the trouble with acting on instinct. It only gets you so far. I hoped it would be enough to get me through whatever happened next.

Jake Godfrey

Kate

Dazed from the kick, she shook her head and forced herself onto her back, enabling her to free her other leg. This was hampered somewhat by the incessant kicks being rained down on her. Once both feet were free, she hooked her left leg under the chair and flung it to the side before flailing them wildly, catching my captor in the stomach. With a gasp, she stumbled to the wall for support, clutching her belly and wheezing. Wasting no time, Kate sprang to her feet and kicked her captor in the back of the legs twice in quick succession, forcing her onto her knees. She wrapped her arm around her neck, positioning herself behind the woman for the best leverage. This meant that she was in complete control of the headlock and could bring about unconsciousness almost instantly if she wanted.
'Why me?'
'You … I … we both work for The Agency. I'm the woman on the other end of the drafts folder.'
Kate frowned.
'What do you want?'
'Jess … My fiancée.'
This shocked Kate for a split second, just long enough for Sam to jam a finger into her right eye.
Sam wriggled out of her grip as Kate rubbed her eye furiously. Picking up the guitar, Sam swung it round in a great arc, a percussive twang echoing round the basement as it connected with Kate's skull. Sprinting for the stairs, Sam was suddenly yanked backwards by Kate clawing at the hem of her jeans. Kate's pull was so strong, Sam's body actually became parallel with the floor before slamming to the ground. Winded, Sam spluttered as she kicked fruitlessly at air, Kate being ready for her this time. No more questions.
Kate's slim figure belied her muscular arms, which she used to grip Sam by the back of her shirt and the waistband of her jeans to toss her away from the stairs. Sam landed in the corner, a lump of limp limbs. Kate advanced, fists clenched.

Sam

Well, that could have gone better.

You see fight scenes in films or on telly, but sound effects can only convey so much. What they can't get across in the pain – the sheer, unrelenting agony. My tendons were trembling, and my knuckles were red raw.

'Can this basement be locked?'

Kate's tone did not inspire my inner hero to lash out again, so I nodded. 'Key.'

I nodded towards the door at the top of the stairs, where I always kept the key in the lock for fear of losing it.

'Spare?'

I could have lied, but I figured that would not have ended well. 'Bedroom. Desk drawer.' I mumbled, panting and cradling my arm.

Kate

It took Kate all of a minute to lock the door, race upstairs, find the key and get back. To an empty basement.

Sam

So, the threat of it ending badly for me was still there, but my sense of self-preservation prevailed. The second I heard the lock click after Kate left, I retrieved the real key from the bookcase (I kept it in a safe behind my John Dickinson Carr collection – locked room mysteries were how I reminded myself about the key).

It took all my energy to heave myself up the stairs, but I knew I only had about thirty seconds before she returned. I knew, in my heart of hearts, that this was only going to end one way. Me or her. I had to get ahead of the game.

Which was why I started the fire.

Kate

The acrid smell nearly knocked Kate on her back. The blaze was spreading quickly from the kitchen. She tried the front door. Locked. She threw a bronze paperweight at a window, which bounced off. Double glazed. She rushed towards the fire, which seemed like a stupid move, especially in an unfamiliar house, but Kate knew there had to be a way out.

Covering her eyes with her arm, she peered round the door. The entire kitchen was ablaze, smoke spewing into the rest of the house. It wouldn't be long before it spread into the hallway in which she was currently standing. Already the heat was unbearable, and she was sure her eyebrows had been singed. Remembering a report she had seen on television about fire safety, she dropped to the floor and crawled past the staircase back towards the front door.

Which was when the cupboard under the stairs sprang open as Sam charged towards her.

Although Kate was caught by surprise, she managed to deflect Sam's blow as she rolled over, taking the momentum out of the attack. There was no finesse to the fighting, not anymore.

Rolling together on the floor, a barrage of knees and fists, neither could see for the smoke. The hallway now felt like a furnace, flames licking the doorframe of the kitchen.

They had minutes.

Seconds.

As they were wrestling on the floor, not even knowing why anymore, Sam's hand fell upon the paperweight. Raising it high above her head, even though she couldn't see, she brought it down and heard an almighty crack.

Silence.

She sat back against the door, panting, quickly followed by coughing. A strange calmness enveloped her then. No more murders. No more machinations.

Peace.

It would be Christmas morning by now. She thought of the firefighters who would spend Christmas morning sifting through her molten memories and began to cry, not out of sorrow or shame.

Joy.

Because the plan, at least on the face of it, had worked.

Epilogue

So, now you know my story.

I write this down not as a confession but as – I don't know … penance? Or maybe it comes back to that issue of ego. I can't actually believe it worked, and I still won't believe it unless I see it written down in black and white.

I may have been the assassin's assistant, but I could have been one hell of an actor.

Because Jess Bancroft doesn't exist.

Oh, all those stories about us going to Stoke and proposing underwater were all true. Just not with her.

I knew that if I wanted to get out of The Agency for good, they would never allow me to simply leave. You never know when they're watching, and as Hans Gruber explained so eloquently in "Die Hard", they *will* find you unless it appears that you're already dead. So that's the plan that I came up with. Well, Kate helped of course. We're engaged and what's mine is hers, including half of the legwork. We had to play the long game, and we had to play it for real, completely straight, just in case they were watching. All those hard knocks? Ouch.

Burning down the house was Kate's idea. Any other way and they might have suspected the truth, but if our bodies were burned to a crisp then they would have nothing to go on. Obviously, I had to fictionalize things a little on the off chance anybody finds this. That stuff about us never having met. If I had the inclination, I'd write a screenplay and fly to Hollywood. But why would I want to? Because here we are, sipping cocktails under the stars in a Parisienne Walkway.

Well, if you can't splash out at Christmas, when can you?

Jake Godfrey

Christmas and Cocktails

Jenny Bromham

Oh God, I'm in the wrong country, aren't I?

From my prime sea-view table, in the dappled shade of the beach bar, I groan into my "Christmas Cocktail". This place is literally everything I'd dreamed it would be when I booked my ticket: white sands, sapphire ocean, palm trees, sun. But here I am, having a Christmas Day epiphany that where I *should* be is back in Billinge with Mum. I should be wearing my Christmas jumper over my Christmas pjs, watching Mum unwrap the new Rudolph slippers I got for her. I should be pouring Tesco-special Cava mixed with long-life orange juice into our festive wine glasses. I should be peeling parsnips in front of "Elf", whilst Mum rings Auntie Jane to remind her to put the turkey in the oven.

Instead, I'm here, in Thailand, on my own, because for some baffling reason I thought that coming here for Christmas would symbolise me taking control of my life before I hit thirty.

With renewed desperation I make a fresh attempt to draw a sip of cocktail through my heavily chewed straw. Eyes wide, cheeks drawn, I suck – a full-on fish-face. My lips lose purchase, resulting in a loud kissing noise just as a six-foot, bare-chested gym-junky swaggers by on the beach. He pauses and raises his eyebrows at me, flashing a film-star perfect smile. Really? He thinks that noise was a deliberate come-on? His ego is as blatant as that pale band of skin on the fourth finger of his left hand. Judging by the way his smile slips, I'm guessing my glare is appropriately damning. He stumbles as he attempts a quick get-away, the sand falling away around his feet. Ha. Not looking so slick now, Mister!

Honestly, where do these creeps keep coming from? There's been a steady stream since my mortifying encounter with the man who I've subsequently renamed "Scumbag", on my first night. Can't they all see that I'm very busy wallowing in my failings here? The most immediate failing being that I'm twenty-nine and I'm going to have to ask a waiter for a new straw because I've chewed up the current one … Unless … I could deconstruct the cocktail, and drink from the glass. There are only four umbrellas, six pineapple chunks and one grimacing, impaled plastic monkey to contend with.

A massive sigh escapes my lips as I meet the monkey's manic gaze. I ordered *this* drink in *this* bar because, as I walked by, the live performer was singing Mum's favourite, "White Christmas", and the board outside advertised "Christmas Cocktails". For a brief moment I'd thought it was a sign – the universe wanted me to enter this bar to find festive happiness. But now the singer is doing a James Blunt cover, and my cocktail has turned out to be this bright pink fruit concoction laced with vodka, gin and grenadine – not a drop of Baileys or mulled wine in sight. This is what happens when you get so desperate you start looking for signs from the universe when you don't even believe in signs from the universe. Yes, Manic Monkey, you have every right to give me that look.

'Do you mind if I sit here?'

It takes a split second to realise this is not the monkey's response, but instead a question from – oh, yes – yet another presumptuous, too-handsome-for-his-own-good creep gesturing at the empty wicker chair at my table. I restore my tried-and-tested glare.

'I do mind, actually,' I say. 'Just because I'm wearing a bikini and sitting in a bar, doesn't mean I want to be mithered by smarmy strangers. It means I want a tan. It means I want a drink. It means Christmas clearly isn't happening here, and I'm not about to make things worse with another one-night stand. Got it? Not interested.' Wow! If only I'd had that speech prepared for Scumbag on my first night here. I inwardly gloat at my verbal prowess whilst maintaining the glare.

But instead of scarpering, the creep fixes me with a piercing look – all dark, brooding eyes and dishevelled, beach-waved hair. Neither are going to help him.

'That's so much more information than I expected,' he says. 'I mean I get the "mithered" bit – I interrupted you and your drink – but "*smarmy*" … for asking to sit in a chair?'

He clearly believes that I'll fall for this affronted act and invite him to join me. I fold my arms and raise an eyebrow to get my message across. I've said my piece. It just needs to register with him.

'I meant "sit" in the literal sense,' he continues, those eyes so intense, as if he's trying to convince me I'm the only woman in his world. 'It wasn't meant as a euphemism for a one-night stand. I'm interested in the chair. Not you.'

'Yeah, and I've heard that one too – it's as if all you creeps have got together to agree a script. Honestly, it's Christmas Day, I don't need this,' I say. 'If you want that specific chair, you can have it, but take it to another table and bother someone else.' Any second now, his act is going to fall away, and the inevitable "smooth" smile will appear at the corner of his full lips.

But instead, he frowns. 'You've been getting a lot of hassle from guys? Okay, I'm sorry.' He actually looks like he means it, holding up his hands and stepping back. 'Listen, the only reason I asked to sit here is because this is the only space left with an unbroken view. I don't even need to angle the chair towards the table. I'd turn it to face the sea. If you're really uncomfortable with me sitting here, I get it, it's not a problem, I can go. But I'm guessing if I sit here, no one else would hit on you because they'd think we were together. It could work for both of us. And I can promise, hand on heart, that I will ignore you the whole time.'

Am I being sucked in by that faint "honest" Brummy accent or the fact that he genuinely doesn't look like he's coming on to me? No puffed out chest or pulled in stomach. No over-flexed biceps or fingers tousling his waves. He's even taken an extra step back as if to give me room to consider his proposal, although his eyes are flicking longingly towards the chair.

'Hand on heart, you'll ignore me the whole time?' I ask.

He puts a hand on his chest, covering the Santa hat worn by the Darth Vader on his t-shirt. If he does turn out to be a creep, he deserves top marks for creating this convincing "Mr Integrity" façade.

'Hand on heart,' he says. There's no ring-mark on his finger.

Making sure to keep my expression neutral, I nod for him to take a seat.

'Thank you,' he says, giving a business-like nod, then he shifts his attention to the chair as promised. He turns it ninety degrees to face the sea, pulls a notepad and pen from the back pocket of his shorts, then he sits down, propping one ankle across his knee. After flicking through the pages, he perches the pad on his lap and proceeds to gaze out to sea with the pen hovering over the page.

He clears his throat. Oh – I'm staring at him – and he can clearly sense it.

Flustered, I pick up my phone and give an elaborate 'ooh', in an attempt to suggest I've just been inundated with fun and festive messages and have absolutely no time to continue staring. I'm not sure why I bothered because a quick glance confirms Mr Integrity is being as good as his word and is ignoring me. What my phone actually reveals is a total absence of messages from home. This seven-hour time difference is rubbish. Mum, and everyone else I know, will still be tucked up in bed with the whole of Christmas Day ahead of them. I suppose this could be a good time to send some "Merry Christmas" messages ready for when they all wake up. I hold out my phone for a selfie, raising my cocktail as if I'm ready to clink glasses with the recipients. I smile and take the shot, then zoom in on the photo to check it.

How pictures can lie! I look like the independent woman I came here to become. I've got a healthy sun-kissed glow and my dark hair looks salon-great, falling into carefully blow-dried ringlets (I mean, how else was I supposed to fill what would usually be the present opening part of Christmas Day?) The bikini top is flattering, suggesting a little more cleavage than reality delivers, and my smile looks expensive – the tan making my teeth look so much whiter. The sunglasses pushed up into my hair and the raised cocktail make me look like a relaxed tourist, totally at ease in these exotic surroundings. This isn't a girl who still lives at home with her mum. This isn't a girl who has worked in the call centre for the last six years, avoiding all opportunities for promotion. This isn't a girl who settled for 5k Park Runs, instead of aspiring to marathons, and this certainly isn't a girl who makes unforgivable mistakes with married men. No – this is a woman winning at life.

I type, *Merry Christmas from sunny Thailand*, and send it first to Mum and Auntie Jane, and then to the "Drinks At The Crown" group chat – the default chat for me and my mates since a random Friday night sometime last decade. Hopefully, I'll start getting messages back before *my* Christmas Day ends.

As I put the phone down with a sigh, a familiar flash of orange catches my eye over by the flower-strewn bar. It can't be. Scumbag is over there, wearing the same conversation-starter orange shorts he was wearing on my first night here. I'd headed into the hotel bar that night planning to grab life with both hands – but instead, all I grabbed was the full attention of his disarming charm. Unfortunately, I didn't become aware of the whole

Scumbag thing until I saw his wedding ring on his bedside table the morning after. It was a failing to top all failings. Never again.

He looks over. He grins. Surely, he's not about to try his luck again after I bolted whilst he was in the shower? He picks up his drink and makes a move in my direction. No, I can't face him! I lurch across the table and grab Mr Integrity's arm.

'Quick. Stop ignoring me and pretend to flirt with me,' I hiss as he jumps in surprise.

'But the deal was,' he begins—

I cut him off. 'This is an Incoming Creep Alert!' I say. 'The deal was that you deter further come-ons. You need to look like you like me —'

Mr Integrity clocks Scumbag, and then ever-so-casually takes my hand from his arm, lifts it to his lips and kisses it. Scumbag stops dead in his tracks. Mr Integrity locks his gaze in to mine, his kiss still warm on my skin, his fingers firm, yet gentle, around my hand. I feel like a Brontë character being saved by a gallant hero and my cheeks flush with heat, my breaths quickening. Wow, those dark, brooding eyes are so dark and so brooding!

'Has it worked?' he says, without looking away or raising his lips more than a breath from my hand.

It takes a moment to register that he means "Has the kiss stopped Scumbag?" rather than "Has the kiss made you notice me?" I force myself to look over towards the bar. Scumbag's back is already turned. He's retreating towards a table of middle-aged women.

'Yes,' I breathe, not taking my hand away.

He does it for me, guiding it down to the table and letting go. 'I'm sorry about the kiss. It seemed like the easiest way to make him back off,' he says. 'Please don't think I'm a creep too.'

'I don't,' I say. 'You've done nothing but ignore me since you sat down. The kiss was ...' I feel my cheeks double-flush. 'The kiss was highly effective.'

He puts his hand on his chest over Vader's Santa hat once again, and gives a nod. A renewed pledge to ignore me. Then he turns back to his notepad.

Well, I'm not quite sure what to do with this situation. It's a Catch 22, isn't it? Mr Integrity only has integrity if he continues ignoring me, but now I don't want him to ignore me. Does that mean I want him to be a creep? I go to take an exasperated sip of my cocktail. Aaah! The mangled straw strikes again. Well, there's no way I'm asking the waiter for a new one in front of my debonaire Brontë-esque hero. My only option is to give up on the drink, keep chewing the straw, and contemplate my situation.

As discreetly as possible, I allow my gaze to wander back to the man sharing my table. He's immersed in his writing, as promised. I take in the stroke of the pen in his strong, tanned hand. I follow the flex of his forearm and linger over the way his loose t-shirt skims his biceps and his chest. I track up to the profile of his face. His cheeks are relaxed, his darkly lashed eyes lowered towards the page, his lips look soft. He's got a good profile – as handsome from the side as he is from the front. I like the faint line at the corner of his mouth, as if he'd smile easily if he wasn't committed to ignoring me. I like the way his sun-streaked hair curls, instead of waves, at the nape of his neck. And I like how perfectly content he looks – lost in his own peaceful world of words.

I suffer from a constant overflow of words – if my mouth isn't over-talking, my thoughts are over-thinking. How amazing would it be to learn to harness ideas into a gentle stream of words across a page, or to simplify them into a single gesture, like the kiss on my hand? I can still feel that kiss. I'm pretty sure that, had I been standing up, I'd have swooned. And I'm a northerner; I am not a swooner. Surely all this means I should find a way to boycott the deal for him to ignore me?

But how to do it without seeming desperate or pathetic – considering I lectured him about not being a creep, and considering I'm stuck in the wrong country due to my own stupidity, and with a chewed-up straw … I steal another look at him and inspiration strikes. Maybe if he thinks I'm a writer too, he'll be so intrigued he'll break his pledge and speak to me. This might just work.

I bend and rummage in the beach bag at my feet, pulling out the small hotel-branded notepad and pen from my room. The sole reason they put them there is so guests can steal them, right? As I straighten up, I notice Mr Integrity glancing across. His eyes dart from my notepad to my face. Is my plan already working? Is he going to ask if I write too? I will him to speak, but instead he simply nods and returns to his work.

I huff, perhaps a little too loudly. I need to make it clear that I mean business – so I turn my chair to face the sea. Is he paying attention? I'm pretty certain I catch a glimpse of movement, as if I've just missed him looking again. The line at the corner of his mouth has definitely deepened, his lips slightly lifted with a hint of a smile. He still isn't speaking.

Now all that's left is to start writing. But what to write? "What's Wrong With My Life? A Christmas List", springs to mind. Plenty of subject matter there. But if I'm feeling down on Christmas now, a list like that might just turn me into a full-on Grinch. How long can I leave my pen hovering before

More Than Mistletoe

Mr Integrity realises this is all a façade? These seconds are stretching out too far. I need a distraction in case he's noticed …

As if reading my mind, the waiter springs up behind me drawing a printed sheet of A4 from his tray. 'Will you both be dining from the Festive Menu today?'

Mr Integrity instantly shakes his head, clearly dead against the very notion, so I blurt out, 'No! We're not together. He's ignoring me.'

The waiter's eyebrows pinch and I can practically see him translating and re-translating the words.

'He's only interested in the chair. Not me,' I add to clarify.

Mr Integrity's eyes are lit with amusement, and it hits me how totally desperate I just sounded. Is he mocking me?

'Well, perhaps I'll just leave this here in case it tempts you,' the waiter says, placing the menu on the table, his attention snaring on my glass.

Oh no. I know what he's looking at.

Before I can whisk it away, the waiter reaches towards my cocktail and plucks out the mangled straw, brandishing it like a symbol of all my failings in front of my debonaire hero. Pathetic is now confirmed alongside desperate.

'Let me replace this for you,' he says as the straw droops, pitiful and rejected, in his hand. He discards it on an empty edge of his tray and picks a new pink one from the pile next to his menus. He plops it into my drink and then he jaunts off, leaving me triple-flushed, facing Mr Integrity.

My heart skips a beat, because apparently that's my new reflex reaction to this man's gaze, but I'm not going to let that stop me from defending myself.

'Okay, if you're about to tell me I gave the waiter more information than he asked for, or make a smartarse comment about adults chewing their straws, you're going to be in for a very short relationship with that chair,' I say.

Mr Integrity doesn't reply. His amusement is still sparkling like sunbeams on the sea, but there's also something else. It's like he's looking into me, trying to read me. I take a self-conscious sip of my cocktail and shudder at the blast of the booze.

'The truth is,' I say, pushing the glass away. 'I should have given that waiter a lot more information than I did.' I'm not quite sure where I'm going with this, but the words are overflowing. 'First, I should have told him that this drink does not come close to being a Christmas Cocktail. I mean, where's the Baileys?' Deflection. That's what I'm doing here, isn't it? *I'm* not the one who's pathetic and desperate, the *bar* is! I pick up the printout from the table to continue. 'Second, I should have told him that king prawns, followed by Catch of the Day, followed by piña colada cake, do not constitute a Festive Menu.' I shake my head. Why isn't Mr Integrity shaking his head too? Surely this is beyond a valid point. 'And the music,' I say. 'The Blunt cover was one thing, but a Chaz 'n' Dave cover sung by a single artist attempting both parts! It's verging on a liable offence.' Why is he still staring at me like that? What does the laughter in his eyes mean? Are my powers of deflection too weak to disguise my pathetic desperation? 'Well, I don't care what you say,' I say, crossing my arms firmly. 'If anything, I think I was pretty restrained. I mean, I didn't even point out that – crimes against Christmas aside – the waiter needs to stop letting smarmy scumbags into the bar.'

Mr Integrity says nothing. In fact, his face has closed now, as if he's read all he needs to read in my eyes, and heard all he wants to hear from my verbal overflow. His amusement has vanished. He shuts his notepad, stands up, presses his hand over Vader's Santa hat – as if that's a good enough way to excuse himself – and he walks off to the bar without a backwards glance.

Oh, so that's it then. Catch 22 case closed. Mr Integrity has kept his integrity because I am the human equivalent of a mangled straw. I could try drawing a small amount of comfort from the possibility that maybe he was never interested in the first place, but it's hard to believe that the chemistry when he kissed my hand was completely one-sided.

My phone buzzes against the table, the screen lighting up with a message. Mum. Perhaps she's sensed my need for her across the oceans. I unlock the phone and swipe to read: *Merry Christmas, Cassie, love. Beautiful photo! I'm so proud of you. THIS IS YOUR CHRISTMAS! Love you lots with festive sprinkles. I'll call from Auntie Jane's later x x x*

A fresh pang of homesickness aches through me as I think about Mum typing this in bed. In a few hours she'll be heading over to Auntie Jane's, laden with presents and parsnips and pudding. I can picture every moment of their day ahead without me, like Scrooge with the Ghost of Christmas Present – from their cackles at the cracker jokes, to their inevitable conga around the Christmas tree. My thumbs move over the keyboard, typing a reply: *I want to come home*. But then I delete it. Mum's always had this eternal, unwavering, unjustified pride in me. If I turn up back at home in the early hours of Boxing Day morning, she might finally see my failings. I'm not sure I could take that.

Instead, I re-read her message imagining her voice saying the words: "This is your Christmas." Whilst I find it easy to ignore my own voice of reason no matter how loudly it bellows, I can't ignore Mum's. She's right, isn't she?

More Than Mistletoe

This Christmas might be my own terrible mistake – it might have led to me sleeping with a married man, spending Christmas Day alone and a confirmed status of "Queen of all Failings" – but this *is* my Christmas, and it's not over yet. I need to make the most of it – no – I *will* make the most of it. Somehow.

Through the chatter and clatter of the bar, a chord strikes. Followed by a second and a third. Hang on … did the Ghost of Christmas Present just hear my pledge? Because this new song isn't a random cover, every note of this song shimmers with festive magic – "The Christmas Song" – and despite the lack of chestnuts roasting or Jack Frost nipping, a Christmassy feeling stirs inside me.

'Your Baileys, madam.' The waiter springs up beside me again and places what has to be a quadruple shot of Baileys on the table. I feel a tentative thrill, like seeing a present from Santa as a kid.

'But … I didn't order it,' I say.

The waiter smiles as he presses a folded piece of lined paper into my hand. 'I'd say a certain someone was interested in more than the chair,' he says, and turns away.

I open the note: *Hoping the correction of music and drinks lifts your Christmas spirits. If I could sort the menu for you, I would.*

Mr Integrity is behind this sudden Christmas magic? After four days totally alone, this kindness is almost too much. I'm not soppy, but my eyes well up as I keep reading: *I'm sincerely sorry if I came across as a smarmy scumbag. I won't mither you again. Merry Christmas.*

Oh no. He thought I was talking about him! I turn my chair back to the table and look around, blinking my tears away. On the opposite side of the bar, Scumbag is still attempting to score with one of the middle-aged women – luckily, she appears to be immune to his charms so far. And then I spot Mr Integrity, propped on an uncomfortable-looking stool attempting to write as the speaker blasts out beside him.

I raise my hand to get the waiter's attention.

'Straw?' he asks, smirking.

'Not funny, Mister,' I say. 'Actually, I'd like you to take a message over to the man who sent me the drink. Please will you tell him that smarmy scumbags wear orange shorts, not festive Star Wars t-shirts, and that I'd like to extend an offer of full use of the chair, however, without the obligation to ignore me?'

The waiter's lips move as he tries to remember and recite the message, then he heads off to deliver it.

It's hard not to stare. What if Mr Integrity still rejects me on account of my mangled straw syndrome? I message Mum to distract myself: *Have a fun morning. Hope you like the pressie. Speak later. Love you lots with festive sprinkles too x x x*

There's a familiar clearing of the throat across the table, and the clink of another glass being put down. Mr Integrity has returned, and for the first time, I see his full smile. It's quite simply mesmerising. He extends his hand across the table to me, and I take it, anticipating the warm press of his lips against my skin again. But I'm forgetting that this debonair, thoughtful, Brontë-esque hero is also the personification of integrity. Instead, he shakes my hand. To be honest, this could be a fist-pump and I'd still semi-swoon.

'If I'm allowed to stop ignoring you, I should introduce myself,' he says. 'I'm Jamie.'

'I'm Cassie.' I hope my smile isn't too Manic Monkey right now.

Jamie gives my hand a squeeze before letting me go. 'I don't want an over-long handshake to put me on your smarmy scumbag list.' He angles his chair to face me and sits, leaning towards me.

'Between the festive Darth Vader, the Baileys and "The Christmas Song", I think you're exempt,' I say. 'Unless you invest in orange shorts.'

His eyes flick across to Scumbag – thank God he's understood the reference – and his amusement is back, not mocking at all. 'Thanks for inviting me back over here, Cassie,' he says, locking his gaze into mine.

I like the sound of my name on his lips. 'Thanks for the corrections to the Christmas drink and music,' I say. 'Honestly, if I was going to make one song request to inspire some Christmas spirit, I'd have chosen the same one.' As I speak, the final line of the song wishes a me-rry Christ-mas to me.

'Oh, I didn't just request one song,' Jamie says, his eyes sparkling as the performer launches directly into "Last Christmas". 'It seemed like your Christmas spirit needed a full playlist to revive it.'

Is this real? A few minutes ago, I was festively destitute, and now my favourite Christmas song is playing and I'm drinking Baileys with Jamie the Swoon-monger. I hold up my glass, and he clinks his against mine.

'What are we drinking to?' he asks.

'To this moment,' I say. 'The best Christmas gift I've had all day.' I no longer care that I'm beaming. But a softening in Jamie's eyes dims it down. Oh no, no, no. That's sympathy, isn't it? He's feeling sorry for me! 'No! I didn't mean poor Cassie's got no presents!' I say quickly. I want festive flirtation, not pity. 'I did have presents, actually. My mum smuggled two into my hand luggage before I left. It wasn't her fault that the fancy tanning

More Than Mistletoe

oil was confiscated at the airport because it was over the liquid allowance. And at least they let me unwrap it before they took it off me. And the other present, which I *did* open this morning, was a Christmas jumper – which I would be wearing right now if it was twenty degrees cooler in Thailand. So, no need to look sorry for me, Mr! Sharing a Baileys with you is actually only the second-best gift I've had all day and would be firmly relegated to third place if I had my tanning oil.'

During the course of my speech, he's gone from pity, to confusion, to a smile, and now he laughs. Flirtation and amusement back on track. 'What happens if I tell you that was so much more information than I expected?'

'I'd say get bloody used to it if you're going to sit here.'

'I'll drink to that too then,' he says, and we clink glasses again. Honestly, the way he's looking at me. If someone showed up with a sprig of mistletoe, we'd be ... I try to tame my thoughts.

'So, I've got a question,' I say. 'What were you writing about earlier?'

Jamie takes a slow sip of his drink and shuffles a little in his seat as if he's uncomfortable. 'I'm a very private writer,' he says. 'What about you? What were you going to write about?'

Okay, that was a quick deflection. There's a tiny "hmmm" at the back of my mind – the kind that makes wild guesses, like he's a mass murderer who enjoys a written plan-of-action, or a wildly off-track trainspotter – but "hmmms" like that are best ignored. 'I was considering writing a sort of twisted Christmas list based on the things I need to change in my life,' I say. 'I had some great material but was worried it was so anti-Christmas, it might have Grinchified me.'

'Grinchified?' he says, smiling again. 'I'm relieved you didn't write it then.'

And, I've got to say, I'm relieved too. Wallowing wasn't a solution. But this whole "making the most of my Christmas" thing is already working out pretty well.

There's a cheer from across the bar, and Jamie and I turn to look. The performer is up on his feet, carrying his guitar, serenading the table of middle-aged women – leaving Scumbag with a satisfying absence of attention. The performer extends the song, looping back to the second verse, and now he's making his way towards us.

Jamie grins. It's a smile laced with mischief, and it makes me several degrees hotter.

'Dance with me?' he asks.

If I properly swoon this is going to be embarrassing, but I'm willing to risk it. He takes my hand and we rise from our chairs, meeting in a single step. His other hand finds the bare skin of my lower back, just above the line of my bikini. My senses ignite. He draws me closer and our bodies are almost touching, moving together, his breath in my hair, his broad shoulder beneath my hand, the smell of his warm, sea-salty skin filling my senses. And, as much as I love "Last Christmas", it's not my passion for the song that makes me want the performer to keep it going for the rest of Christmas Day.

The rest of Christmas Day? Hang on. I'm breaking my own rule here, aren't I? After what happened with Scumbag, I promised myself I'd always complete a full interrogation before giving anyone else a chance. But I haven't asked Jamie anything about himself. I've let his actions speak instead. Maybe he's not free to spend the rest of Christmas Day dancing with me. Maybe – and I feel bad even thinking it when he's already proven himself to be integrity personified – maybe, he's not actually free at all …

I draw back a little and look up into those dark, brooding eyes as we continue to sway.

'I'm so sorry, Jamie,' I say, 'but I've got to ask you: are you here on your own?'

His smile falters. 'I'm here with you.'

There's a second "hmmm" at the back of my mind, and this time I listen to it. 'I don't mean here in the bar. I mean are you here on holiday on your own?'

His eyes dart away from mine. His cheeks redden.

Oh no. I pull away from him. I'm about to ask the killer question, "Are you single?", but I don't even get the chance to speak. A beautiful brunette in a blue bikini appears behind him and prods him on the shoulder.

'Bloody hell, Jamie. I've been looking for you everywhere. I had to leave the kids outside on their own to come in here. It's time for Christmas dinner.'

As she speaks, Jamie's blush deepens. The singer stops singing.

'I was just …' He can't even think of an excuse to finish that sentence, can he? He turns to me and holds up his hands in an apology. 'I'm sorry.'

Creep, Creep, Creep, Creep, CREEP!

The brunette gives me a look somewhere between contempt and pity, and she yanks Jamie's arm.

'Come on!' She starts to walk off, but he pulls his arm away and looks at me.

'Go buy yourself a pair of orange shorts,' I say, grabbing my beach bag and tossing back my hair. And I walk out the bar through the opposite exit to a scattered applause.

More Than Mistletoe

To the spectators in the bar, I must have looked like the controlled, independent woman that I came here to become. But inside I'm reeling. I could so easily have made the same mistake twice. These creeps must have a gullibility radar or something. I lean against a palm tree trying to slow my breathing. Over on the beach, the brunette is storming off ahead, with Jamie ushering two kids in her wake.

A flash of orange catches my eye. A super smug Scumbag saunters towards me carrying my Baileys – he clearly thinks I'm easy prey.

'That was a dignified exit, Kayleigh,' he says, holding out my drink. 'Most girls would have slapped the creep, or at least—'

I don't know if it's the fact he called me Kayleigh, or the pot/kettle creep thing, or the fact that *this is my Christmas* and I'm not going to let him ruin another moment of it – I grab the Baileys out of his hand and sploosh it in his two-timing face.

As he steps back, blinking Irish Cream from his eyes and swearing, the table of middle-aged women cheer from the bar, and one calls out,

'Nice one, love – saved us a job! Now that's what I call Christmas Spirit!'

I raise my glass to toast them, knock back the final sip, press the empty glass into Scumbag's hand, and then I turn and walk away.

And I'm smiling – I can't help it. I know that wasn't dignified or thirty-year-old mature, but I feel like I've just passed all the guilt about the other night back to its rightful owner, and now I'm free. I took control – my way! As I cross the beach towards the sea, the women's laughter still pealing behind, I let the heat and the light and the beauty of the scene ahead fill me. The sun scatters glitter through the sand and decks each wave with tinselled silver. The palm trees sway with their coconut baubles and the breeze carries the distant notes of "Santa Claus is Coming to Town" from the beach bar.

'Cassie!'

For God's sake! Just as I'm about to congratulate myself for doing something right. I spin towards Jamie's breathless voice. He's running towards me and I consider rekindling my tried-and-tested glare, but I'm no longer willing to let him, or any other creep, dampen my Christmas spirit.

'Please, let me explain,' he pants, stumbling a little as he stops before me.

'What is there to explain?' I ask. 'We shared a table and we had half a dance. We don't owe each other anything. It was nothing.'

He steps towards me, his palms turned up in a plea to be heard. 'It wasn't "nothing" though. It was something more – I felt it, and I thought you felt it too.'

Honestly, he deserves more than top marks for this "Mr Integrity" façade; this is Oscar-worthy. Unfortunately, my instincts are acting of their own free will, trying to force me to move closer to him, to believe his shallow words. I have to stay in control.

'I'm going now, Jamie,' I say, stepping back. 'Go and spend Christmas with your family or writing your trainspotting notes or your murder plans. Please don't follow me again.'

'You think I was writing trainspotting notes or murder plans?' he says as I start to walk away.

I keep going. No need to engage. I return my focus to the glittered sands, the tinselled ocean, the baubled palm trees, the shining possibilities of my Thai Christmas.

Jamie's voice follows with the breeze. 'Until this moment, I've never believed in the guiding hand of fate or signs from the universe—'

Okay, I know I was struck by a similar thought earlier, with the whole "White Christmas" drawing me into the bar to find festive happiness thing, but I'd never share such pretentious musings out loud – especially with a fleeing stranger. I speed up.

'—But something drew me into this bar, and it wasn't the bad Blunt cover,' he continues, his voice rising with my distance. 'I thought for a moment that the "something" was the chair with the perfect view, the chance to sit and write on Christmas Day, so I asked the woman already sitting at the table if I could join her. And she looked at me.'

Hang on. Is he speaking in prose?

'She was beautiful,' he calls after me. 'With long, dark hair and eyes full of stories. And I knew, there and then—'

I turn. Jamie is standing where I left him, his notepad open in his hands, his long lashes lowered towards the page as he reads. He clears his throat. His cheeks have reddened. 'And I knew, there and then, that she was what fate wanted me to find—' He must feel my eyes on him, because he stops reading and looks up and our eyes lock.

This isn't fair; this is cruel. Because whilst my head is screaming "CREEP!" yet again, everything else in me wants the connection in his words to be real. 'Why are you doing this?' I call.

He lifts his notepad as if it's an explanation. 'I'm sorry. I know it's bad writing,' he replies. 'And I know I told you I was only interested in the chair, not you. That's why I didn't want to share it. But it's not trainspotting notes and it's not a murder plan. I meant what I wrote. I mean it now. I think we're destined to—'

'We're destined to rip up that page and go our separate ways,' I say. Honestly, he doesn't know when to stop. If I didn't have a newly deepened reserve of Christmas spirit, I don't think I'd be nearly as restrained.

His notepad falls to his waist as his shoulders sag. 'Okay. I get it.' His voice is so soft I barely catch his words across the distance.

'Just go home to your wife and kids, Jamie,' I call, already walking away. 'It's Christmas.'

'No, wait!' he calls. 'Sister and two nephews!'

I stop in my tracks. *Sister and two nephews?* I turn. He's already walking towards me, and I'm drawn to him.

'I'm here with my sister, Sam, and her boys and my mum,' he says. 'Not very cool, I know, but hopefully better than being an adulterous, murdering trainspotter?'

There's no smile on his lips. He's posing this as a genuine question!

'Do you know,' I say, feeling my own smile stretch, 'my new Christmas jumper might have to be relegated to second-best gift of the day?' He's so close now, I can see his confusion pinching his eyebrows. 'I think the words "sister and two nephews" have just snatched the first-prize gift position.'

Jamie's eyes light up. He's just an arms-reach away. I close the gap and take the notepad, pressing it to the Darth Vader Santa hat on his chest.

'How about going back to our table for a sparkling wine and orange juice, and you can read this to me again?' I say.

His fingers lace around mine and he moves so close I think he's going to kiss me. My heart stills in anticipation and I lift my face to meet his soft, full lips … but he really is Mr Integrity, isn't he? He smiles his incredible smile and lifts my hand to receive his kiss.

'How could I refuse my muse?' he says. 'Christmas and cocktails with you were meant to be.'

Jenny Bromham

Christmas at The Little Blu Bookshop

Sarah Shard

'Out of all the crazy ideas, this is by far the stupidest.' Ben shrugged as he slammed the fourth dust-covered box of books onto the countertop just in front of his friend. 'Never mind that you are doing it on Christmas Eve.'

'With best friends like you who needs enemies?' Michael said sarcastically whilst waving like a crazy person trying to disperse the dust cloud Ben had created. The dust settled but unfortunately, it settled mostly on him. His small, circular, brown-framed glasses were almost as dusty as the handkerchief he removed from his tweed blazer pocket to clean them.

'We are in the prime of our lives.' Ben turned his attention to the window as he spotted two sets of pretty eyes peeking through the gaps in the newspaper. 'Come on. You should be coming out with me living life to the max, not getting yourself tied down to this place.'

'By place, do you mean the shop or the village we both grew up in?' Michael continued to check through the mountain of book-filled boxes that were taking over the shop floor.

The eyes belonged to two pretty blonde women and Ben's peephole flirting approach had worked because he was now patting the dust off his leather jacket and running his fingers through his long and wavy dark hair which he insisted was "all the rage" – although the accompanying dusty sheen wasn't part of his usual go-to look.

As he gave a thumbs-up to the giggling women outside the window, he gave Michael one last chance to join him. 'Both. So, you gonna pause the dork and come check out the bunnies with me?'

'Thanks, but I'm kinda busy right now.' He pointed to the pile of boxes next to him. 'And it would go quicker if you were helping me.'

Ben shook his head, already out the door as he waved goodbye.

Michael knew it was probably for the best. Ben was useful lugging boxes and signing for deliveries, but the actual organisation of the stock was not in his skill set. Plus, it was Michael's favourite part of opening a bookshop. As he opened a new box, he took each book one by one, checking to ensure there was no damage and then placed it in the piles by genre and author name. Every now and then, he would recognise a book he had read, hold it close, squeeze his eyes shut and inhale the history of each page – something only true book lovers ever did. He would reminisce about the first time he had read that particular book, and if it was one he had read multiple times, it went on the special "Recommended Reads" pile that was growing with each box.

Michael was the epitome of the term "book worm". Growing up, he would split his spare time between the bookshop in Windermere, the library in Applewood, or locked in his bedroom either reading or writing. In the book shop, he would sit for hours in the corner reading every book he couldn't afford from cover to cover, from the classics like "Treasure Island" or "Nineteen Eighty-Four" to "Slaughter House Five" when the owner wasn't looking.

He carried on into the night, emptying each box and filling the shelves with a mixture of his personal collection (well, the ones he was happy to let go of) as well as the few hundred he had managed to get at a bargain price from a shop in nearby Whitehaven at their closing-down sale.

As evening crept closer, and the dulcet tones of Tony Blackburn excitedly announced (from the old radio Michael had found under the counter) that Pink Floyd had retained the number one single slot for the fourth week running, Michael was overcome with tiredness. As soon as his body hit the old armchair in the corner of the store, he dozed off and remained dead to the world until the early hours of the morning when the clang of the milk bottles being delivered stirred him awake.

Realising the time, he jumped from the chair, grabbed his jacket, satchel and keys, and rushed out of the shop. Tripping over the corner of an empty box, he fell face-first at the feet of Bert, the milkman. The contents of his bag were flung under the milk float, his glasses landed on Bert's boots and the keys fell onto the grid at the side of the road.

'Sugar!' he yelled, watching them land and slowly, one key at a time, fall over the edge until he heard the sound of the dreaded splash. He managed to reach under the vehicle to grab his bag.

'Morning, Michael lad. Need some help down there?' The portly, red-faced and balding man, dressed in a white jacket and overalls, leant down and offered him his hand. Embarrassed Michael grabbed it and was yanked quickly to his feet.

'Thanks, Bert. Don't suppose you can rescue my keys as well, can you?'

'Well, this could be your lucky day.' Bert reached into the back of the float and grabbed a long metal hook. 'If I had a pound note for every time I dropped my keys down a grid I wouldn't need to be delivering milk.' Within a few minutes, he had rescued the keys and dried them off before handing them back to a dishevelled and flustered Michael.

'You're a lifesaver. If you ever want a book, it's on the house.'

'Not much of a one for reading, but I'll always take a bag of those liquorice sticks – if you have any.'

'Sorry. Mrs. Clifton emptied all the sweets before I took over the shop. Just be selling books, I'm afraid.'

'Shame that. The Mrs has to go all the way to Windermere for them now and she gives me a right earache when I ask for some.' Bert placed the stick back on the float and climbed into the driver's seat. 'You looked in a rush but no point giving you a lift. You could run faster.' Bert laughed, quite proud of his attempt at milkman humour.

'Sugar, yes. I gotta run. Thanks again.' Michael quickly locked the shop door before running off down the street.

He managed to get home, changed and make it to the library just before the first class of pupils from St Cuthbert's visited, as they did every Monday at ten a.m. sharp. The teacher opened the door and the children marched in one by one. As soon as they were all inside, the order turned to chaos as they dispersed across the children's section throwing their book returns towards the desk where Marjorie was waiting. She and Michael made a start on the returns, whilst Lydia sorted the bottles of milk and biscuits ready for the eleven a.m. story time.

'Excuse me, do you have any new books? I've read all of these,' asked a young girl as she straightened her glasses, held together on the bridge of the nose by white tape.

Marjorie smiled at the disappointed girl. 'Jessie, you know we don't get any new books until the end of the month. Why don't you look on the returns trolley round the back? I'm sure I saw one of the Enid Blyton books on the bottom shelf. One of the Famous Five series.'

Jessie raised her eyebrows while she considered the option and then smiled before running off to track down her next adventure. As she did so, Lydia came to help her two colleagues sort the books and library cards ready to stamp the next lot out.

'So, have you heard about the new girl?' Marjorie asked Lydia but ensuring Michael heard her.

'Oh, yes. Bert said he saw her last night on her own in the pub.' Michael was never surprised that the revelation of a young lady alone in a pub would continue to draw attention, even in 1979.

'What is she here for? Did she say?'

'Bert said she told Betty – you know, that new bargirl – that she was looking for a friend but wouldn't say who as it was a surprise. She's foreign. Got one of them foreign accents. French, no doubt.' Lydia spoke in a hushed voice.

Michael could still hear what they were saying but as he often did, chose to act obliviously. He took himself off to the far corner of the library where he had begun re-organising the encyclopaedias the previous Friday. He was eager to get it finished before he left at the end of the week. This job had been a stopgap whilst he worked on his writing, which he had intended to pursue more vehemently before the old sweet shop had come up for rent. He knew the library didn't need the three of them full-time but he had been grateful that Marjorie had taken him on when he'd finished university. His time working at the library had given him the right kind of insights into books he needed. He had learned what to stock based on what the customers asked for and, more importantly, which books they were prepared to pay for.

As he sat on the floor pulling the final few books from the bottom shelf, a wave of perfume filled the air and instantly captivated him. His senses awoke with a familiar scent of hyacinth and vanilla. He looked up, eager to see who the owner of such an aroma could be but there was no one nearby. Hypnotised by the familiarity of the scent, he stood up to investigate further. His nose led him to the main area again where he found Jessie gleefully spritzing herself.

'May I take a look?' he asked her politely. The young girl reluctantly passed him the delicate heart-shaped bottle which had an arrow through it. The closer he got, the more intense the wave of familiarity became. 'Is this yours?'

More Than Mistletoe

'Yes. I didn't steal it. That nice lady gave it to me.' Jessie pointed towards the door and the back of a woman with long dark hair, who was disappearing out of sight.

Michael handed the bottle back to Jessie, who had followed Marjorie's advice and was clutching one of Enid Blyton's Famous Five books in her other hand.

'Do you know who the lady was?' he asked.

Jessie just shrugged as she popped the small delicate bottle in her coat pocket and ran off to join the queue of children ready to get their new books checked out. Dissatisfied, Michael returned to the corner of the library, but his mind kept rushing back to that smell and trying to remember why it was familiar. He knew he would figure it out eventually, but for the same reason he liked to write stories of mystery, his brain wouldn't give up until the mystery had been solved.

*

Another day passed, and still Sofia had been unable to find him. She sat staring out of the window of the smallest bedroom at the Sunflower Bed and Breakfast on the edge of Applewood village. The walls were decorated in sunflower-covered wallpaper and the bedding was yellow and brown, all matching. This amount of chintz was a far cry from her bedroom at home in Calcata, on the outskirts of Rome where Sofia had lived with her family. Her mother had passed away a few months ago, and whilst sorting through her belongings, Sofia discovered that her parents had been very good at keeping secrets.

For Sofia, it was the discovery of his last letter and the realisation that her father's intervention had been the real reason her teenage heart had been broken. She felt deeply betrayed, but with both her parents now gone, her focus shifted to his last letter; it ignited a spark of hope that her teenage fantasy of falling in love with the boy from England could become real. However, she couldn't help wondering if she had made a mistake. Her grand gesture was not turning out exactly as she had hoped so far.

Knock, knock.

'Only me, love. Got you a nice brew and some digestives.'

Sofia opened the door to Mrs Potts, the owner of the Sunflower, who was the only friendly person she had encountered so far.

'You're so kind.' She smiled as the short, rounded lady in her sixties, with rollers in her hair and a scarf covering them, placed a tray on the small dressing table.

'Not at all, love. Any luck today?'

Sofia shook her head. 'No. I found the library but couldn't see him. It was busy so I didn't ask. Your village reminds me very much of my home in Calcata. We have just a small number of shops and one school.'

'Oh, isn't that a coincidence. Not many new businesses open up round here, usually go into towns like Windermere.'

'It's nice here. At the library there were lots of children in there. One sweet girl said she liked my perfume, so I gave her a small bottle I keep in my purse. I always carry two, anyway.'

'Oh, yes. I forgot the school children go to the library on Monday mornings. Well, don't lose hope, dear. I'm sure you will find your Mickey. It's a shame you don't know his surname. "What's meant for you won't pass you by" as my dear grandmother used to say.' Mrs Potts gave her arm a comforting squeeze before leaving the room.

Sofia recalled the little girl and how wide her smile had been when she'd handed over the little bottle of perfume. Growing up, she was not allowed perfume, so she would sneak into her mother's bedroom to use it when she was working. She would have loved someone to gift her even the smallest of bottles. Seeing her own envy in the young girl's eyes, she couldn't resist the opportunity to make someone else smile. As she poured the tea from the sunflower patterned teapot into the matching teacup and saucer, her thoughts shifted to the object of her teenage affections. Sitting back on the little chair by the window, she felt consumed by the words from the letters she had read so many times as a love-sick teenager. Letters her parents had destroyed, although, when she found the last letter, she realised that her mother had secretly held onto it but had never told her. There was no envelope, the top part of the page was torn off and what remained was crumpled. The words had faded, and the handwriting smudged but it didn't matter to Sofia. The three words that remained undamaged were his nickname for her, "Mi Piccolo Blu".

As she sat clutching the letter from her case, she overheard Mrs Potts talking to another lady outside her window. She knew she shouldn't listen to other people's conversations, but they were far from quiet. Whilst English was her second language, besides a slight accent, she loved to listen to local dialects.

'Our Bert saw him at the weekend. He's turning it into a bookshop of all things.'

'Always did have his nose in a book, that young Bennett boy.' Sofia's interest piqued and she paused as sparks of excitement and hope began to rise inside. Could this be him? A bookshop certainly would suit her pen pal.

More Than Mistletoe

'Oh, didn't he just. Our Betty had eyes for him at one time but no girl ever turned his head. Always reading or writing, that one. Went to university, too. Not many around here have one of those degree things, that's for sure.'

Mrs Potts sensed she had an audience. 'Yes. Whoever does turn his head will be a very lucky lady. Thinking about it, have you ever heard anyone call him Mickey?' Sofia was now fully invested in the answer and smiled down on the landlady, who averted her eyes to the window briefly in acknowledgement of Sofia.

'Mickey? No, never heard him use that name. Don't know of a Mickey round here. Why you asking, Lil?'

'Ah, no reason. Not one for gossip, me. Better get back at it, getting on.'

As the ladies said their goodbyes, Sofia sat back against her chair, clinging to the letter with renewed hope this might be him. A mixture of emotions swirled in her stomach, butterflies of hope battling dragonflies of doubt at the possibility that a bookshop could hold the key to finding him.

*

Michael had been in the shop an hour before Ben turned up to take over the morning shift.

'You're late! It's my last week in the library. I promise after this week I won't need you to cover or help out as much.' Ben looked tired, his shirt was untucked, and his hair was more Bob Marley than Mick Jagger.

'Well, you owe me big time. I had to leave the arms of a beautiful woman to come here and wait for your deliveries.' Ben opened a bottle of milk from the counter to make himself a brew. 'Where are the teabags? Can't function without a brew, you know that, Mickey.'

Michael went over to his satchel and took out a small white box of PG Tips.

'Here, and don't call me that. No one has called me that since junior school. Right, the stationery order is due today and the sign guy is coming to finish it off and cover it up, ready for the reveal.'

'Oh, yeah. Still think it's a stupid name for a shop.'

'So you told me before. It means something to me and that's all that matters. Now, can I trust you to not go wandering off if a pretty blonde walks past?' Michael put his hand on his friend's shoulder, squeezing it tight and looking for a positive response.

'Well, if the ladies come a-knocking, who am I to deny them the pleasure of my company? Anyway, think I'm more into brunettes than blondes now. I know they say blondes have more fun, but brunettes can be feisty.'

Ben's cheeky wink did nothing to instil confidence, but after twenty years of friendship, and despite their apparent personality differences, he was one of the only people Michael trusted with his life – including his bookshop dream.

It was a quiet morning in the library, so Michael took the time to clear his stuff from his locker and review his list of things he had left to do before opening. Marjorie peered over his shoulder.

'You selling Christmas ornaments, too?'

'No. It's for the display. I'm opening Christmas Eve aren't I? It would look a bit "bah humbug" if I didn't have any decorations. I am hand making some, just nothing over the top.'

'Do you need any help? I can pop over on Friday afternoon as we're closing early, and it is your last day. Can't do it all on your own, can you?'

'That's so kind of you. I'll save the tree decorating for then if you like. Not my greatest skill, is it?' They both looked at the library tree, stunning from the front with perfectly co-ordinated baubles and tinsel that Marjorie had done, versus the purposely hidden side which she insisted Michael do, much to their mutual regret. The baubles were sporadic, the tinsel falling off. As they looked, the third bauble of the week fell and smashed on the floor.

'Well, everything comes in threes, so they say.' She laughed before handing him a dustpan and brush.

As he swept the red sparkly shards from the library floor, he looked up at the tree. The red and gold tinsel was perfectly balanced between the branches, which were dotted with gold, red and green baubles of all shapes and sizes. Above his head were the coloured paper chains made by the local school children, which brightened up the dreary old building and the shiny lantern-style decorations placed along the bookshelves.

He noticed a paper snowflake had fallen to the floor. Picking it up, he was transported back to the memory of the first and only girl he'd ever had a crush on. As he touched each corner of the paper, he recalled how it was just like the one he'd created when he was twelve years old. He remembered how his class had been matched to another school class in Italy. The pupils were tasked with sending Christmas cards to their new pen pals. Michael thought about how he was the only one who didn't send a normal card but instead cut out the snowflake to send. At the time, he didn't know who he would be matched with, but he was excited to get a Christmas card back from Italy, a country he had read so much about but could only dream of visiting. He smiled at the thought of the delicate handmade card he'd received from a young girl named Sofia. After that first Christmas exchange, they had become pen pals, and this time of year always reminded him of her and that first card. He smiled to himself as he whispered, 'Buon Natale, mio piccolo blu.' (Happy Christmas, my little blu.)

*

Sofia stood across the street from the old sweet shop. A man she didn't recognise stood outside signing for a delivery as another man stood perilously on a ladder, removing the old sign from above the door. She observed from afar as he carried the large box in through the shop door, bantering with the other guy before returning to the pavement. She spotted a pause in their conversation, and seeing an opening, quickly crossed the street.

'Hello?' she said to the man on the pavement, before nervously biting the right side of her bottom lip and holding out her delicate hand.

'Well, hello, there, beautiful.' The man took her hand, and his face lit up in a smile before he gently placed a kiss on top of it.

Sofia couldn't help but smile back at him. No one had ever kissed her hand like that before.

'I'm looking for someone.' She nervously bit her lip again before continuing. 'Mickey, are you, my Mickey? Spiacente, I mean, sorry.' She shook her head as she felt her cheeks becoming hot with embarrassment. 'Not my ... I mean, just Mickey.'

'I can be anyone you want me to be, darling.' She watched as he looked her up and down as if taking in every inch of her but without looking directly at her face. His gaze hovered over the perfection of her hourglass figure and tiny waist. She tilted her head to the side, reaching to lock eyes with him. As they did, she felt disappointed that she didn't get the butterflies she always imagined she would. She had dreamed of that moment for over ten years and all the scenarios she had played out in her mind had a magical moment when their eyes would meet and there would be a spark; butterflies would spiral inside them in perfect synchronicity, and they would both *just know*. The connection she felt to the words on the paper didn't seem to be coming to life as her teenage self had dreamt of a thousand times.

She pulled her hand away and stepped back a little. 'Are you Mickey?' she repeated.

'Mickey, well, erm, hard to say really.' The man looked uneasy as he fidgeted with his jacket collar and rubbed the back of his head. 'Why don't you let me take you for a drink on Friday? We could get to know each other a bit more.'

'I'm Sofia,' she continued, but he still didn't seem to recognise her.

'Sofia? What a beautiful name for a beautiful woman. Shall I pick you up about seven-thirty?'

'Erm, well.' She scrunched her lips, unsure of how she felt. Considering how long she'd waited to meet him, she had to see it through. 'Yes, okay. I am staying at The Sunflower, do you know it?'

'Oh, yes. Lilly Potts' place.' He walked inside, popped the box down and returned outside. Taking her hand in his again, he kissed it. 'See you Friday, beautiful.'

Sofia smiled back before walking away. She felt frustrated that he didn't seem to recognise her name. After so much waiting, the teenage love they'd declared all those years ago seemed to have eroded over time. *Was I that easy to forget?* she thought, longing to hear him whisper, "Mi piccolo blu".

When she arrived back at the bed and breakfast, Mrs Potts was polishing the brass door knocker.

'So, did you go to the bookshop?' she asked eagerly.

'Sí. I met him, I think.'

'You think?'

'He wasn't who I expected. I don't think he remembered me, but he is taking me out on Friday. Hopefully, it will feel different then.'

She smiled, but she could see her own concerns reflected in Mrs Potts raised eyebrow and suspicious-looking smile.

*

Friday came round quickly; Ben held the fort in the shop during the day and Michael worked late into the night every night to get everything ready for the opening on Christmas Eve.

'Well, mate, we're almost there,' said Ben. 'Shelves are stocked, and I managed to fix that old till so it will last a little longer. Nearly lost a finger in it yesterday.'

The men stood next to each other looking around with pride at the transformation of the little sweet shop into a fully stocked and almost ready bookshop.

'You should be proud of yourself, Michael; it couldn't have been easy,' added Marjorie as she was placing the blue and white paper chains in layers on the tree. Ben had already helped her to hang the bigger white snowflakes from the ceiling as well as the odd sprig of mistletoe, which Michael had argued against, but Ben had insisted, "In case any pretty young lady finds herself underneath some"'. Marjorie reluctantly agreed thinking it might add a bit of festive fun.

'I couldn't have done it without both of you. So, thank you so much. I hope you'll both be there on Monday. I have the brass band coming at around one to play Christmas carols outside and the school choir will be here shortly after for a sing-a-long.' Michael straightened one of the blue wooden hand-painted star ornaments on the tree.

'For someone who isn't mad on Christmas, you sure went to a lot of effort making all the ornaments yourself.'

Michael ignored his friend's remark. 'I thought you said you had a date.'

'Yes, I do. A beautiful exotic brunette is waiting for me to sweep her off her feet.' Ben winked at his friend before heading towards the door. 'Or hopefully, she will sweep me off mine.'

'Where did you meet this mystery brunette again? You didn't say,' enquired Michael.

'I dunno. She was looking for some guy called Dickie or something but found me. Must be destiny.'

'What do you *mean*, Dickie or *something*?'

'Yeah, but she couldn't have said Mickey, could she? You ain't used that name since you were in junior school, mate. As you keep reminding me.'

'Guess not. There's only one person who might call me that but I can't imagine that it was her.'

Ben's avoidance tactics continued. 'Anyway, mustn't keep the lady waiting. I'm at my sister's place this weekend so will be back for opening on Monday. Nice to see you again.'

Ben nodded at Marjorie, who waved back before repositioning the star that Michael had added.

Michael locked the door behind his friend and turned to Marjorie. 'That mystery woman in the village, what was her name again?'

'Oh, I don't remember, love, but sounds like she might be keen on young Benjamin, doesn't it? No doubt she'll realise what a mistake that is soon enough. Why, do you know her?'

'Erm. Probably not.' Michael shook off the ludicrous notion that she might be someone he once cared for. 'Anyway, back to business. So, do you think the shop's looking good enough to open yet?'

'Once we finish the Christmas decorations then I think it is ready to open. I do have to ask you though, why is everything blue?'

'You'll see.' He touched his finger to the side of his nose, not ready to reveal anything quite yet.

'Can't wait to find out. And I am really looking forward to Christmas Eve, now more than ever. It's going to be such a special one this year. I can feel it in my water.' It was an expression Michael had never understood but he felt it, too. This would be his first Christmas at the bookshop, and the start of a whole new chapter in his life. He was eager to turn that page.

*

'Hello, Ben. What brings you here?' asked Mrs Potts as a shy Sofia hid from view behind the door of the small dining room.

'Oh, how do, Mrs Potts? I'm here to pick up … erm, Sofia.'

'Oh. You changed your name, have you? Funny that, lad. I'm sure I never heard anyone call you Mickey.' Sofia could just about see the back of the landlady, standing with one hand on her hip, the other holding the door halfway closed as she tapped her foot waiting for an explanation.

'Erm, well,' answered Ben awkwardly. His voice lowered and became too muffled for Sofia to hear.

Mrs Potts said intentionally loudly, 'Well, sorry but you will have to take yourself out. She won't be going out with you tonight.' He mumbled something to her which Sofia strained to hear. She could only make out the word, "Monday".

Mrs Potts closed the door behind her and made her way into the dining room. Sofia didn't know whether to feel relieved that it wasn't him, upset that she had been mistaken or annoyed that she had been deceived.

'I'm so sorry, love. That was Ben Bradshaw, not Michael or Mickey as I think you know him as.'

'Michael? Is that his name?'

'Yes, Michael Bennett is the owner of the new bookshop. It seems young Ben saw a pretty face and forgot his own name. No harm done though. He said the shop is having a big opening on Monday. You can see if Michael is the one you have been looking for. I think he is. Now, do you want some dinner? I made some cottage pie earlier.'

'No, thank you.' Sofia had no idea what a cottage pie was, but she didn't feel hungry. 'I think I will get changed and go to bed early. Thank you so much for speaking to him.' Sofia smiled as she left the dining room and headed up the steep, creaky old staircase to her room. Once inside, she walked over to the window and could see Ben walking away from the house. She closed the curtains and picked up the letter again, holding it to her chest, and whispered, 'Presto amor mio, presto.'

*

Michael stood at the door of the closed shop. A small crowd gathered outside. With his hands shaking, he took a deep breath and looked upwards as if waiting for some divine permission to signal he was ready. When he opened the door, it triggered the ping of the old-fashioned bell that had been there since before it was even a sweet shop.

He stood back to greet the familiar faces of the villagers who were stepping in one by one to explore his new little empire. Marjorie was there with her husband. After hugging Michael, she headed for the tree to check everything was exactly as she'd left it. The school children with their parents all ran straight to the Children's Adventure section, eager to pick up another Christmas gift. Bert and Lydia were looking around to see what changes he had made and Betty from the pub seemed to be hovering under some mistletoe trying her best to catch Ben's eye while he stood talking to a pretty, auburn-haired girl.

Michael looked around and smiled. His dream of one day owning a bookshop had come true. The hard work, relentless saving and bravery it had taken to accomplish his dreams all started to feel real.

When he saw his first customer approach the empty counter, he quickly shuffled through the small crowd to serve her.

'Hello, Mrs Potts. How can I help you?'

'I wondered if you had one of the books in that my niece hasn't read yet. She likes Enid Blyton and I know she's asked Santa for one.'

'Oh, yes. Jessie's been wanting this one.' Michael took a book from the shelf next to the counter. 'And I know we haven't had it in the library yet, so she'll love it.' He'd suspected young Jessie would convince someone to buy it for her, so he had put it to one side.

'Oh, I wish I had come to you for all my presents. Would have made it so much easier,' sighed Mrs Potts as he delicately wrapped the book in white paper and tied it with a blue ribbon. 'Well, isn't that perfect? Can I ask though, why blue and white?'

'Well, you are not the first person I have heard commenting on the blue theme, so I suppose it's about time I revealed the reason. And the band are here now, so it's perfect timing.' As he finished the transaction with Mrs Potts, he waved at his friend. Ben nodded before taking a book from the shelf and banging it a few times on the counter. The shop gradually fell silent.

'Everyone, can I have your attention, please? If you would all like to follow the man of the hour outside.'

Once outside, the brass band started to play "Oh Come All Ye Faithful". Everyone gathered around them but all facing the shop, eagerly waiting for the big reveal. Ben moved to the side of the shop window and held a rope that was attached to the blue sheet covering the sign.

Michael stood in the doorway. He was fidgeting with his dickie bow as he tried to calm his nerves. Public speaking wasn't something he usually did and so he had practised his speech a hundred times over the weekend leading up to the day.

As the music came to a pause, Michael cleared his throat. 'Firstly, I'd like to thank everyone who has helped to make my bookshop dream come true. We all have many happy memories of the sweet shop over the years, and I hope you will all enjoy the bookshop, just maybe without the liquorice sticks, I am afraid, Bert.'

'Bloody shame. My favourite sweets,' added Bert.

His wife hit him on the arm. 'Shush, Bert. You and those bloody sweets.'

The crowd laughed, more at the comical marital outburst than his original quip. 'So, many of you have noticed there is a lot of blue in the shop. Well, there's a reason for that. Ben, if you will do the honours.'

His friend pulled the rope and the cloth dropped. Unfortunately, they hadn't practised the reveal moment and he was caught by surprise as the cloth shrouded him, causing a small round of applause and laughter.

'The Little Blu Bookshop? What kind of name is that?' called out Bert looking confused by the sign.

'They spelt it wrong, didn't they?' Everyone laughed at the young boy at the front and his observation of the apparent mistake. Having escaped from the attack of the drop cloth, Michael recomposed himself.

'No, not a mistake. This is The Little Blu Bookshop, and the word blue is spelt without an "e". It's my reminder of the first person I ever told about my dream to own a bookshop who didn't laugh. So, the name is to honour her for her encouragement to a nerdy teenage boy with a dream.'

'But what does it mean?' added the boy in the front row, still confused. Before Michael could answer, a voice came from the back of the crowd.

'Bella Luminosa Unica.'

The crowd fell silent with intrigue. Gradually, mumblings of curiosity could be heard taking over like the flow of a Mexican wave.

Mrs Potts knew.

Ben knew.

Michael caught the odd glimpse but was eager to see the woman behind the voice. Like the parting of the Red Sea by Moses, the crowd started to step to the sides, one by one until only one person remained. Her long hair was dark and wavy, her blue, belted coat was the perfect colour to showcase her Mediterranean complexion. Her large dark brown eyes sparkled as they met the crystal blue of his.

'Sofia?' he asked.

She smiled as she nodded ever so slightly.

His heart thudded so loudly in his chest, he was convinced everyone could hear it. 'Mi piccolo blu?'

The young boy, oblivious to the magic of this momentous encounter, shouted, 'But what does it mean?'

Forcibly snapped out of his gazing, Michael turned his attention to the inquisitive youngster. 'Blu is a very rare Italian girl's name. Each letter has a meaning. Bella Luminosa Unica means beautiful, vibrant and unique.'

'So, it's a girl's name, is it? Well, that's stupid,' scoffed the young boy whilst Michael, and a few of the crowd, laughed at his innocence. Michael's nerves now lifted, along with his smile as he continued to address the audience.

'Anyway, I now present properly to you all, The Little Blu Bookshop. I hope that you enjoy shopping here and visiting me as much as I will enjoy helping you all – hopefully for many years to come.' Applause broke out before he continued. 'Now, if you will all excuse me, I have a little catching up to do.'

Ben and Marjorie proceeded back into the shop to help serve customers. The band started playing and the children started singing along with many others. The spirit of Christmas was truly alive in the little village of Applewood.

Michael and Sofia made their way across the street, just out of sight from prying eyes. Here they were, at last, just inches apart but their smiles were as wide as any ocean. Butterflies swirled inside them, and the scent of her perfume filled his senses.

'Was it you at the library? Did you give Jessie the perfume?'

She nodded and added, 'Your name is Michael; I was looking for Mickey.'

'I don't use that name anymore. What are you doing here? Why, after all this time?'

'I'm sorry. My father destroyed all your letters years ago and told me I wasn't allowed to write. I never received another letter, so I thought you had stopped. It was only when my mother passed away that I found this, a letter I never received. I think it was your last letter.' She held out the folded paper and he took it in his hands, their fingers touched, sending a jolt of electricity that made them both jump.

'I remember this letter. I asked you to come to England when you finished school, but you never replied. I thought I'd scared you off for good.'

'Not at all. When I didn't hear from you again, I tried my best to forget you. It was only when I found this letter that I realised it was not your fault and I just knew I had to find you. I needed to meet you but all I knew was that you lived in a village named Applewood in what you called the Lake District.'

She reached out her hand to touch his, and they both felt that spark again. He put the letter in his pocket and took both her hands in his. Lost in her eyes again, he prayed this was not a dream.

He smiled as he watched a delicate tiny snowflake fall between them and land on the end of her nose. More followed. They both looked up to see the sky filling with snow.

Sofia knew this was the moment that she had dreamt of but the reality far surpassed any dream. With the laughter and joy coming from the shop, the sound of "Silent Night" was a perfect backdrop to this perfect moment between the two long-lost souls, their search for each other now over.

Michael felt so overwhelmed with joy, he wanted to pick her up and spin her round in his arms, never to let her go. This woman, who he had never met, but whose soul he felt so connected to, more than any romance novel he had ever read.

Their grip tightened as he leant in towards her, their bodies being pulled together as if string around their hearts was tightening. Their lips touched softly for the first time, their eyes closed and they both became lost in each other. Their hands parted only to wrap their arms around each other.

Their first look, their first touch, their first kiss – all here, on their very first of many Christmas Eves together at The Little Blu Bookshop.

The End ... *or is it just the beginning?*

December for Dad

Michael and Sofia had a wonderful marriage with four children they love dearly; Ben, Sam, Bella, and Michael Junior. Unfortunately, the last few years had been plagued with constant sibling squabbles and the family was broken. When Michael became ill, he had an idea of how to fix his family but he quickly ran out of time. On his death, he leaves the family with some important final requests.

In the Christmas novel, "December for Dad", we meet the Bennett family forty years after the opening of the bookshop in what becomes their saddest moment; where they come together for the passing of a wonderful husband, father, and friend. The novel tells the story of the family long ago broken but it is through another of Michael's letters that they are forced on a journey of reflection to the many Christmases of their past and we catch up on the goings-on at The Little Blu Bookshop.

Can re-living the magic of the past re-ignite hope for the future for not just Sofia and her children, but the future of The Little Blu Bookshop in the not so sleepy village of Applewood, nestling between the lakes and the mountains of the Lake District.

Sarah Shard

Not Today, Santa

Martha May Little

Izzy hurried through Waverley station as if she were training for the Olympics, although, laden with shopping bags, a suitcase and wearing wildly inappropriate footwear, she was more likely to break her ankle than any world records.

'This is the last call for the replacement bus service to Inverness. Can all passengers please make your way immediately to the concourse. This service will depart in three minutes,' a disembodied voice boomed over the tannoy.

She clutched her ticket and said a silent prayer as she rattled down the escalator, muttering apologies and 'Merry Christmases' to those she jostled on the way. Her heels clacked rapidly on the tarmac as she turned the corner, hoping the bus was still there. She was never late. Ever. It was not in her makeup to keep people waiting, and she was determined not to start tonight.

She arrived just as the driver had shut the last luggage compartment. Her luck was in; as he took pity on her, and reopened one to safely stow her bags away.

He climbed onto the bus, gesturing for Izzy to follow. 'You seem like you've had a day of it, hen. Come and get yourself settled.'

The kindness in his voice almost buckled her. 'You could say that. Not the best time for a signal fault, is it?'

'Aye, I'm not sure there's ever a good time for these things to happen, but Christmas Eve must be about the worst one, I reckon. Never mind, you're here now, and Pat here will get you home, safe and sound.' He punched her crumpled ticket and handed it back with a smile.

'Thank you. It's nice to know I'm in safe hands.'

'You may not thank me when you hear the Christmas playlist I've selected,' he grinned.

'I need all the Christmas spirit I can get. You bust out those Christmas crackers, Pat.'

'Will do,' he said with a chuckle, and Izzy set off to find her seat.

It was clear the journey would not be a quiet one; groups of merry revellers chatted to each other across the aisles, and Izzy's hopes of sitting next to someone antisocial were scuppered as she discovered her seat – right at the back, of course – was next to a tall, chatty Santa, deep in conversation with the couple in front.

She sat down, checked her phone, and groaned when she saw it only had ten percent charge left. She rifled through her handbag and cursed – the bag containing her charger and earbuds was in the luggage compartment below. Well, if that wasn't the icing on the stale Christmas cake! She knew her sister, Jasmine, would be busy with the kids and, not wanting to disturb her with a call, shot off a text with her estimated time of arrival to Inverness. How she would get to Brackenbogle after that was a different matter. As the bus trundled into motion, Izzy closed her eyes and attempted to relax.

'Hmm?' she said as someone gently jostled her shoulder.

'Your phone. It's ringing.' Santa pointed to the gap where her phone had slid between the seats. "The Imperial March" from Star Wars rang out, telling her it was Jasmine calling.

'Oh crap, I must have nodded off.' She grabbed the phone and answered it. 'Jazz ... sorry, I was sleeping.'

'I can't believe you're not home yet!' Jazz's voice was so loud Izzy had to check she hadn't left the speaker on.

'You have Ben to thank for that,' Izzy replied. 'He was super late, as usual! Then they couldn't find the toys I'd ordered for the twins, and I had to visit three shops and—'

'Bloody Ben, I hope you gave him a good kick in the nuts.' Jazz was never one for subtlety.

'I'll be sure to give him a hefty boot from you the next time I see him.' Izzy sighed and rested her forehead on the seat in front.

'Did you manage to get the presents?' Jazz asked, her tone softer now.

'Yes, I got them, but I missed my train and by the time I got to Edinburgh my connection had already gone. Oh, and it gets better! Then they cancelled the last train out of Waverley, and I got the last space on this bus!'

'What a nightmare. It could only happen to you, couldn't it? Have you eaten?'

'No, I'll get something if we stop somewhere.'

'Not just—'

'—not just crisps and chocolate, I'm not a toddler. Jasmine, please don't worry, I'll be home for Christmas. I promise.'

'Okay.' Said Jazz, somewhat placated. 'Love you, sis.'

'Love you too. Bye.'

Izzy tucked her phone into her pocket, hoping the background chatter and driver Pat's playlist had prevented her from being overheard.

'Sorry you've had such a bad day,' Santa said.

She shrugged, hoping to appear nonchalant, and went back to ignoring him.

'I'm not surprised that Ben is continuing to act like a bell-end though.'

'I appreciate the concern, but …' His words struck her, and she whipped around to face him. 'Hold on, you know Ben?'

'Santa knows everyone on the naughty list,' he replied with an infuriating wink. His voice was incredibly familiar, but she couldn't quite place him.

'Look,' she growled, her patience at an all-time low, 'I'm sure this is all very amusing to you, but I'm not in the mood – not today, Santa. And maybe Mrs Claus – or Mister Claus – if there is one, forgot to tell you this, but it's rude to eavesdrop.'

'I can assure you this Santa is single. And you can't call that eavesdropping. I'm sure they heard you whinging up front.'

Izzy balled her fists in frustration. 'Oh wheesht! I think not! Mariah Carey is on and there's no chance I'm louder than her!'

'Maybe not on a normal day, but you're getting dangerously close right now. And your pitch is almost as high. The dogs around here must be wondering what is going on.' He replied, with a smirk that only added to her ire.

'I'm sure this is all very amusing, but you've already heard how abysmal my day has been and I'd appreciate it if you wouldn't try to make it worse, okay?'

Santa stroked his fake white beard and Izzy considered for a moment how satisfying it would be to shove it down his throat. Part of her felt bad for being snippy. It was unusual for someone to annoy her so quickly, but this man pushed her buttons with the glee of a toddler destroying a toy. She hadn't been this annoyed simply talking to anyone since her ex, Ben, and his friends. Specifically, one friend …

No, it couldn't be – could it?

'Chris?' she asked, crossing all her fingers, and hoping she was wrong.

Santa removed his hat and beard and grinned broadly. 'Tada! The one and only! Live and in person!' he said with a flourish. 'I'll try not to be offended that you didn't recognise me.'

'I couldn't see your horns beneath your Poundland fancy dress, and the nylon beard must have masked the smell of sulphur,' Izzy said, calculating just how bad she must have been in a previous life to deserve this rotten luck. She eyed the beard again. It would be so easy to grab it off him and – no, she would never hear the end of it if she spent Christmas in a police cell. Jazz would probably make t-shirts to commemorate it. She sat on her hands and resolved to behave.

'Oh please, I'm wearing the hell out of this little ensemble. It's proved quite the hit today.'

'I'm sure it has; however, the bar's set rather low at the moment.'

'Meaning?'

'Just that it's almost a scientific fact that people are more welcoming – or forgiving, depending on your perspective – at Christmas. You could be adorned in strands of the straggliest tinsel known to man and still receive a rousing public reception.'

'I see you haven't lost your ability to dish out those famous backhanded compliments,' said Chris, shaking his head.

She studied him for a moment. That same stupid, charming grin that had melted many hearts when they were teenagers was still there. How dare he age so well when she had gained nothing apart from eye bags and frown lines?

'What can I say? It's a skill, although sadly, not a marketable one. I see, you're as irritating as ever. Did you know it was me right away?'

'Nah, you were fast asleep before we hit the West End, all cooried in like a little dormouse. I wasn't sure until I heard Jazz's dulcet tones.'

'She's hard to mistake, that's for sure. I didn't snore, did I?' Izzy asked with a wince.

'As much as I would like to say you snored like a sedated warthog, you did not.'

'It's just as well. I'm not sure what little is left of my pride would have survived that.' Izzy yawned. All this talk of sleep wasn't making it easy to stay awake. 'Urgh, I can't believe we're actually stuck here together. What are the chances?' She scraped her hair into a messy bun and secured it with a scrunchie, all the time aware of Chris watching her. The intensity of his gaze sent a flush creeping up her throat, and she rubbed her neck, hoping he wouldn't notice.

'I reckon it's fate,' he said. His eyes twinkled, enjoying himself far too much for Izzy's liking. 'Your luck has just changed for the better with me – your very own Santa – at your side.' There was that smile again. He *had* noticed. Swine.

'I can think of some other four-letter words that are more apt, but I'll be polite. What's with the outfit, anyway? Are you trying to earn a few extra quid as a low-rent stripper?'

'You wound me, Isobel Watson!' Chris gasped, placing his hand over his heart in mock outrage. 'I've never dressed up or removed my clothes for money! And I assure you that, if I did, I would charge a princely sum for it.'

'As much as I admire your confidence, you should keep a hold of your day job; I doubt even you would survive an ego-crush like that,' she said, with a wry smile. 'So, the costume?'

'It's a long story.'

With his hat and beard off, Izzy noticed his eyes were red and puffy and his shoulders slightly hunched. She felt a twinge of sympathy; she knew he wasn't the sort of man who showed weakness easily. Izzy had spent many evenings in Chris's company before she and Ben got together. He had been enigmatic and charming, with a biting wit similar to her own. They found common ground in a mutual love of 80's synth music and John Hughes' films, but when she and Ben became a proper couple, Chris withdrew even further. When she thought about it, this still saddened her. She had once felt very differently about him and had often wondered how things could have been, if only … She shook the memory of those feelings away before they could creep further in, stealthy little critters that they were.

'You've heard the headline version of my terrible day,' she said, in a bid to re-focus on the here and now. 'It's only fair you share your woes with me. I might even be sympathetic.'

He raised a sceptical eyebrow.

'What?' she protested. 'I could have mellowed since we last saw each other. I could be a Zen master by now, for all you know. Except on days like today, that is. Spill.'

'I'll believe that when I see it, but okay. Have you heard my mum's unwell?'

Izzy nodded. Her mother's specialist subject on Mastermind could easily be about the comings and goings of the population of Brackenbogle and there wasn't a birth, divorce, or retirement that Izzy hadn't been told about in painstaking detail.

'Well, I've not been home much these last few years, and it's been rough for her without me around. I know it's inconceivable to you, but some people actually enjoy my company,' Chris said with a half-hearted laugh, which made Izzy feel rotten for being hostile. 'Anyway, I've tried to get back more, but I had to work in Australia for a couple of months and wasn't sure I'd get home for Christmas until about a week ago. Then I did what every sane person would and booked flights with ridiculously long layovers to get back in time. I haven't told her I'm coming. I thought I'd surprise her by pitching up on her doorstep on Christmas Eve dressed like Santa.'

'Of course – the logical choice. You don't seem enthused by the whole notion now, though.'

'It was a great idea when I assumed everything would go to plan. I should have arrived in the UK yesterday to get some kip and organise myself. Instead, I had to deal with a last-minute crisis meeting and the journey home turned into a massive game of snakes and ladders: you think you're getting closer to the end then somehow, another six hours of travel are added to your journey.'

'How long have you been travelling?'

Chris checked his watch. 'Thirty-three hours and twenty-seven minutes. Give or take.'

Izzy's mouth fell open. Here she was thinking her ten-hour-long day had been challenging. 'Hang on, were you dressed like this the entire time? Why don't you smell like the bottom of a hamster cage?'

'Who says I don't?' He chuckled, wafting the air under his arms at her. She wrinkled her nose in disgust and batted his hands away. 'I picked this bad-boy up in Perth and packed it in my suitcase. Not even I can do long-haul in 100% nylon. I did a quick change in a toilet cubicle at Heathrow. That got me a few funny looks, I tell you.'

'Wow. I have to admit, I admire your dedication. You must be desperate to get home.'

'Yeah, I am. It's been hard being away. It'll be worth it to see her face, though,' Chris said with a faraway look on his face.

'I'm sure having you around will be the best present.' She said, remembering how close his family was. 'Good luck getting her to take it easy, though, you'll have a battle on your hands just trying to keep her out of the kitchen. How is she keeping?'

'My life wouldn't be worth living if I tried to cook. I could weigh twenty-five stone and she would still load my plate with second helpings. Feeding people is her "love language", apparently. Whatever that means.' He laughed quietly, but the smile didn't quite reach his eyes. 'Ach, you know how she is. She's not one to complain, but the strain of dialysis three times a week takes a toll.'

'It must be tough, especially as she's so active and used to treating patients – not being one. Is the dialysis permanent?'

'Until she gets a transplant.' He rubbed his hand over his face and stifled a yawn. 'And that isn't a quick process. We hoped either Ashley or I would match, but we didn't. There are a few people still to be tested. We'll see. It's a waiting game.'

'Someone will be a match soon. I can feel it.' Instinctively, Izzy took his hand and gave it a reassuring squeeze, but he flinched, and she withdrew as if scalded.

She stared past him and out of the window at the cloudless, ink-black sky and took a deep breath, trying to ignore the white-hot embarrassment coursing through her. It was half-past ten now. They would be in Inverness in around an hour. Surely, they could stomach being next to each other until then? She considered asking one of the other passengers to swap seats, but everyone was now either asleep or butchering Boney M's "Mary's Boy Child".

'Anyway,' said Chris, interrupting her plotting, 'enough about my woes, tell me what Ben's been doing to get in your bad books.'

The mere thought of Ben made Izzy's temper flare. She considered being diplomatic for a second before breaking into a rant.

'Nothing new, really. You know how he's always late?' Chris nodded. 'Well, I waited over two hours for him to drop his key off this morning; the one he's been too busy to return for the last ten months.' Her hands danced in the air as she talked. 'I was proper Hulk-smash-angry by the time he rocked up and he even brought his new girlfriend just to wind me up – as if him moving on would bother me!'

She took a breath; aware she was getting riled up again. This happened with impressive speed when focussed on this particular topic. Jasmine called it "the Ben Effect".

'Anyway, turns out, his girlfriend's lovely – far too good for him, of course – I think it annoyed him that we got on. That's one positive thing to come out of today, I suppose.' It wasn't until she finished speaking that she noticed Chris's quizzical look and wondered if her rambling had finally tipped him over the edge. 'Why are you staring like that?'

'You and Ben split up?' he asked, shocked.

'About a year ago now – you didn't know?'

He shook his head. 'What happened?'

'Nothing major. He wasn't cheating or anything. It sounds like a total cliché, but there was simply no future for us. Once I realised that, there was no point in dragging it out and delaying the inevitable.' Izzy shrugged. 'I can't believe this is news to you. I thought he would have mentioned it when he moved out. He's such an arse.'

Chris remained silent and continued to study her.

'You're creeping me out. Can you say something instead of boggling like that?'

'Sorry. It's just … I'm surprised. That's all.'

'He really didn't tell you?'

'We don't talk much anymore, Iz.' Chris rubbed his temples and shook his head sadly. 'Since when?'

'Not for a couple of years. Maybe three.'

'What!?' Izzy exclaimed, louder than she intended. 'How is that possible? You're best friends!'

'We haven't been close for a long time. I mean, I've been out of the country a lot and things change. We're in a few WhatsApp groups, but beyond that, we're not in touch.'

Izzy was floored. She may not have been on good terms with Ben recently, but surely, she should have known he and Chris had fallen out three chuffing years ago.

'I can't believe he didn't tell me. Was I such an awful girlfriend he couldn't share that?'

'Don't blame yourself. Ben is pretty good at telling people what he wants them to hear. He isn't as happy to admit something could be wrong in his perfect world. Anyway, I didn't see the point in broadcasting it either, so it's not entirely his fault.'

'What did you fall out about?' Izzy tensed, knowing it must have been something serious to cause a rift that big.

'I think we hadn't been real friends for a long time.' Chris paused and seemed to debate whether to continue. 'I found out he lied about something important that happened a few years ago. He thought I would be okay about it because a lot of time had passed, but I couldn't get past it.'

'I'm really sorry to hear that,' Izzy sighed. 'I'd like to think he only changed for the worse in the last few years, but he hasn't. It's just taken us this long to realise who he actually is.'

'You could be right. Mind you, it amazed us that he moved down to Manchester when you went. We thought he would be a Brackenbogle boy forever – give him his due, he has changed a bit.'

'I'm not sure where you got that idea from. Manchester was all his doing – he couldn't wait to get away. He'd applied to colleges long before I came around to it.'

'Seriously?' Chris's voice was barely louder than a whisper.

'Absolutely. I wouldn't have considered studying down there if not for him. I was happy to go to Aberdeen or Dundee – anywhere close to home. His mind was made up though, and I traipsed after him like a love-struck eejit. It all worked out okay, but it was his dream we followed, not mine. Look,' Izzy said, irritated by the mistakes of her younger self more than anything else, 'can we not talk about him anymore? It's destroying the smidgen of Christmas spirit I have left.'

For a moment, she thought Chris might protest. She set her jaw and furrowed her brow at him, and he conceded. They sat in silence for a few minutes and Izzy relaxed again, although she was careful not to get too comfortable for fear she would fall asleep and wake up drooling on Chris's shoulder.

'Can I ask you another Ben-related question?' Chris asked, disrupting her calm. 'I promise it'll be the last.'

'Fine. Make it snappy.'

'If you didn't insist on him coming with you to Manchester—' He put his hand up when she protested. 'I believe you; I do. Did you ever ask him not to come back for holidays or weddings? He always said you didn't want him being led astray by us. Was he lying?'

Izzy felt like someone had kicked her square in the gut. The wind flew out of her lungs in a comically loud braying noise. Heads swivelled around to her, and she surprised herself by laughing. She waved apologetically to her audience and eventually regained her composure, with tears of laughter streaking her cheeks.

'Oh, I'm sorry,' she said to Chris, wiping what little mascara was left from her eyes. 'I don't know why I'm laughing. It isn't funny at all.'

'So, that's a yes?'

'I promise I never asked any such thing. I wanted to come home loads and Ben always had an excuse not to. For a while, I came alone, and that was okay, but even that tailed off as we settled into our new life. As for me not wanting him around you all – or whatever nonsense he spouted – I swear, I've never once even *thought* that. Why would he lie?'

'He must have had his reasons.'

'I can't imagine what they were.'

'I have a couple of ideas.' Chris said cryptically.

'Such as? Actually, don't tell me. I'm not sure I can cope with any more blood pressure fluctuations today.' She stared at her hands, which were clasped firmly in her lap, and tried not to think about what else Ben may have said. 'Is it any wonder you've hated me for all these years? I would have too!'

'I don't hate you.'

'You've done a grand job of acting like you do for the last eight years.'

'I'm capable of many things, Izzy, but hating you will never be one of them.'

Something in the tone of his voice told her he was being sincere. Pulse racing and palms clammy, she closed her eyes and tried to make sense of it all. If Chris didn't hate her, what did he feel? As she opened her mouth to speak, a loud bang emanated from the front of the bus, and it veered sharply left before groaning slowly to a halt in a small layby.

'What was that?' Izzy grabbed the armrest.

'Whatever it was, it didn't sound good. I'll go and see if I can help.' Chris squeezed past her and made his way down the bus.

The man from the couple in front, Tom, joined him and his partner, Lucy, kept Izzy company.

'Tom's a mechanic. If he can't fix it, he'll be able to identify what's gone wrong.' Lucy said. A reassuring smile accompanied her broad New Zealand accent and her calm, confident air put Izzy instantly at ease. 'Plus, it gives us time to get acquainted. It's not all bad, is it?'

Lucy told her about the time their minibus broke down in the centre of the Australian Outback two hundred kilometres away from the nearest garage, and Izzy listened intently, never more grateful for Scotland's much more diminutive scale.

'The way I see it, if we don't end up cooking roadkill on a makeshift Barbie tonight, we're winning.' Lucy concluded with a big grin.

'I can't argue with that.' Izzy laughed as Pat clambered back onto the bus.

'Folks, could I have your attention, please.' He waited for the chatter to subside. 'I'll start with the bad news: one of the front tyres has blown, and it looks like an axle has snapped. Someone's coming to repair it, but it could be a while. We've arranged taxis to drop you off in Inverness or as close to your homes as we can get. The good news is that the engine is working fine so we can stay warm while we wait – and the excellent news is we can still listen to my playlist!'

This was met with cheers and applause, and Pat took a bow. 'You can stretch your legs if you like, just mind and keep close to the bus. It's very dark out there and we want everyone getting home for Christmas in one piece.'

Half an hour later, Izzy and Lucy stood at the roadside watching as Pat opened one of the luggage compartments and Chris rummaged through the bags.

'What on earth is he doing?' Lucy asked.

'Not a clue,' Izzy said as Chris emerged, raising a rucksack aloft like a trophy, before handing Pat and Tom some of its contents.

'I think it's food,' Lucy exclaimed in delight. 'What a legend!'

Izzy rolled her eyes. *Of course, Chris would be prepared for this sort of thing. He probably had a three-person tent in there somewhere.* He jogged over and handed Izzy a bag.

'Here. Eat something.'

'Couldn't you magic up a Mars Bar, or a packet of McCoy's?' Izzy grumbled, peering at the selection of protein bars, apples and water.

'I can't incur Jasmine's wrath by encouraging you to eat like a toddler, can I?'

'You're wise. I wouldn't recommend unleashing that kraken,' she said, secretly pleased he remembered she hadn't eaten. 'Thank you.'

'You're not going to lecture me about eavesdropping again, are you?' He blew on his fingers, his breath puffing out into the chilly night air. Lucy plucked an apple out of the bag and pretended to bow down to Chris.

'No. You're safe for now, since you've brought me food.' Izzy said, laughing at Lucy's display of reverence.

'Well, that's a relief. I thought you might use the apple for target practice.' He mimed wiping sweat off his brow, and she smacked him playfully on the arm.

'Thanks for this.' Lucy took a large bite out of her apple and crunched happily. 'I'm famished.'

'You're more than welcome. It's just as well I stocked up at King's Cross. You never know when you might need supplies,' Chris said. 'Right, I'd better head back, don't stay out here too long.' He doffed an imaginary cap and returned to Tom and Pat.

'He's great, isn't he?' said Lucy.

'I suppose, he's not awful,' Izzy admitted. 'You all seem pretty friendly. Did you meet him on the bus?'

'We just met on the train up from London, but it feels like we've known him longer – he's just one of those people, you know? It's our first Christmas in the UK and our accommodation fell through at the last minute, today. Complete nightmare. Chris was a hero and sorted it out – we didn't need to ask – he just offered. He's such a sweetheart.'

Izzy took a swig of water, slightly unnerved at further proof of Chris's innate decency. The feelings she had worked so hard to quell were blooming again, and she was surprised to discover that she didn't really mind.

'What about you?' Lucy asked. 'Do you go way back?'

'Sort of. He's a friend of my ex. We've not spoken for a while.'

'Until tonight? Wow. Why haven't you spoken – because of the ex?'

'Something like that,' Izzy said.

'This is the perfect chance for you to bury the hatchet. Fate has brought you together!' Lucy practically vibrated with enthusiasm, and Izzy wished she would dial down the sunny disposition a notch. As if she had read her mind, Lucy moved closer and continued in a hushed tone, 'What's she like, the girl who broke his heart?'

'Whose heart? Chris's?' Izzy coughed, inhaling a mouthful of water. 'I have no idea.'

'You must know, the one who chose his friend instead of him?'

Izzy shrugged. 'I moved away a while ago. It must be someone I haven't met.'

'I don't think so. It seemed like they went to school together. Oh well. Sorry for being nosy. Tom says I get too invested in other people's love lives, but I can't help it. I want everyone to have what we have – everyone deserves that kind of happiness.'

'There are worse things to wish for, that's for sure.' Izzy said, envious of the certainty Lucy clearly felt about her relationship. Izzy couldn't remember ever having that with Ben.

'I think so, too. Tom doesn't agree, but that's why we work together. We balance each other out.' She gave a loud whistle and Tom instantly turned towards her. She blew him a kiss and, even in the darkness, Izzy could see how red his face was turning. He gave a shy wave and signalled he was about to get back on the bus. 'See? He's the salt to my pepper. Well, if you do meet Chris's mystery woman, tell her she's missed a good one there.'

'I will.'

'Jeez, it's cold, I can hardly feel my face!' Lucy wrapped her coat around her slight frame. 'I'm heading back. Are you coming?'

'In a bit. I'll have this first,' Izzy said with a grimace, waggling a protein bar in the air.

Izzy stood for a few minutes, rooted in place. She wanted to push Lucy's words to the back of her mind, but a niggling voice grew louder each time she did, forcing her to question who the source of Chris's heartbreak could be – and whether the nervous, twisty feeling in her gut was right.

Before she could process this, the first fleet of taxis arrived. A cheer emanated from within the bus and Pat unloaded the luggage as the process of organising who was going where, and in what order, began.

Chris walked over. 'There's a couple heading up Brackenbogle way with a space in their cab. You should be home in less than an hour.'

'You really are playing the part of Santa tonight, first delivering food and now good news.'

'It's lucky I wore this, then, isn't it?' he said, gesturing to his costume. 'Best thirty bucks I've spent in a long time. Tell me, are you staying at Jasmine's or with your parents?'

'Is this so you can drop my actual presents off, Santa?' Izzy asked, her skin prickling with goose bumps that she told herself were a product of the cold and not the thought of seeing Chris again.

'I'll need to check if you're on the nice list, first. It might be just a lump of coal for you. No, it's so I can tell the driver where to drop you off.'

'Ah. Fair enough. I'm staying at the Bogle Inn.'

Chris tilted his head quizzically and she explained.

'My family is fabulous, but if it's a choice between a quiet hotel room with a lovely en suite, listening to infants wailing in stereo all night or the annual family talent show, the hotel wins every time.' Izzy shivered at the thought of the alternatives.

'A talent show!' Chris clapped his hands with glee. 'How many people take part?'

'Too many. I usually get out of it by volunteering to do the dishes. Sadly, you can't ever avoid Uncle Eric's rendition of "Delilah". You can hear him three streets over – it's the stuff of nightmares.'

'It sounds amazing. What's your talent, except washing dishes?'

'I can't possibly tell you that. It'll spoil the surprise if you ever have the misfortune to be invited.' Izzy scuffed her shoes on the gravel, and tried to conceal the hope in her voice when she asked, 'Are you not coming in the taxi with us?'

'I said I'll stick around until the end, help Pat with the luggage and whatnot. He'll give me a lift when this is all sorted. Can I see your phone for a minute?'

'Here, it's nearly out of juice, though.'

Chris quickly typed something and handed it back. 'I've added my number. Let me know when you get to the hotel.'

'I will.' she said. 'Thank you, for the food and the taxi … and the company.'

'It's been my pleasure, Iz.'

After saying her goodbyes to Lucy, Tom and Pat, Izzy watched Chris wave goodbye as the taxi pulled away and a feeling of melancholy swept through her. She closed her eyes and allowed herself to accept that she wasn't ready to part ways with him yet.

Maybe she never had been.

*

After a shower (that was easily one of the best she had taken), Izzy flopped onto her hotel bed, exhausted but awake. She grabbed her freshly charged phone and scrolled through her contacts. Willing herself to be brave, she searched for Chris. He wasn't listed under "C" – of course, that would be too simple. Continuing to scroll, she cackled when she eventually found him and quickly penned a message.

Izzy: *I'm at the hotel. Safe & sound. How's the rescue mission going?*

Santa/Satan/Hero: *All done. Pat is driving us back now. I'm nearly home.*

Izzy: *Fantastic. He's a star. Tell him happy Christmas from me, please.*

Santa/Satan/Hero: *He wishes you a Merry Christmas too. So do I.*

She propped herself on her elbows. Her nerves fizzed in a way they hadn't since well before Ben.

Santa/Satan/Hero: *Lucy said she spoke to you earlier. About me.*

Izzy: *She did. It was enlightening. And a little confusing.*

Santa/Satan/Hero: *What was confusing?*

Izzy: *I didn't know your heart had been broken.*

Santa/Satan/Hero: *I always thought you knew, back then.*

Izzy: *Nope. Didn't have a clue.*

Santa/Satan/Hero: *How do you feel now?*

Izzy: *That depends.*

Santa/Satan/Hero: *On what?*

Izzy: *On whether I'm the woman who broke your heart.*

She watched the dancing dots that showed he was typing. The dots stopped and she waited anxiously until they started again; her stomach lurched as if she was sitting at the highest point of a rollercoaster, waiting to drop.

Santa/Satan/Hero: *You are.*

Her heart thudded fiercely in her chest.

Izzy: *I wish you had told me this eight years ago.*

More Than Mistletoe

Santa/Satan/Hero: *Would it have made a difference?*
She didn't hesitate to reply.
Izzy: *Yes.*

*

'What the—' Izzy fumbled in her bedsheets, trying to locate her phone while its alarm blared. 'How is it that time already?'

She forced herself out of her warm cocoon, knowing she was expected at Jasmine's house by seven a.m. to witness her niece and nephew open a sled's worth of presents. Checking her phone, she was disappointed to find there was nothing from Chris. She had been certain there was something between them. Maybe she had read it all wrong. Either way, she had neither the energy nor inclination to chase him if he wasn't interested.

She grabbed the gifts and her room key and headed out, knowing she would need to be quick to get one of Jasmine's famous Christmas breakfast rolls before the rest of the gannets descended. She was so preoccupied with thoughts of bacon and hash browns as she left the hotel, she didn't notice the patch of ice on the pavement and skidded straight into someone waiting outside, dropping her bag of presents in the process.

'I'm sorry, I wasn't watching where I was—' She picked the presents off the ground and the figure handed back her bag as she straightened up. 'Chris … what are you doing here?'

'I thought I'd pay you a visit. Make sure you're okay. You don't seem happy to see me?' He asked, nervously.

'Well, you didn't reply to my last message.'

'I know. I'm sorry about that. I figured some things are best said in person and didn't think turning up at your door at two a.m. was wise.'

'Excellent decision. The jungle drums would have been beating at full force if you had. Anyway …' she rifled through her bag to make sure nothing was damaged, suddenly unable to look him in the eye. 'It must be important then, for you to visit this early?'

Chris thrust his hands in his pockets and stared at the ground. 'This might be weirdly intense, but there's a lot I need to say. I'm just going to get it out before I bottle it – is that okay?'

'Sure.' Izzy gave a nod. 'Do you want to chum me to Jasmine's house? You talk and I'll listen. No snarky comments, I promise.'

They walked in silence until he was ready.

'Right. Here goes. You know the night you and Ben got together – at his party? Well … he overheard me telling Ashley how much I liked you and that I planned to tell you that night. Going back, there had always been a bit of a rivalry between us. Usually it was friendly enough – if I got new trainers, he got a better pair – that sort of thing. As we got older, he took it more seriously and became really competitive. I just got on with things and tried not to let it bother me.' There was an edge to his voice, a rawness she hadn't heard before. 'I searched everywhere for you that night, but you were already with him when I found you.'

'I didn't see you that night.' Izzy said, perplexed. She definitely would have remembered him being there.

'I left. Said I didn't feel well. It wasn't exactly a lie, either. I don't think I've ever felt as gutted as I was in that moment. But what could I do? You seemed happy and he was my mate. I had to swallow it.'

Izzy frowned, her mind working overtime as she tried to piece the fragments together.

'So, you were fine with everything until three years ago – what changed?'

'Believe me, I was never fine with it. Never,' Chris said, shaking his head. 'I'd been working abroad, thinking the distance would help me move on and be happy for you both. But the last time I came home, he wasn't happy to see me. He was drunk and angry about everything and nothing, shouting that he knew I had feelings for you and had since Ashley's party. He told me he only –'

'Pursued me out of spite? That we were together for eight years because he wanted to get one over on you?' She shook her head, defiantly. 'No. We wouldn't have lasted that long if his feelings weren't real.'

'I'm not saying that. He was interested, but knowing I liked you appealed to his competitive side.' He winced. 'I'm sorry, that makes it sound like you were a prize to be won. I promise that's not how it was.'

'Thanks ... I think.' She knew only too well how competitive Ben could be. 'What was the lie that stopped you from being friends?'

'He said you made the first move at Ashley's party, that you'd liked him for ages. He also said you only bothered talking to me to get close to him.'

'That never happened,' Izzy hissed. 'I thought he was nice enough – a bit of a poser and a chancer – but never boyfriend material. I even said I was interested in someone else, but he was persistent, and I gave him a chance.'

'I know that, now. He knew how I felt and did his best to make sure nothing would happen between us. I spent years watching you two together, trying to get over you.'

'By being a dick – how did that work out?'

'Not well. I thought it'd get easier, but it never did. I had all these things I wanted to say and couldn't, so I was as mean as possible and ended up pushing you away instead.'

'And I gave it back to you with both barrels.' Izzy shook her head. 'I'm sorry.'

'You've got nothing to apologise for. None of this was your fault.'

'Maybe, but we spent ages being horrible to each other. Bloody Ben.' Izzy stopped walking and turned to face Chris. 'Tell me now.'

'What?'

'All the things you couldn't say before – tell me them now. We've wasted enough time already, don't you think? Unless you don't feel the same way …'

He took a step towards her and tenderly cupped her cheek. 'You are the funniest, most clever, beautiful and infuriating woman I have ever met. You care so much, and I love how passionate you are about everything you believe in. I could listen to you talk about anything, even when you're calling me out on the most ridiculous little things. You admit when you're wrong and always push yourself to do better. You—'

Izzy reached up on her tiptoes and, sliding her hands into his hair, pressed her lips softly to his. He froze for a moment, before returning the kiss with an intensity she felt right down to her toes. He was the first to pull away, and Izzy was left dizzy and aching for more.

'Do you have anything to say to me?' he murmured, snaking his arm around her waist, and drawing her closer.

'Such as?' She rested her head against his chest and breathed him in. He smelled familiar and new, all at once, and she felt a thrill as the certainty – the rightness – of being there with him struck her.

'You never said who you liked when Ben tried it on. Care to share?'

'Oh, him? He's selfless and caring and helps other people at the drop of a hat without being asked. He's wise and witty, and I want to be around him even when he pisses me off – which is often.'

'He sounds terrible.'

'The absolute worst.' She teased. 'And he may, or may not, look ridiculously good in a Santa outfit.'

'Is that so? Play your cards right and you might get to see him in it again.'

'I look forward to it.' She reached up again and kissed him, relishing the feel of his smile against her lips. 'Now, onto more important business. How do you feel about bacon rolls on Christmas morning?'

'I feel positively about bacon rolls at all times.'

'Correct answer! Come with me and one shall be yours. Be prepared to be interrogated by Jasmine, though.' Izzy stopped suddenly. 'Wait a second, shouldn't you be at home with your mum?'

'I've got a few hours free. She's still recovering from my arrival – and cooking enough food to feed the entire town.' He grinned at her, his eyes bright. 'There were a few tears shed.'

'I can imagine. Are you sure you're okay to come with me? I don't want to mess up your mum's plans.'

'You won't be – she'd love to see you, later.'

'You think?'

Chris nodded. 'She's always had a soft spot for you. And she's been dying for me to bring a girl home for Christmas.'

'You've brought no one home before?' Izzy asked, her voice nearing Mariah Carey-like levels again.

'I've been holding out for the right one. Now …' He took hold of her hand as they walked. 'About this talent you're keeping secret?'

'Not today, Santa. All in good time.'

'Spoilsport. Merry Christmas, Izzy.'

'Merry Christmas, Chris. I have a feeling it'll be one to remember.'

Sealed With a Christmas Kiss

Bláithín O'Reilly Murphy

1
~ *Getting her tinsel in a tangle* ~

As the snowplough shuddered to a halt Avery's stomach tightened. The Swiss chalet looked peaceful and idyllically romantic, framed by fresh snowfall. She exhaled sharply. Avery was about to be stranded alone with a man who was not her boyfriend for the next few days. She kept telling herself that she had nothing to be nervous about, that it was just Everest. But as she looked out the plough's window and watched the beautifully carved doors open, glimpsing Everest's tall muscular frame filling the door, a jolt hit her. It was the first time she'd seen him in a year.

'Thank you so much for the lift, Lars, you really saved me!' Avery said to the snowplough driver. 'I didn't fancy camping at the airport for the next few days.'

'Anytime! Give me your hand. It's a bit of a drop-down from the cab.'

The snow was softer underfoot than Avery expected. She sank a little as Lars let go of her.

'Lars! Thank you!' called Everest from the doorway. 'I don't know what we'd have done without you!'

Avery felt a tingle as she heard his voice. She really had missed him.

'You're welcome, Mr White. I'm sure you're all okay here but if you need anything just get on the radio, and I'll be right over!'

Avery smirked a little at someone calling Everest *Mr. White*. He was 20 years Lars' junior. But she supposed when you're the heir to billions, people call you Mr White!

Avery and Everest both waved as Lars and his plough chugged on down the road. As he pulled out of view, Avery was caught off guard by the scent of Everest's aftershave. His eyes twinkled as he smiled down on her.

'I didn't think you'd ever make it!' he said. 'I take it your mobile died on the way here? Poor Nik's been calling every 15 minutes. I'd be surprised if he hasn't started swimming here. You best call him now; my phone is inside. But first, give us a hug! It's been a long year. I missed you.'

Everest wrapped his arms around her. Despite the thick layers she had on, she could feel his heat. He smelt of sandalwood and an open log fire and she thought she'd lose herself in the aroma. Being in his arms again awakened something in her. She broke away hastily.

'You look well, Ev.' Avery looked at him – she was having a hard time keeping her eyes off him.

'It's good to see you, Avery.' He looked deep into her eyes. The intensity of his gaze almost made her uncomfortable … almost. 'Come on, come inside, it's bitter out here. C'mere, hand me your bags.'

'Thanks,' she said.

He lifted her two bags with ease and headed inside. Avery was left bewildered on the doorstep. She took a moment before she followed him. What the hell was going on? She was over Everest and very much in love with Niklaus. She shook off the tingling sensation that had lasted since their hug.

As she walked through the door the scene before her caught her breath.

'Wow, Everest. This place is gorgeous.'

With all the stress of trying to catch an earlier flight, she'd actually forgotten it was Christmas week. The chalet was decorated for the season and looked so magical. Outside everything was so snowy and white, but inside, the chalet was filled with festive colour and twinkling lights. Avery took a deep breath, filling her lungs with the scent of pine from the three Christmas trees she could see from where she stood, and the floral swags and garlands that adorned the stairs and fireplaces. Well, she thought, if she had to be stranded somewhere at Christmas, this was the dream. It was like being stuck in a Christmas card.

'I thought you'd like the decor,' smiled Everest, walking in from the kitchen carrying a steaming mug. 'Here, there's something a little extra in your hot chocolate. I'm sure you need it after the day you've had. Dinner will be ready in about 30 minutes, and there is a bath ready for you if you want it. But first, please call Nik.'

Avery took the hot chocolate and outstretched mobile phone. She wandered into the open-plan lounge and stood in front of the roaring fire. She drank deeply and sighed. Ah, brandy, her favourite. It added just the right amount of spice to an almost perfect winter's drink. She watched Everest as he left, then looked down at the phone. Nik's name flashed before her. Her cheeks lifted as she saw his name.

'Nik! Hi!' Her voice caught in her throat.

'Avery, thank God! I've been trying to get through to you for the past two hours. When did you arrive? Are you ok?'

'Yes, literally just through the door, I was just about to call you. My phone died on the way here. Where are you?' Avery was glad to hear his voice.

'Still in Chicago. All the airports near you are closed. I'll be here until the morning at least, then I'll get a flight to London. I'll take the Eurostar into France and make my way to you from there. They say the storm should only last a day or so and things will open back up.'

'That sucks! You must be exhausted?' She was disappointed. He'd been away on a photography assignment for weeks.

'Ah, I'm grand, now that I know you're okay.'

'I'm good, a little tired. Drinking spiked hot chocolate and Everest has a bath drawn and I smell beef bourguignon from the oven … I'm living the dream!'

An awkward silence filled the phone line. Avery watched as the glow from the fairy lights danced across the wall behind the Christmas tree. She preferred coloured lights herself, but the warm white was soothing.

'Avery, I love you.' Nik's voice was barely audible.

His declaration of love brought Avery back to their conversation. He always told her as often as he could how he felt. It usually made her so happy. But right now, he sounded sad.

'I love you, too,' she replied. Why was her chest tightening?

'How's Everest been since you got there?'

'Everest? He's Everest. Hasn't changed a bit. But I've literally just arrived so I haven't heard of any of his adventures yet.' She couldn't talk to Nik about Everest. Not after the way he'd made her tingle. 'Babe, I utterly stink. Do you mind if I call you later once I've had a bath?'

'Sure, give me a call when you're going to bed. I've not much to do today other than edit a few photos.'

'I will. Talk to you then. Love you!'

Avery hung up the phone and bit her lip. Nik seemed odd. She should have taken the time off work and gone to Ecuador with him for his assignment. Then they'd both be travelling here together, and she would not be in a Swiss chalet alone with Everest. Why did she feel so uneasy? Their teenage love triangle was well and truly over. Was it because this was the longest the three of them had ever been apart since they were thirteen, and now that she and Nik were coupled up, she didn't know how to be around Everest? She stared at the crackling logs, the flames wrapping themselves around what had once been a neat pile. She frowned. Or was it that she still had feelings for Everest, and his gap year abroad had not been the space they needed after all …

Avery walked into the kitchen to hand back Everest's phone. She watched the muscles in his back flex as he lifted plates from the press.

'Glass of wine?' he said as she placed his phone into his hand. Her fingers brushed the palm of his hand as she moved them away. His hands had always been so soft.

'Yes, I'd love one.' She moved to the other side of the kitchen island. Touching him had sent shivers down her spine. She needed to put some distance between them.

'How's Nik?'

'Frustrated. He's stuck in Chicago for now.'

'Yeah, this storm really has screwed everything up!'

Avery smiled; she could barely breathe. She needed to leave the room. 'Ev, I'm just gonna take that bath. But then I wanna hear all about your adventures. That ok?'

'Of course, dinner can be served whenever you're ready. Your room is the second on the right at the top of the stairs.'

Avery carried her luggage upstairs. She was breathless, and she told herself it was from the weight of her bag – but she was worried that it was for a completely different reason. She threw her bags on the bed and went into the adjoining bathroom. Locking the bathroom door behind her, she hesitated a moment before laughing and peeling off her jumper. Stuck to the large picture window that framed the roll-top bath were the words "It's a one-way window". Braver now than she'd been as a teenager, she stood naked in front of the window looking down over the crisp white landscape. Even if it had been a two-way window there wasn't a soul in sight to see her. She slipped into the jasmine-scented cloud of bubbles and lay there trying to steady her racing mind, watching as the light of the candles Everest had lit flickered on the chrome fittings. She desperately wanted to relax, but she couldn't.

They say absence makes the heart grow fonder, and in a way, she supposed that was true, but in the year that Everest had been away on his belated gap year, Avery had thought she'd gotten over him. In the almost decade they'd been friends he had declared his undying love to her three times. And she had looked deep into his emerald eyes and broken both their hearts on each of those three occasions by putting him firmly in the friend zone. Best friend zone, but friend zone none the least. Avery didn't want the heartache that would come with a relationship with Everest. But friend-zoning did not stop the longing. That same longing that had hit her repeatedly in the twenty minutes she'd been here.

She and Everest had only ever shared a brush of the lips. She couldn't even call it a kiss. Their only intimate moment had happened at the end of their last school recital when they had danced a duet together. A slow rumba. It was the most sensuous and alive Avery had ever felt, before or since. Even though they had practised the routine for months, that night, the night of the one and only public performance, there hadn't been a sound in the auditorium as they danced. At the end, with their bodies pressed together, it had felt to Avery like they were the only people in the world. Everest had leaned down, ever so gently, to her lips, and brushed his to hers. To this day, she had never felt a thrill like it. The audience had erupted in applause at that moment and jolted them back to reality to take a bow. Avery sighed heavily, remembering. But she and Everest could never be together. And why was she even thinking about this again? She was very much in love with Nik!

Avery leapt out of the bath and stood in front of the bathroom mirror, wrapping herself in a berry red bath towel. She felt refreshed after the soak. As she watched the water droplets drip from her hair to her neck and down her chest, she reminded herself that she and Everest were, and would only ever be, friends! Avery dried herself and put on some festive loungewear. Putting on a bra was the last thing she wanted to do. But not wearing one in front of Everest seemed too casual, so she suffered the discomfort.

As she made her way back downstairs, she was surprised to smell extinguished candles, and when she arrived at the doorway to the kitchen, Everest had his back to her, surrounded by faint clouds of smoke.

'Jeez, Avery,' he said, turning around. 'You gave me a shock. I wasn't expecting you so soon. Did you enjoy the bath?'

'I did thanks. I really needed it. The pinot is delicious. Any more?'

'Sure, give me your glass.' He reached out, and as she passed him her glass, their fingers touched, and she felt that same thrill again.

She took her hand back quickly. 'Need a hand with dinner?'

'No, it's all done. Do you want to take a seat, or eat in front of the fire?'
'The table is fine.'
Two linen napkins with embroidered wreaths hung from beneath the charger plates. Two sets of cutlery were carefully placed equidistant from everything else. And she could still smell the smoke from the dripping candles – Everest had evidently changed his mind about those.

Avery took a seat and Everest placed a steaming plate in front of her. She inhaled deeply. The aroma of the beef bourguignon was tantalising. Everest was an excellent cook.

Avery had grown up on beans on toast and chicken nuggets. Unless it came in a TV dinner that her dad liked, she hadn't tasted it. Her world and taste buds were opened at thirteen when she'd secured a scholarship to the best boarding school in Ireland. It was there she met Everest and Niklaus. In fact, Everest and Avery had first bonded over food. At thirteen, crudités were a new dish for Avery, and she'd thought the hummus was gone-off mayonnaise. She'd looked down, horrified at the platter placed in front of her and her classmates. Some sniggered at her, but Everest had kindly agreed that the hummus did look a bit dodgy today. Since then, and as Niklaus' family owned one of the most exclusive restaurants in Dublin City, she had eaten some of the best food in the world. She couldn't cook to save her life, so it was just as well she was surrounded by so many exquisite chefs.

'I've got Nik on a train from Paris to a station about an hour away,' Everest was saying. 'Provided they're running he should be here inside of three days. A combination of car and Lars will take him the rest of the way. Don't worry, he won't miss Christmas.' Everest looked away quickly as he said it.

Avery smiled, 'Thanks, you're always so good with that sort of thing.'

'Can't have you without your man on your first Christmas together.'

Avery paused. *Your man* hung in the air. Her mouth twitched. 'Everest ... are you really okay with Niklaus and me? We've never had a chance to talk about it. Alone.'

He didn't say a word until he sat down. His shoulders slumped as he did. 'I'm happy that you're happy.'

Avery digested the words. A million things said and unsaid lingered between them.

'It would never have worked between us, Everest.'

'You never gave us a chance to find out.'

Her heart ached. 'I couldn't.'

'Why?'

'Because your family would have forced you to end anything as soon as they found out.'

More Than Mistletoe

Everest looked up. 'Why did you say that?' He didn't seem hurt or upset, just genuinely surprised.

Avery lowered her head, reliving some of her worst memories. She looked away to gather strength. 'I heard your mother say as much. Twice.'

Everest swallowed hard. 'What did you overhear?'

'That even though I was perfectly accomplished and that I had risen well above the challenges of being a motherless, illegitimate child of a recovering alcoholic, I was not right for you. She said we would be doomed.'

Everest looked genuinely hurt by his mother's words – but no longer looked surprised.

'I was there the night she said it to you, Ev,' continued Avery. 'In the hallway before dinner.'

'I didn't know. Avery, I'm sorry you heard that. Why did you never say?'

'What would that have achieved? Besides, it wasn't the first time I heard your mum say something like that about me.'

'What do you mean?'

'I overheard her talking to your father about me, years earlier, when we were about fifteen. She said I wasn't right for you then, either. I remember it distinctly, 'cause I'd only just realised that I …' Avery hesitated, 'that I was in love with you. And I'd come to your house to find you, I suppose to tell you. Or see you or something. I don't know what I was thinking, I was fifteen and well, instead of you I stumbled upon them in the lounge. So, I left.'

Everest paled. 'Avery, I'd no idea. I just always thought you were too focused on school to admit your feelings for me. I knew how important getting through school and college was to you. I'm sorry you heard that. But Avery, does that mean you did love me?'

'I do. I mean, I did.'

He nodded.

'But honestly, Everest, I couldn't face being rejected by the only person I loved, and so I rejected you all those times. It broke my heart.'

Everest's face looked pained. 'What makes you think I would reject you?'

'Because there is more at stake than just us and our relationship. You marrying, even dating, someone who is less than perfect and without the support of your family can affect stock, jobs, economies …'

'Avery, to me, you are perfect.'

He held her gaze, and she wanted to look away but couldn't. Everest let out a sudden laugh.

It shocked Avery. 'What's so funny?'

'The irony – that my grandfather was dead set against my parent's marriage, too.' Avery looked at him confused. 'Yes, Allegra White was not deemed good enough, even though she came from an equally wealthy family and was top of every class she ever attended, if she's to be believed.'

Avery took a gulp of her wine.

'My grandfather told me recently that it took some time before he was convinced she was right for the family.' Everest took a sip from his own glass thoughtfully.

'Makes me sad that your mother would treat another person like that, even more so now.' Avery traced the rim of her wine glass with her finger as she mulled over this revelation.

Everest cleared his throat. 'Look, Avery, there was a reason I asked you and Nik to come out here and spend Christmas with me. Something I wanted to tell you both. I'd intended to do it when we were all together, but I think it would be best if I do it now.'

Avery got an awful feeling in the pit of her stomach.

'I'm moving to New York. Relocating in the New Year. I'll be heading up the Marketing Team there for the family business.'

Avery looked at him in utter shock. 'New York? But you love Dublin! You hate the round-the-clock nature of the New York office!'

'I did. Well, I probably still do. The truth is, Avery, I'm happy for you and Nik but I need some space and distraction to give my heart some time to get over it. I'd kidded myself into thinking those stolen glances between you two when we were younger meant nothing. That it was always me and that it was only a matter of time before we would be together. There are no hard feelings. I love you both and I'm happy you are both happy. I just need time and space.'

Avery closed her eyes. Tears pricked her eyes.

'Are you okay? You've gone very pale, Avery.'

'I don't want you to go.' Avery couldn't bring herself to look at him.

'What do you mean?'

'Everest, I just got you back and you're leaving …'

'Avery, I—' He was up and over to her side of the table, with his arms around her, and she sobbed into his chest. She held him tightly, not wanting to let go. The sobs finally slowed, and they parted slightly. They looked at each other; a sweet kiss hung between them.

'We can't Everest. I'm sorry, we can't.'

They drew apart and sat back down. Everest poured more wine and they both drained their glasses in silence.

'Shall I open another bottle?' Everest said, rising and heading to the counter where another bottle waited.

'No, not for me. Wine and all this emotion won't make for a great head in the morning. If you don't mind, I think I'm going to go to bed. I'm exhausted.'

'No, of course not.' He looked after her longingly as she got up from the table.

'Everest, I wish you weren't going. I just hope you won't stay away forever.'

As she crawled into bed, Avery fell into a heady, fitful sleep. She completely forgot to charge her phone to call Nik.

2
~ *How to be a cotton-headed ninny muggins* ~

'Avery, wake up.'

She could feel herself being shaken awake through her slumber. 'What? No, five more minutes.'

'Avery, Nik's on the phone. Wake up.' Everest's voice interrupted her sleep.

'What? What time is it?'

'It's about 6.30 a.m.'

'Christ!' Avery sat up in bed and took the phone from Everest. He was only wearing boxers. His chiselled body still sported a faint tan. A line of hair trailed down from his belly button. She blushed when she realised he saw her looking, and turned away. 'Nik, is everything okay?' she said into the phone.

'You never called. I was worried.'

'Called?'

'You said you'd call when you were going to bed. I tried your mobile.'

'Sorry.' She felt bad. She *had* said she would call. 'I crashed pretty early and forgot to charge my phone. It must be still in my bag. Nik, I'm fine. It's so early, babe, can I call you later? I'm still exhausted.'

'I'm headed to sleep now myself and then I have my flight to catch. I'll try you from the airport.'

Already laying back down, a wave of sleepiness taking over her, Avery barely managed to say, 'Speak to you then,' as she fell asleep clutching Everest's phone.

When she woke a few hours later, feeling more refreshed, Avery opened the curtains to find her bedroom window completely blocked by snow. She panicked. Were they literally trapped in the chalet now? A phone buzzed behind her. She uncovered it from the depths of the duvet and realised she still had Everest's phone. "Mum calling" was flashing on the screen. She hesitated, then answered it.

'Hi, Mrs White. It's Avery. I'll get Everest for you now.' Avery hurried out into the hallway. The smell of bacon wafted up to meet her.

'Avery, where is Everest?' came Mrs White's agitated voice.

'He's in the kitchen making breakfast.'

'I see, and why do you have his phone?' she persisted.

'I was talking to Nik.'

'So Niklaus didn't manage to arrive yet?'

'No, he should be here in two days if the storm lets up.' Avery almost tripped on the last step of the stairs in her rush to get off the phone with Allegra White as quickly as possible.

Everest looked up from reading his iPad as she entered the kitchen.

'Everest, your mum is on the phone. Goodbye Mrs White, have a lovely Christmas if I don't speak to you before then.'

'Oh, you'll be seeing me before then, dear,' Avery heard her say from arm's length as she passed the phone to Everest.

She poured herself a large cup of coffee, trying too hard to hear what was being said. Was it too early to add whiskey? She felt she needed it, as she was pretty sure that Everest was about to tell her his parents would be joining them for Christmas after all. Harold White, Everest's father, she quite liked. Allegra White, on the other hand – well, Allegra White was work, hard work. Everest finished speaking with his mother, then hung up the phone and turned slowly around.

'Your parents are joining us, aren't they?' Avery looked at him pointedly.

Everest nodded his head. 'I'm sorry.'

'It's okay. As soon as I answered the phone, I realised I should have let it go to voicemail. I knew your mother was already telepathically booking flights when she heard my voice. But perhaps the storm won't let up, and you and I will be cocooned here alone for Christmas …'

A longing passed between them. In another life that would actually have been the perfect Christmas. But their reality was very different.

'Hungry?' Everest said in an attempt to change the subject. 'I've made bacon and waffles and there are strawberries and cream in the fridge.'

'Oh yum, any maple syrup?'

'Of course, it's already on the table.'

She salivated a little as she saw the breakfast spread on the table. It was her favourite meal of the day. There was bacon and waffles like Everest had said, as well as scrambled eggs, soft boiled eggs with soldiers, grilled mushrooms and sausage and a plate piled high with Danish pastries. Last night's vase of roses had been replaced by a garland of green and white flowers that wove its way around the platters of food set on the table. This morning, the linen napkins were embroidered with vintage Santa Clauses. Avery wondered if the invisible housekeeper changed the flowers as she pleased or if she was on a strict schedule. She suspected it was the latter.

'How many people are you expecting for breakfast? Are you going for the host with the most Mr White?'

'Please don't call me "Mr White."'

'Sorry.' She knew he hated it. She lowered herself into a chair.

They sat in silence for a moment until Avery piped up, 'Is it normal for the snow to be up past the windows?'

Everest laughed.

'What's so funny?'

'Your bedroom is on the second floor, Avery. The shutter is closed.'

'Oh. But it looked white?'

'It is; mum had the insides painted white. She thought it was nicer to look out on when they were closed but the curtains open.'

Avery nodded. Of course, she did. Allegra White always thought of everything. Avery sat thoughtfully as she ate. The next few days were not going to be the Christmas break she'd imagined.

'Penny for them?'

'Well, I was thinking, in a way your mum is probably right.' Avery put down her knife and fork.

'What do you mean?'

'I probably wasn't right for the role of Mrs White. Or even the girlfriend of Mr White. I'd never think of the things your mum does. My brain doesn't work like that. Standing next to you in the boardroom, that's where I'd excel. But taking care of your life and home – well, homes – that's what you need. I'm not that person.'

Everest looked at her thoughtfully.

Later that day, wrapped in a chunky blanket in an armchair by the open fire, Avery was engrossed in a book she'd found in the study. How the Whites managed to have the latest bestsellers stocked on the shelves of their ski chalet that was only used seasonally was clearly a secret trick of the insanely rich. She looked across at Everest. He was dozing opposite her, his book resting on his chest. It felt nice to be this relaxed together. The Christmas tree lights flickered and danced across the wall behind them.

Avery had never really enjoyed Christmas, especially not as a young child. Her father was a possessive drunk. He didn't want her, but he didn't want her grandparents involved so Christmas had always been a fibre optic tree and whatever cheap plastic toy the petrol station or off-licence sold. But here, with Christmas music playing softly in the background, a crackling fire, a good book and a goblet of mulled wine, Avery finally got the appeal. She'd even taken a thrill in adding her small selection of Christmas gifts for Niklaus and Everest to the pile under the tree earlier. She'd had a sneaky peek at the beautifully wrapped presents already there, expecting them to be empty decorations, but they were all labelled individually.

Her phone buzzed beside her on the table. She picked it up eagerly. 'Nik! Did you arrive at the airport?'

'Avery, hi! Not exactly.'

'Oh? Was the flight cancelled? Oh – Nik, there's a knock at the door. Everest's asleep. Can I call you back in a moment?' She said getting up from her comfy chair.

'Avery, hold on a sec.'

'Sure, I'm still here.'

'Keep me on the line while you answer the door.'

'Okay … what are you up to?' Avery asked, struggling to keep the phone to her ear whilst opening the large locks on the unnecessarily big double doors to the chalet. As she opened the doors Avery felt strangely suspicious. Before her stood a very small delivery man wrapped in layers of coats, holding a very large bouquet.

'Oh my gosh, Niklaus Snow,' she said down the phone. 'Did you have something to do with this?' She could barely believe her eyes.

'Ms. Avery Duff?' said the delivery man.

'Yes, that's me.' Avery was almost giddy with excitement; she had known even before she'd asked that they were from Nik.

'Here you go, Merry Christmas!' The small man handed her the bouquet and trekked back through the snow.

'Nik, are these Pear Blossoms?' she said into the phone.

'On the first day of Christmas, my true love gave to me, a bouquet of pear blooms instead of a tree!'

Avery laughed. 'Nik, you're crazy. How on earth did you get Pear Blossoms in winter – and this many?! The bouquet is enormous!'

'It is spring somewhere, darling.'

'I miss you, Nik. I wish you were here.'

'I am.'

Avery's heart skipped a beat. 'What? Where?' She looked from left to right. Her woolly socks wouldn't offer much protection from the snow-covered porch. She stuck her head around the doorframe to see if she could see him, and when she turned back around, there was Nik, smiling, and on bended knee. Avery swallowed sharply.

'Avery,' he said, 'I can't bear to be away from you a moment longer. Will you marry me?'

She looked down in stunned silence at Nik, holding an open ring box. A solitaire diamond twinkled back at her. She didn't know what to say. Her breathing became erratic, and she thought she was going to pass out. She stumbled a little and dropped the bouquet in an attempt not to fall over, but her knees buckled, and she sank into the snow filling the porch. She felt she was having an out-of-body experience.

'Everest, are you there, mate? Come help me!' Nik shouted into the chalet.

'Nik! What happened?' Everest exclaimed as Nik carried Avery haphazardly into the sitting room.

'I don't know, her knees just buckled, and she dropped to the ground.'

'Jeez! What did you say to her?'

'I, well, I asked her to marry me.'

'What? Here, lay her down on the couch.' Everest instructed.

Avery could hear their back and forth, but she couldn't – or didn't want to – open her eyes.

'Should we call a doctor?' Nik asked while placing a pillow beneath her head.

'Give her a moment. Might just be shock. I'll get a glass of water,' said Everest.

Reluctant to face the situation, Avery opened her eyes. Nik's forehead was creased. She could smell cinnamon from the candle burning on the table beside her and she was reminded how peaceful and happy she'd felt moments before.

'There you are. Are you okay, darling?' Nik reached his arm out to help Avery into a sitting position.

'Nik, sorry. I don't know what happened.'

Everest returned and handed her the water. She sipped it slowly. Her mind was racing.

'Are you okay?' asked Nik again.

'I'm fine. Honestly. Just, wow, Nik, you just took me by surprise.'

He laughed. 'That was kinda the aim.'

Avery smiled weakly. 'No, it was lovely. I-I just wasn't expecting it.'

And she wasn't. They'd never once talked about marriage. The future, yes. But how it related to careers and travel. Never something as "forever" as marriage.

'So should I ask again, or is that a "yes"?' He laughed nervously and sat down beside her.

Avery looked at him, it only just occurring to her that she needed to give him an answer. She opened her mouth, but nothing came out. She closed her eyes. She wasn't prepared for this. 'Nik, I need some time. I really wasn't expecting this. We've not even been together a year.' Avery looked at him, wondering what the hell she was supposed to say. 'I just can't give you an answer right now. I'm sorry.'

He looked at her, stunned. As did Everest.

Nik got slowly to his feet. 'Is there something going on between you two?' He looked from Avery to Everest and back again.

Avery sighed. Nik had long promised her he was over his jealousy of Everest. 'No, there isn't,' she said. 'I just need time. Marriage is such a big step. I didn't think we were at this stage yet. And, honestly, I don't know how I feel about marriage. I need some time to think. I'm going to lay down for a bit.' She left the room and ran up the stairs before anyone could say anything more.

The soft wool blanket that had been casually thrown across the chair in Avery's bedroom gave her little comfort as she wrapped herself in it. Her head began to throb. Ten years of unresolved feelings and emotions filled the room as she stared out the window into the snow. Why was love so complicated? As a child, she had believed you could only love one person. After all, that was the very reason her mother had died from a broken heart when the person she'd loved simply hadn't loved her back. The thought had utterly terrified Avery in her youth – the thought that you could choose so wrongly. It had also helped a young girl understand why she had never felt loved: she simply hadn't met that one person who would love her yet.

She had been drawn to Everest from the moment she met him. When they were in a room together, they naturally orbited around each other. She felt more confident and alive when he was there. His smile or even a casual glance would send a thrill through her body. It had taken her a couple of years to realise she was in love with him. But she'd always known that she had to be sensible. She couldn't let herself get derailed by a relationship, especially one that was doomed. She had a very concrete life plan to start before she was ready for that. And so, she'd kept him at friend's length.

Niklaus and Everest had always come as a package deal. She'd always liked Niklaus; he was fascinating. At school, they'd spent hours together reading and looking at wildlife photography, his greatest passion. But she had never been attracted to him in the same way she was drawn to Everest. Not until the day she'd looked at him from the side as he talked so animatedly about the lighting technique used to capture the image of two lions chasing each other. That's when she first wanted to reach out and kiss him. Her feelings for him seemed to come from nowhere. She had tried to hide them, but it was obvious even to the blind mice in the Science Lab that she was in love with both Everest and Niklaus.

As Avery watched the snowflakes flutter against the windowpane and drop to the growing mound on the sill, she realised that "teenage Avery" had been much more resolute than she was feeling now. She really had thought she was over Everest and happily in love only with Niklaus. How was she so conflicted again? She looked down at her hands. In some parallel universe, she would be wearing a sparkling diamond right now, freshly placed on a finger that desperately needed a manicure. Did she want that? Did she want to be Mrs Avery Snow? She'd never thought about marriage. Love yes, a family — she'd always dreamt of one. But for some reason, she, Avery Duff, actually being a married woman, hadn't factored.

Until now.

3
~ *All I want for Christmas is ...* ~

The night sky darkened outside the window as Avery lay on the bed. It was so peaceful here, and she could see stars start to dot the night sky. She closed her eyes and let sleep overtake her, unable to think about Nik and Everest anymore.

She woke, hours later, to a pitch-black star-filled sky. She rolled over to turn on the bedside lamp. Nothing happened. She got up off the bed and felt for the light switch. It clicked, but the room was still in darkness. She opened the bedroom door and found the hallway filled with flickering candlelight. The power must be out, she realised.

She made her way to the stairs, and as she descended she caught sight of Everest below her, standing in front of the fire. The flames crackled, illuminating his silhouette. It was then that she heard the faint notes of the tune.

Dada, dada, da, da, da, da ... the opening notes to "Only You", a cover sung by Kylie Minogue and James Corden, filled the air.

He turned around and saw her.

'It's our song.' He smiled.

She nodded.

'Do you remember the dance?' He reached out his hand.

Avery hesitated a moment. She knew she shouldn't, but she wanted to capture that night one last time. She took his hand and he twirled her gracefully into his embrace. The steps came effortlessly, as if they'd only practised yesterday, and not over five years ago. The notes of the song wrapped around them.

As she turned back into him for that final finish their lips met and for the briefest of moments Avery's body exploded with joy.

'WHAT THE HELL IS GOING ON?' Nik's voice struck through the chalet.

They both spun around.

'Nik? I?' Avery thought she was going to faint again.

'Shit! Nik, sorry,' said Everest. 'It was just the heat of the moment. Honestly, it meant no—'

'It meant what exactly? Cause we all damn well know it did not mean "nothing"!' Nik spat the words out. 'I can't believe you would do this to me. Both of you. The whole bloody time you both said *nothing* was going on. Did you both take me for a fool?'

'Honestly Nik, nothing has been going on between us, I promise!' Avery pleaded with him.

'What do you call this then? Just a nice trip down memory lane and a little kiss for old time's sake?'

Avery and Everest looked at each other. They really weren't sure what that had been.

But it had definitely been something.

'Should I give you another few days alone shacked up here to decide exactly what you want to tell me?' demanded Nik.

Avery looked at him, hurt. 'Nik, please, nothing happened. You clearly saw the dance and the kiss, that was it. Nothing else.'

'I'm not stupid, Avery. You two have been on and off again for years. For most of the past decade!'

'Nik, we haven't,' said Everest. 'You know we haven't. Avery has always been very firm with me. This, this – it was just a momentary lapse.'

'A "momentary lapse"?' Nik laughed, but it was contorted.

'It was, Nik, that – that was our first kiss.' A tear rolled down Avery's cheek.

'I'm sick of this. Always worrying about what's going on. Avery, you have to choose once and for all. Is it Everest or is it me? What do you want?

Tomorrow's Christmas Eve. Put us both out of our misery for Christmas and let us know – by the end of tomorrow!'

Avery was shocked by Nik's ultimatum. His tone was vicious. She looked at the man she thought she was in love with and saw him in a new light. He looked wild. She swallowed hard. 'Okay, Nik, if that is what you want. I'll let you know tomorrow.' It came out much more confidently than she felt. She left the room and walked straight into the kitchen. She needed a drink.

Avery stared down into the glass she'd poured and finished the brandy in one gulp. What did she truly want? That was the issue, wasn't it? It had always been the issue. Their messy teenage love triangle had spilt into their adulthood. She turned to leave the kitchen – she could hear Nik's raised voice from the lounge.

'She's mine, Everest! Was mine first. Just wait and see. She'll choose me.'

'Nik, please! Calm down. Nothing is going on between us.'

'Things would be a little different if it was me kissing the woman you love.'

'Nik, you have been kissing the woman I love, all year,' Everest said exasperatedly.

'Yeah, well, just wait. Tomorrow, when she chooses me, you just stay away then! Right?'

Avery watched horrified from the doorway as Nik jabbed Everest in the shoulder with his index finger.

'Nik just please, stop!' Avery stood at the edge of the room utterly frustrated.

'Avery, I was—'

'Nik, just stop,' she said, exasperated.

There was a knock at the door. Avery turned to open it to find two smartly dressed waiters standing there, laden down with bags that smelt delicious.

'Hej, Miss, we 'ave arrived with your celebration dinner.'

Of course, you have, Avery thought. And perfect timing too. 'I'm not hungry,' she said.

'Of course, Miss.'

She looked at Everest and Niklaus. 'I'm going to my room. I need to think. Please leave me alone – I don't want to see or hear from either of you tonight. I will come out when I'm ready.' She was very calm. And as she climbed the stairs, she felt like she was taking back control of her life. Now, she just had to figure out what the hell that meant.

It was 3 a.m. before sleep finally came to Avery. She woke the following morning strangely refreshed, despite the lack of sleep. She walked downstairs to find the chalet silent. Everyone must have been sleeping. She made coffee, and took two of the freshly made pastries that miraculously appeared every day, and sat outside on the balcony looking up at the snow-capped mountains. She still had no idea what she was going to do. But she felt calm. Maybe it was the postcard scene in front of her – the calming effect of the perfectly still snow, the trees sprinkled with white flakes, the sunlight dancing over the fresh landscape.

A movement inside the chalet caught her attention. To her relief, she saw it was only the housekeeper, silently making up the master suite – making sure all would be perfect for the imminent arrival of Allegra and Harold White. Wouldn't their presence make this shite situation all the more festive, Avery thought. As the housekeeper moved out of view, Avery's eyes settled on a framed quote just in view on the wall, *"Everything you want, is on the other side of fear. ~ Jack Canfield."* She repeated it twice.

Avery was very much for pushing yourself past your comfort zone. She'd spent her whole life doing that, securing the best scholarships for school and college, and going for her dream job that realistically, she was probably five years too early for. But getting to the other side of her fears? Well, that was just terrifying. Nik's ultimatum last night had made it seem like she was about to lose everything. And it was making her face her biggest fear: being alone. But actually, she reflected, sipping her coffee, it was allowing her to discover what she really wanted.

As Avery descended the stairs that evening, having spent the day alone with her thoughts, she found Nik and Everest in the lounge by the fire. Both matched each other in height but were utterly different in features. Everest's chocolate hair framed his face, and she could see his emerald eyes looked stoic. Nik's strong Korean features were tense and strained. Despite the atmosphere, the scene looked perfectly festive. They looked like two rather tall kiddies waiting for Santa. Except they weren't waiting for Santa. They were waiting for her. As they heard her on the stairs, they both looked up at her expectantly.

She didn't say a word until she stood in front of them, then took a breath. They both opened their mouths to speak. She held up her hand to stop them.

'This hasn't been an easy decision,' she began slowly. 'But it's the one I want, and I hope you'll both understand and respect it.' She took a deep breath. 'I love you both. I have for a very long time. But I love you both differently. I'm not even sure what that means. Only that what I feel for you both is different.' She turned to Nik; his face was full of hope. She swallowed hard. 'Nik, I'm not ready to get married. Not for a while at the very least. There is too much I want to accomplish first. I'm sorry. Maybe one day I will get married, but right now it's not something I want.'

Nik looked at her in complete shock. 'You're choosing *him*? Well, I hope the two of you will be very happy!' He stormed out of the chalet.

Avery looked after him, not knowing how to react. But she needed to continue while she still had the courage. 'Everest.' She took a deep breath. 'Everest, there is so much I want to say. So much to talk about – about our futures. But before we do …' Avery hesitated. She stepped forward and leaned herself up towards Everest's lips. In the candlelight, his eyes really were the most terrific green. The spice of his aftershave was intoxicating. She lifted her hand to his face; his skin was like silk. She lowered his head towards her and kissed him.

It was a gentle kiss, but little by little, it grew passionate and hungry. Her body came alive. As lust flooded through her veins, she finally confirmed what she had suspected for ten long years – that her feelings for Everest were real.

But she had to stop it before it got out of control. Suddenly, reluctantly, she withdrew from his lips.

'Everest, I've always been in love with you. Always will. But right now, I'm not ready to be with you. I know that's probably not what you want to hear. And it's not me trying to string you along. Or even asking you to wait. It is you I want to be with.'

Everest's face washed with emotion. Joy, confusion and the realisation of what she was about to say.

'But first,' Avery went on quickly, 'before I can truly love you, I need to learn how to love myself. I need to focus on me. I've been focused on all the wrong reasons why we should or shouldn't be together. You know I desperately want to be a part of a family because I've never had that, but it needs to be right; for everyone. I never thought I would say this, but your mum saying I'm not right for you has merit. I'm not saying I wholeheartedly completely agree, but she has a point. We both have big futures and right now I don't think either of us should have to take a back seat for the other. So right now, I'm choosing myself.'

She turned away from him and walked upstairs to collect her bags.

~ *Not the End* ~

Dying to know what happened our love struck trio? Be sure to check out the novel "It Started with a Gift" coming late 2022 and set ten years into their future.

Bláithín O'Reilly Murphy

Our now restauranteur, Niklaus Snow, and the ever-mysterious Everest White find themselves, once again in love with the same woman. Holly Clementine thinks she's sworn off love; that is until she meets our two dashing leading men! She falls madly in love with one and marries the other – but all is never as it seems. As a festive celebration brings their lives colliding, they are all forced to face the stark reality of the choices they've made.

It is then that Avery Duff makes her return. But is she too late for the happily ever after she now wants?

Find out in – "It Started with a Gift", coming late 2022.

Love, Forever

Donna Gowland

Love, Forever

The café was empty. The last customers had left only minutes before the pale December clouds burst open, pelting the Edinburgh pavement, and bouncing off the brightly coloured umbrellas Katie had laid out for unsuspecting tourists. Her favourite song played in the background – a perfect antidote to the dreary day – and Katie hummed along. When the chorus hit, she belted out the lyrics, losing herself completely until a cough from behind interrupted her. Embarrassed, she turned to see her brother Clive waiting for her at the counter to collect the day's takings for the bank. Not that there was much to take. Tracks and Snacks hadn't exactly been doing a roaring trade lately.

'You always get words wrong,' he chided.

Katie's bright red lips erupted into a wide grin. 'No, I don't. I just prefer my version.'

'If it's impossible for anyone to "Live Forever", surely it's as improbable that someone can *love* forever?'

Katie sighed. 'What can I say? I'm an old romantic.'

Clive rattled the half-empty takings bag.

'If it carries on like this, your optimism might be all we have left.'

'Urgh, Clive, way to kill the mood,' Katie replied, slumping into an unstacked chair.

Clive took a seat next to her. Though Katie was the epitome of vintage with her carefully curated outfit, impossibly high heels, and flame-red hair (with its one perfect vanilla streak in the front), Clive was every bit the stereotype of the word "accountant". Still, despite their differences, their resemblance was uncanny.

'I'm just looking out for you.' He shrugged. 'If you keep running through your inheritance like this, you'll have none left. Is Tracks and Snacks really worth it?'

'You could always invest your inheritance in it?' Katie said sweetly. It had worked well at getting him to change the channel or give her his sweets when they were children; she doubted it would work as well now.

'Mine's all tied up in property, as well you know. I've got a family Katie; I can't afford to waste it …'

Katie shot up, her Achilles heel well and truly scratched.

'You think I'm wasting my life?' she fumed. 'That this is – what, exactly – a hobby? I'm a trained chef, Clive!'

He sighed. 'It just isn't what you dreamt of.'

Katie gaped at Clive's dismissive attitude. The café was her heart and soul: each decision painstakingly made, from the duck-egg blue walls to inspire calm and joy in her customers, to the carefully selected pieces of art, and shelves packed with books and vinyl records. It wasn't some hollow building; it was a living breathing museum of her. Why couldn't Clive see that?

'I'm sorry.' Clive sighed. 'I know how important it is to you, but the café can't survive like this. You need a fresh approach, some fresh ideas. It's nearly Christmas – why not put some festive events on? Do some office parties?'

'I'd need entertainment and alcohol licenses for events and the council are already circling like vultures. They'll deny any applications if it means I close down sooner.'

'Just think about it. Jen and I are happy to help however you need it – everyone's rooting for you.' Clive stood and wrapped Katie in a bear hug, instantly putting her at ease.

'Right, I'd better pay this in. See you soon.'

'Try not to get mugged on the way to the bank,' Katie laughed, her smile fading with every step he took away from the café.

Though she'd never admit it, Clive was right; she had taken the café on as a distraction after their parents' death. It had been easier to throw herself into this business than wallow in her grief; afraid that letting that grief in would open the floodgates to other griefs – the expected and then the unexpected. Her biggest loss.

Dickie's sudden exit from her life had split it into three acts: Before Dickie, With Dickie, and After Dickie – this third act stretching out like flexing an old injury – bearable day-to-day, but capable of flaring up at any small reminder.

In their short time as a couple, their infatuation had marooned them together, on an island of love, drifting away from anyone, and anything else that mattered. His disappearance left Katie alone and desperate, stranded so completely that she could never make it back to life on the mainland.

Twenty-five years had passed since Dickie vanished. So much easier to disappear in the '90s, she thought, before the days of social media, mobile phones and Google. Back then, there had been no way of getting in touch with him, no-one answering her repeated calls to Dickie's landline, no home address for the letters she wrote but could never send. It was as if Dickie had just walked out of her life.

Once her anger and hurt abated, Katie had thrown away every trace of their life together, only to spend the next decade hunting it back down, re-assembling their romance through other peoples' possessions: using their memories to recapture her own.

She tapped her fingers to her lips, kissed them, then placed them gently on the glass cabinet containing a slowly fading gig ticket. Their last night out before Dickie had abandoned her. Many years later, the ticket had fallen out of "The Female Eunuch", opening the floodgates of painful memories. Now, both book and ticket were housed in a glass cabinet, proudly displayed next to a bust of Oscar Wilde and a mural of sunflowers. Pride of place. Love forever. She would.

A gust of winter wind broke into the café, and Katie startled to see Clive in the doorway. The grave expression on his face made her heart sink. It wasn't like him to come straight back from the bank; there was no way he was bringing good news.

'Katie.' He started, voice strained and hesitant. 'If you don't make a profit this month, the bank's stopping the business overdraft. You've got to do something.'

*

Richard Hall was tired of waiting for the train. It seemed to be all he did these days. Prior to his move to Edinburgh, he had hoped that the city trains would be more reliable than the rural ones. That would teach him. He yawned, rubbed his eyes, yawned again. The sky was black: the day as reluctant to get going as he was.

Coffee, he needed coffee, but none of that station rubbish or the stuff in plastic cups from coffee chains. No, he wanted a proper coffee from a place that could become a second home. Sweat bristled at the cruck of his shirt, despite the cold. Why did his new office insist on a shirt and tie? The shirt's collar would surely asphyxiate him before the train arrived!

When the train finally pulled into the station, the windows were steamed by the passengers packed inside like sardines in a tin. Richard sidestepped the deluge of people pouring out to their next destination and slid to a space by the door, ignoring the angry tut of the woman whose bag he'd tripped over. He closed his eyes and counted down the stops.

Once he arrived at his destination, Richard reluctantly opened his eyes, allowing the cold air from the parting train doors to refresh him as he stepped onto the platform. His calm was soon shattered by the unwelcome sight of an early morning busker outside the station. Pulling up his collar, he walked past briskly. Even the *thought* of music brought him out in hives. Richard couldn't remember any music from the time before his accident, and anything he'd heard afterwards had given him nothing more than a splitting headache. Music was overrated – except Christmas carols. He could tolerate those.

The cathedral bells rang out as he exited onto the high street. He didn't have time for a coffee after all. The council buildings were grand and imposing, a world away from the small-town office he'd been used to in Droitwich. He took a deep breath; this was the start of his new life, the chance to live a life in the present day – not clinging to a past he didn't remember or a version of himself he didn't recognise. Time to be brave. Richard strode into the buzzing reception with a confidence he did not feel and dived towards the lift just as the doors closed.

'Going up?' A sandy-haired man called from the lift, holding the doors for him.

'Thanks.' Richard panted gratefully. The man had a kind face, inviting him to ask, 'Do you know where licensing is?'

The man held out his hand. 'I'm Carl. Environmental Health – we're on the same floor.'

'Richard.' He returned the shake, feeling bad about his sweaty palm. 'Good to meet you.'

'First day?'

'Yes.' Richard laughed nervously. 'It's a lot bigger than my last place, but I'm sure I'll find my way around soon enough.'

More Than Mistletoe

'I'm sure you will.' Carl smiled. 'Well, I'm down this corridor and you're at the bottom of that one.' He pointed to the right. A row of indistinct doors leading to identical offices, Richard thought. 'Good luck Richard, we'll have to go out for a coffee sometime.'

*

'Blimey, you've got a tree up already?' Clive hovered at the door, bringing the cold air in with him. 'It's certainly looking twinkly in here.'
The café was decked out in multi-coloured fairy lights and paper garlands hung from on every inch of the walls. Baubles and Christmas wreaths adorned the painted figures on the mural of '90s Indie icons on the far wall. To passers-by outside, it looked like a Christmas edition of NME, glowing welcomes in the dim dusk. It was a shame no one had stopped to admire it so far.

'I needed to inject a bit of festive cheer. Help me with this, will you?'

Katie held out the fairy she had fashioned from an old Barbie, stylishly re-dressed in a mustard corduroy skirt and Fred Perry top. The Barbie's long locks had been unceremoniously cropped to a pixie cut and dyed platinum blonde. Much better, in Katie's opinion, than the generic brand.

'I'm presuming you made this?' Clive frowned, turning it over in his hands.

'Yes, I did. And I've made a different one for every week in the run up to Christmas. Can you guess who'll be top of the Christmas tree pops this year?'

'Hmm, let me see. Who's your top Indie icon? That woman from Sleeper? Elastica?'

'For someone who hates Indie music, you've an excellent memory for their names.'

'Just because I don't like the music, doesn't mean I can't appreciate the women.' Clive winked.

'Urgh. Gross!' Katie grimaced. 'You're wrong. I've got two this year. I'll give you a hint: feuding brothers who share mutant eyebrows – at least by my artistic styling they do.'

'The Gallaghers? That's the first time I've ever heard them described as angels,' Clive laughed, climbing a chair to reach the top of the six-foot Christmas tree that dominated the shop's window. He fixed the Barbie in her regal position, surveying the café below. 'There.'

Katie stepped back to admire the scene.

'Perfect.' She smiled, staring at the tree. 'Tea?' She clapped her hands together.

'Yeah, go on then.'

They sat at the counter drinking their tea, neither feeling the need to make small talk. Katie contemplated the unique Christmas themed menu she laid out each year, but she could tell from Clive's silence that he was mustering the courage to bring up their previous topic of conversation.

'Have you thought about what I said last week?' he finally asked, blowing his tea.

'Yes, in fact, I have, and you'll be pleased to know that I've made a list.' She looked either side of her. 'Now, where did I put it?'

Katie disappeared under the counter, scrambling bits of paper together, then emerging with a Prodigy themed to-do list and flamingo pen.

'Ok, so my theme this year is "Battle of the Bands", as it's 25 years since the chart war between Blur and Oasis.'

'They were both shite,' Clive shrugged. 'Carry on.'

'I'm going to do it with … drum roll, please … the band night at The Krazy Kabin.'

Clive frowned. 'The place where all the underage goths go?'

'The same,' Katie nodded proudly.

'Won't that be noisy for a tiny café?'

'I've thought about that.' Katie smiled smugly. 'I'll host the acoustic night here. Round two will be at The Krazy Kabin and the final will be another acoustic evening here, on Christmas Eve. What do you think?'

'It's one idea,' said Clive, unconvincingly. 'But I can't see it generating much money.'

'It will spread word of mouth and once people taste my cakes, well, they won't be able to stay away.'

Clive grinned. 'Let's hope so, eh?'

'I've asked my friend Lloyd to read some Christmas ghost stories over a couple of evenings, but as he'll be finished by nine, I won't need an extra licence.'

'Give me the dates,' Clive smiled, 'and I'll get Jen to work on some posters for you.'

'No need,' Katie winked. 'I emailed her this morning.'

*

Richard struggled against the crippling winds as he trudged up the Old Mile. Compared to everywhere else he had lived; Edinburgh was all hills and curves. Still, there was nothing more beautiful than Edinburgh Castle, a gold beacon in the distance. The lights from the shops and hotels in the town below shimmered like small jewels in a majestic crown. As one of the first places he'd visited as a boy – and revisited after his accident – it held a special place in his heart. Physically tiring though the climb was, it lifted his spirits.

His numb fingers fumbled in his pocket to fish out his phone, and he snapped a picture of himself in front of the castle, which he sent to his mother. Her reply was instantaneous and brief: an aubergine emoji. Richard laughed but the sound was soon swallowed by a brisk night wind that swept it away. She still hadn't got the hang of them. She'd be horrified if she knew what that emoji meant. Overwhelmed by the urge to hear a familiar voice, he dialled her number and she answered before the second ring.

'Are you enjoying yourself, Dickie?' she asked.

The blood rushed to his cheeks and his heart ached. Richard wasn't sure *why* the nickname evoked such powerful emotions in him, but each time he heard it, it felt as though it belonged to someone else, someone important …

'I'm having a great time, Mum,' he replied through gritted teeth, grateful his mother hadn't graduated to video calls to catch his face in a lie. 'Are you and Dad going to come up to the markets?'

'We'll try to, but your Dad's got a new date for his knee operation and we don't want to jeopardise that. You're still coming home for Christmas?'

Richard sighed. This was the plight of the only child; the perennial expectation of coming home for Christmas. He could never let them down.

'Of course, I am.'

'Hopefully you'll be bringing someone special with you one of these days?' His mother's expectation hung over him like a heavy cloud.

'Yes, one of these days, I'm sure,' Richard bit his lip. When was she ever going to stop pestering him about his love life? 'Right, I'll let you get on. I was just ringing to say hello.'

'Ok, Dickie. Take care of yourself – I love you.'

'Love you too,' he said to the phone's dialling tone.

The cathedral bells chimed, and Richard's stomach groaned in synchronicity; he would stop at the takeaway on his way home – the cold weather always made him fancy some chips. His mother's words rang through his mind, echoed by the couples he passed, hand in hand or arm in arm, huddled together against the bitter December winds. Another year was almost over, another year he had spent alone.

*

Katie balanced her paints and brushes in one hand, sprinkled extra cinnamon on her cappuccino with the other, and sat on a stool in the café window. With her "That's What I Call an Indie Christmas" playlist cranked up, she traced the outline of her vision of two large country houses; giant Christmas trees in the gardens; fancy cars in the driveways and the pièce de résistance – caricatures of the members of Blur and Oasis sticking out of the house windows.

With every note she belted out, slithers of the girl she once was came back to her. This was who she was supposed to be – who she would have been, had life taken a different turn. The dream of being a singer may have faded, but within these walls she would always be a superstar.

She closed her eyes and threw every emotion she had into the song; singing from such a deep place in her soul that when the song finished, she sank into her seat with exhaustion. Katie opened her eyes, blinking them back to reality, and walked over to the Christmas tree. She turned on its lights and was immediately soothed by the warm, tangerine glow released into the room, gently easing her away from the haze of her pretend stardom.

Moving back to the window to tidy up the paints, she noticed someone under the shadow of the lamppost in front of the chip shop. There was something in the slight hunch of the shoulders, an awkwardness of the pose that stirred a long-forgotten hope. It couldn't be.

It looked like Dickie.

Katie rushed to the door, but there was no one there. She shook her head, pushing the thoughts of him away, but they pounded at her heart, flooding every fibre of her being with memories of him. Katie ran out into the street and called out his name, but the word was an echo rolling down the empty street.

She dreamt of him that night; the dream that haunted her for years. Dickie. Forever young. Forever loved. The vision of her younger, carefree self-brought no joy, and the sound of her sobs jolted her awake. Katie stepped downstairs in the early morning darkness, fired up the coffee machine, and tore off a piece of white paper from the doodle pad she kept under the counter. She willed herself to do the one thing she'd spent years avoiding: remembering every detail of his face; his curtain hairstyle; long, slim nose; large brown eyes and thick lips.

By the time the sun had risen, Katie had resurrected him.

*

The coffee shop was new. Or at least, Richard thought it was. Last night, the vivid display had caught his eyes and then the woman creating it. As he watched her, a sense of loneliness enveloped him, and he longed to comfort her. When she looked out on to the road as if she knew him, his nerve had gone and he ran back to his flat, unsettled by her gaze.

Now, he was back in the same position, only the chip shop wasn't open, but the coffee shop was, and he paced along the cold pavement, desperately trying to pluck up the courage to go into it. His mother's voice chastised his thoughts, telling him he'd wear his shoes out like that. Richard inhaled sharply, then crossed the road, stopping in front of the Christmas window, hoping it would obscure him until he'd calmed down and his heart had stopped racing. Panic attacks were an unwelcome side effect after the coma, but he hadn't had one in years and his coping mechanisms were rusty. Pretending to scrutinise the window, he named the reindeers one by one as a grounding technique to regulate his breathing.

Once his pulse settled, he cast his eyes over the rest of the pictures; frowning as he looked at the figures; knowing that he should recognise them. There were signs and symbols he knew he'd seen before, but they may as well have been hieroglyphics.

Then, a flash of red hair streaked the rooftops of the houses in the picture. It belonged to the woman painting the scene last night. Now, she was serving customers, laughing with them about something. She straightened, wiping the hair out of her eyes, and almost caught him staring at her as she did so. Richard scuttled out of sight, then checked himself. He was determined to go in. He closed his eyes, walked over to the door, and opened it.

"Yeah, yeah, yeah, YEAH!" a chorus of rocker vocals screeched out of the open door, the layers of electric guitars and crashing drums thumping at his temples. His foot was barely in the door, but he had to get out of there. No matter how beguiling the red-haired artist was, she wasn't worth the headache.

*

Katie picked up the plates she had just dropped on the floor, mumbled apologies to her customers, and ran to the toilet to compose herself. This was ridiculous.

He wasn't Dickie.

Why did her brain keep tricking her? Why was it playing these tricks after so many years of suppression? There was no way of knowing what he looked like now. They might have passed each other in the street hundreds of times over the years and not known. Katie smoothed her '50s rockabilly skirt, using the motions of her hand to calm her nerves. She was no longer the girl she'd been at university, the shy girl with a love of band t-shirts and flared corduroy trousers – that carefree and easy-going girl had been replaced by one who believed in ghosts and shadows; it had taken a long time to reconcile the parts of herself into one coherent being.

*

'A Battle of the Bands?' Richard shook his head. 'That doesn't sound like a good thing for a man who's had brain trauma and has an aversion to loud noises.'

Carl had sold their current evening out to Richard as a quiet night in a local pub, enjoying a few beers. It was anything but, being match night. Still, the volume would stay at acceptable levels unless one of the teams scored.

'That makes it the perfect thing for you,' Carl laughed, slapping him on the back. 'Seriously, Rich, you need to get out there. Find yourself a woman. When's the last time you had a girlfriend?'

'Well, I can't remember any relationships before the year 2000, but I've had a couple of girlfriends since then.'

'I think you made up the trauma story to cover the fact that you were a cad in your younger days!' Carl picked up his pint.

'With looks like these?' Richard smiled. 'I'm sure I was fighting them off. Cheers.'

They raised their pint glasses and squinted their eyes towards the blurred screen playing the football match. Behind the bravado, Richard was grateful that Carl had taken him under his wing. It was good to have a more confident friend and Carl could talk to anyone – especially women – with a gift of the gab that Richard could only dream of. It would be very handy if Richard was to meet a woman and finally get a girlfriend.

God. Girlfriend. The word sounded lame coming from a middle-aged man. Partner sounded even worse; Lady Friend sounded like a razor for intimate body parts; and no one on earth could convince him that "Friends with Benefits" wasn't a dating app for people on benefits. There had been girlfriends, he was sure of that, but he'd guarded them with the same secrecy he carried with him now. He hadn't been at university long enough to introduce his parents to anyone – friends or girlfriends. There was – to the best of his knowledge – nothing or no one that could fill in those gaps. He was the unassuming man that went unnoticed in a crowd, even now.

'Do you fancy going to a Battle of The Bands? Might help you get over your music phobia.' Carl snickered.

'Can't think of anything worse.' Richard shuddered. 'Where is it?'

'Tracks and Snacks, the café on Broughton Street. The Indie themed one?'

'Indie themed?' Richard's spirits sank. 'Why would anyone want to have an Indie themed place?'

'Katie – the owner – is "mad-for-it" as they say.'

'Mad. For. It.' Richard chewed the words around his mouth. 'Mad. For. It. What does that even mean?'

Carl shrugged. 'Search me. You'd better ask Liam Gallagher about that. He probably remembers as much of the '90s as you do.'

Carl burst out laughing again. Richard was regretting ever telling him about his accident. Or, rather, his parents' version of events; that he'd slipped on some ice, straight into the path of an oncoming car which had knocked him over a bridge and into a river. It was lucky he'd been run over, people told him, otherwise no one would have ever found him. *He* didn't feel lucky.

'Earth to Richard.' Carl waved his hands in front of Richard's face. 'What do you think? Battle of the Bands? Mad for it?'

Richard shook his head. 'No. I don't like Indie music. However quietly it's played. Thanks, anyway.'

He finished his pint and put his coat on.

'Have a think about it. Don't be put off by the music. It could be a good night. You could meet the love of your life.'

Carl turned back to the football. His team scored and he was up on his feet, too wrapped up in celebrations to notice Richard leaving. It wasn't far to the café and Richard walked back to it as if in a trance. The pitch-black of its interior was a relief. He stood outside, using the streetlight to trace the features of the artwork on the window. So much time and effort had gone into it. The work of a proper artist. He turned the handle on the door, not sure whether he was relieved or disappointed to find it locked. Maybe he would venture in one of these days. Richard smiled and walked away.

Band Night 1

'I've never seen it so busy; this was a good idea, Katie,' Clive said, picking up a tray of mince pies to serve to customers.

'I know. I've sold out of most of my mocktails and specialty hot chocolates.'

Katie buzzed around, taking orders, serving others, and loving every minute. She hadn't seen Dickie's doppelgänger for a few days, and she'd brushed aside her paranoia while preparing for her events. The first one – a reading of "Ghost Stories" by her friend, gamely dressed as Charles Dickens, had sold-out. Its success had led her to add further dates and drag in a couple of local drama students to act as Charlotte Riddell and M. R. James. For each event, she'd been elbow deep in pastry, cinnamon and festive fruits and spices and, even better, at each event she'd sold everything she'd made. This one would be no exception.

The evening passed in a blur and by the time the winners were announced, Katie was ready to shut the door and call it a night. As the last of the customers trickled out, Katie filled the dishwasher then prepared for bed – she'd tackle the rest of it in the morning. The tinkling of the doorbell signalled someone's entry – probably a customer searching for a left-behind item. The lights from the Christmas tree cast a haze upon the half-lit room, offering just enough light to see the shadow of a person in the doorway, but nothing more.

'I'm sorry, we're closed now,' Katie shouted from the back of the room. 'You'll have to come back in the morning.'

She nudged Clive to deal with it.

'Oh, I'm sorry.' The stranger stepped into the café. 'I saw the lights on and thought you were still serving. You haven't got any cakes left, have you?'

Clive went behind the counter and repeated the customer's request to Katie. 'Have you got any cake left? Can you check the fridge?'

Katie rubbed her eyes, stepped into the storeroom. 'Erm, I've got a couple of pieces of fruit cake left? Or a Christmas themed carrot cake? I could let you have that.'

'I'll take the carrot cake please.' The stranger raised his voice to her. 'How much is it?'

'On the house.' Katie put the cake in a takeaway carton, tied it together clumsily, and handed it to Clive. He passed it over to the customer who loitered in the doorway for a few minutes before thanking them and closing the door.

'You'll go out of business if you keep giving things away.' Clive chided, turning away from the door, and walking back through the café. 'I'll get my coat and get going. I'll go out through the back if you close the front door.'

'Yeah, thanks Clive.' Katie replied, on autopilot.

She was watching the figure walk away from the shop. There was something in his walk that reminded her of Dickie. Ghosts of Dickie on every corner. How do you charge a ghost for a slice of cake? Had she somehow manifested all these doppelgangers by thinking of him? A peculiar energy swept through her; a desperation to figure out what was drawing her back to Dickie after all this time. Katie stepped into the street, searching all the empty spaces for a sign of him. Finding no answers, she turned back into the shop, closed off the lights and bolted the door, then felt an overwhelming compulsion to pick up her long-abandoned guitar.

*

Richard sat on the bench opposite the castle, sick with nerves. The cake box sat beside him, untouched. Why did he feel like this? This feeling was alien to him; he felt detached from his body, and yet connected to this stranger with the red hair. An invisible thread pulling him towards the shop, towards her. He felt calm, chaotic, and ridiculous – all at once.

Flakes of snow drifted down, tickling his face, and telling him to go home. The cake wouldn't last long if the snow fell any thicker, and he would need a full stomach to help him decide what to do next about this mystery woman.

*

Now that Katie had allowed Dickie back into her thoughts, she could think about nothing else. Her mind replayed the cake scene over and over until she was absolutely convinced that it was him. Now, all she had to do was find him again – find some way of bringing him back to the café. The Christmas Eve final of "The Battle of The Bands" was fast approaching, and there was no better opportunity.

Everything was coming together. She hadn't felt so inspired in years. Lyrics flowed from her like water, and her hands plucked guitar chords like they were stray flowers; she wrote song after song, until finally, she felt confident enough to play at the acoustic night.

She plastered buildings and lampposts with posters bearing her sketch of Dickie, hidden amongst the '90s themed imagery used to advertise the last event. If her mystery man *was* Dickie, she could think of no other way to get his attention – every other attempt had failed.

'Let me get this straight,' Clive started, handing her a poster for the noticeboard in the blue bookshop. 'You've seen this guy a couple of times who bears a slight resemblance to the love of your life, and you've put up posters around town trying to get him to come to the "Battle of the Bands" final.'

'When you put it like that, it sounds odd,' Katie replied, thumbing the drawing pin into the board. 'When I say it, it sounds romantic.'

'I know you've been thinking a lot about life recently, and that's partly my fault for encouraging this introspection and *carpe diem* attitude …'

'Carp and what?'

'Seize the day, sis, seize the day!' Clive grasped the air with both hands. 'But I meant it purely to take risks to save the business. Not stalking men who look a bit like old boyfriends from decades ago.'

'I *am* taking risks with the business and it's paying off.' Katie puffed her chest out. 'And I know you think I'm crazy but *carpe diem*, as you say.'

'I hate to think of you setting yourself up for an enormous disappointment …' Clive put some flyers on the counter, smiled at the bookseller and ushered Katie to the romance aisle, ' … because it can go one of two ways. Either he *is* your ex-boyfriend, and he's ghosted you for twenty-five years – or he isn't … or he's with someone else and you're just setting yourself up for more hurt.'

'That's three ways, Mr Accountant.' Katie smirked. 'I know what you're saying, and I know you're right, but my heart's telling me to do this, and I haven't listened to it in a long time. Worst-case scenario, I'm wrong and nothing changes. As for the best-case scenario …' Katie winked, 'who knows what might happen?'

*

'Doesn't this look like you?' Carl laughed, thrusting the poster for the "Battle of the Bands" night in Richard's face.

Richard snatched it from him, inspecting the drawing closely.

'Got a look of Richard Ashcroft,' Richard replied. He scratched his head, unsure whether he'd remembered the name or whether it had triggered something else.

'More of a look of Rich Hall.' Carl sniffed. 'Perhaps you're the prize? We should go to it. Someone's trying to get your attention.'

'Do you think?' Richard gasped, allowing himself a moment to dream that the woman from the café was trying to get his attention.

'Either you've pulled, or you're wanted for a robbery. See you later.'

Carl went back to his office, leaving Richard with the poster. It *did* look like him, but younger, as he had looked on the school photo in his parents' lounge. Had people told him *he* looked like Richard Ashcroft? The Doctors told his parents that his memory would come back in time; was it coming back now – decades later? It hadn't seemed fair to keep dragging his parents back through it. Perhaps now that he was older, it was time to ask the questions about the accident, fill in the blanks of those empty years, before it was too late.

He folded the poster up and tucked it away in his pocket. If the weather stopped him travelling to his parents, he might go along to the Band night, if he could stand the noise.

Christmas Eve

By Christmas Eve, Edinburgh was knee deep in snow and all trains out of the station were cancelled. Regardless of the mayhem the weather caused, everything felt filled with magic and the aglow with possibilities. The castle shone from its fortress, guarding the old town, as fireworks soared from behind it, casting rainbow arrows into the clear night sky. Katie was as nervous as a hare, hopping in front of the window, hoping beyond hope that Dickie would turn up to her event – giving her happiness or closure, at last.

The café was full, the air infused with the spiced-apple hot toddies she'd made to accompany the free mince pies and Christmas cake. Baking was the best distraction, and the counter was full of cakes and snacks, styled to look like row upon row of presents.

At nine o'clock, she officially kicked off the band night, introducing the first act to make it through to the final. They played a slow, soulful version of her favourite Oasis song "Live Forever", and she resisted the temptation to change the lyrics to "love forever" for fear of tempting fate. When the band finished, the crowd's applause was deafening, preventing Katie from hearing the swish of the door.

Every time an unfamiliar shadow hovered at the door frame, she hoped it would be him, but by eleven o'clock, the bands had finished, and Katie's expectations had worn her out.

Bolstered by the popularity/success of the events, the Krazy Kabin had asked her to join forces and host regular events, so for now the café's future was secure. That was something to celebrate. Being surrounded by musicians and buoyed by their enthusiasm had given Katie the confidence to play here amongst this crowd of new regulars who had come – in a very short space of time – to feel like a community. She was the last act, and she *had* to play if she was going to fulfil her dream of being a musician. Katie finally felt as though she was living the life she'd always wanted to live, almost.

'Please give it up for our final act tonight,' the booming voice of Dave from the Krazy Kabin alerted Katie to grab her guitar and get to the stage. 'Our fabulous and talented host, KATIE EVANS.'

The spotlight on the stage made her eyes water. She swallowed the lump in her throat, sat on the stool and strummed the first chord of "Silent Night". Katie's voice was velvet soft, mesmerizing the crowd below into complete silence, broken only by the standing ovation she received at the end of the song. Clive and Jen whooped loudly, jumping up and down in their prime spot at the front of the crowd. Her heart swelled with pride, and she took a small bow.

'Thanks everyone. Your support has saved my business and changed my life. So, eat, drink and be merry – it's all on the house until we run out of cakes.'

'Best cakes in Edinburgh!' someone yelled from the back, holding up a half-eaten cake as proof.

'Thanks, Eddie,' Katie chuckled, strumming the chords to the next song. 'Okay, here's a song I haven't sung in twenty-five years.'

She closed her eyes, inhaled deeply. She was going in. This was the song she'd written about Dickie, the one she'd performed on the last night she'd seen him. Time to lay the ghost to rest.

'How can you think that I don't love you?
My thoughts rush to you all the time.
You are my soul, my life, my reason,
You are the rhythm and the rhyme.
I wear your shoes, I house your mind,
I hold your blues within mine –'

The crowd fell silent as a voice from the door interrupted the song, singing the next verse.

'I live for your heart,
I'd die for your touch,
Your love is my home, is this real love?
Is this enough?'

Katie squinted past the stage lighting, and gasped as a man stepped under it, his face unmistakably familiar, even after all these years.

'Dickie?' she gasped, the tremble in her voice amplified by the microphone. 'Is it really you?'

Richard weaved his way to the front of the crowd, knocking over Christmas decorations and a Christmas gnome in his haste. He stopped in front of her, sweat smeared his fringe onto his forehead, he pushed it out of the way, blowing air up from the side of his mouth. His brown hair was shorter now and flecked with grey at the temples and scalp, his rich chocolate eyes shone with the kindness and sincerity of his youth. The poster had practically been a photo fit.

Katie's cheeks flushed, and not because of the heat of the stage light shining directly on them.

'So, it is you? I'm not imagining things.'

Katie shook her head. Of all the romantic things to say to the love of your life you've not seen for decades. It was up there with 'you look nice' and 'you've aged well.'

'Yes, I … er … think so.' He looked at his feet. 'My name's Richard Hall.'

Katie held out a shaking hand. 'Katie Evans.'

Richard looked down at the hand, wiped his own on the back of his trousers then grabbed at it. When their hands joined it was as if some great buried treasure had finally been revealed, the room went hazy and golden. His heart beat loudly in his ears, Katie's did the same.

'We were together at university, weren't we?' Richard stammered; the jigsaw pieces of his past were finally slotting together.

'Yes, we were …' She bit her lip, a vain attempt to curb the tears that were pushing up behind her eyes. 'But you left.'

She couldn't hide the bitterness in the words.

'I had an accident; I was in a coma.' Richard stammered; it was impossible to put everything that had happened into one sentence. 'I lost my memory. But hearing you sing … I feel young again.'

Someone turned the lights on. Katie could see him clearly now, could trace the quiet beauty and vulnerability of decades earlier in his face.

'Something brought me here. I can't explain it. I didn't know what it was, but now I do,' he hesitated, stepping from foot to foot. 'It was you.'

Katie let go of his hands and ran backwards, adrenaline and desire coursing through her in equal measure. There was only one thing she could think of doing; she lunged forward, diving headfirst into his open arms, hoping he would catch her.

Her body collided with his and she melted into his arms as they tumbled onto the floor in a tangle of arms and legs that looked like a pulled Christmas cracker. The castle bells struck twelve, and the crowd erupted into cheers and exclamations of "Merry Christmas!" but Katie couldn't hear them.

All she could hear was the synchronicity of their heartbeats, steady as the opening beats of her favourite song. Her lip trembled; she knew nothing about him – nothing about who he was now, at least – but everything about who he had been, once upon a time. She had known him by heart so long ago, now they could know each other again.

Richard's gaze was sweet and intense, even with an audience cheering them on, he didn't look away from her. So much time had passed between them, but in matters of the heart it appeared they hadn't missed a beat.

'If I hadn't come here …' He stammered. 'If I hadn't found you again, I'd have loved you forever, even if I couldn't remember you.'

'Let's not think about that.' Katie pulled him closer to her.

'I'm not very … I mean I don't have that much experience in …' Richard mumbled, his words fading out as Katie tilted her head towards him, closing her eyes and parting her magenta-coloured lips in expectation. He hesitated, bit his lip, excitement and nerves joining forces within him to turn his body to liquid and his mouth to fire.

'That's your cue to kiss me.' She said, opening an eye for a moment before resuming her position.

The crowd started chanting "kiss her, kiss her", their words thudded in his ears as he closed his eyes and lowered his head towards hers. As their lips met, the years slid away, their bodies relaxed into the kiss and found a home there.

'Give the girl some air,' Eddie shouted from the back of the room. Richard and Katie pulled apart though their eyes locked with the promise of a lifetime of catch-up kisses.

The crowd rose to their feet, their second standing ovation much louder than the first.

'I'd never have got that for my singing.' Katie chuckled.

'That's the first standing ovation I've ever got for kissing,' Richard replied, slipping his arm around her waist, glowing with contentment as their lips met once more.

The Last Christmas

S. L. Robinson

Chapter One

Christmas Eve – 1958

Knock, knock, knock!

'Oh, who's that at this time of night?' Mum huffs, buttoning her coat. The whole family – all five of us – are in various states of readiness at the foot of the stairs, and running late for Midnight Mass. My sisters, Abigail and Nancy, appeal to Mum's last shred of patience as they struggle with the laces on their shoes, and I take my time looking busy fixing my scarf and hat to avoid being called on to help.

'I'll get it, love, don't worry,' says Dad, bustling past us.

As soon as the door is a crack-width open, a rousing chorus of "Joy to the World" bursts into our tiny hallway, and Dad's face lights up.

'Henry, come here, son,' he beckons, his eyes glued to the carollers. 'Come and see.'

'Get rid of them if you can,' Mum hisses as I pass, 'otherwise, your father'll have us here all night, and we're already guaranteed bad seats at this rate.'

I join Dad in the arch of our doorway, where a blast of icy air attacks the small areas of exposed skin my clothes do not cover. A cheery sight greets me: a rag-tag group padded out with scarves, hats and gloves, rosy-cheeked from the cold but smiling broadly, singing out to us from the dark. Flurries of snow romanticise our quiet, boring road, blanketing each sleepy house like a frosted cake.

A tall lad with a mop of unruly ginger curls escaping from under his hat, instantly catches my eye as the sole dissenter from the smiling brigade. Sandwiched between the burly shoulders of two other red-headed men – who I assume are older brothers or cousins, perhaps – his porcelain face is illuminated by the glow of their hanging lanterns and would be quite cherubic, but for the mutinous glare etched upon it. Occasionally, his eyes shift from his hymn book to throw a withering look at his counterparts, and it amuses me to no end.

When the carol finishes, Dad claps loudly and I stick my fingers in my mouth to whistle loudly in the way Mum disapproves of.

'What do you think, one more, eh?' Dad asks me with a wink.

He's a hopeless sentimentalist, which Mum says is because of the War, and all those who were lost to it. Displays of togetherness such as this make him nostalgic for the past, and grateful for the future.

'It's me you should be asking,' mutters Mum behind us, but when she joins us at the threshold her face is soft, and her eyes misty at his joy; she is happy to risk our late arrival at Mass – and the poor seats that come with it.

My eyes remain firmly planted on the scowling cherub as he is nudged to the forefront of the group. He deigns to raise his head, and at this precise moment, our eyes meet. I have no words that could justly describe this feeling. I am utterly bewildered by the jolt of electricity that passes from his eyes to mine. I'm sure he feels it too, because when he opens his mouth to sing, all that escapes is a strangled yelp of sorts.

I cannot suppress my mirth and a laugh escapes me, though I immediately feel terrible for it. Nevertheless, it seems to spur him on and with a contemptuous flick of his nose away from me, he restarts, and I am mesmerised.

I know from that first note, that I will never again hear a rendition of "O Holy Night" that could compete with this siren song. His heavenly tones, supported by the low vibrational humming of the backing ensemble, bewitch me. I can feel the goosebumps on my arms raise with each undulation of his voice, and the hairs on the back of my neck stand to attention in respect when he hits a falsetto note so high I'd swear it rang out from the skies above. I'm glad my family are just as entranced by him, as it allows me to hide my fascination behind the intensity of their awe.

The song ends quickly, in that cruel way in which time speeds up when you want it to slow down. I could stay in this moment forever, but we bid the merry band farewell and hurry down the street to Mass. Before we round the corner, I turn around for one last glimpse of him, and butterflies fill my stomach as our eyes meet once more – he's looking back at me, too.

As though annoyed that I've caught him in this act of voyeurism, he flicks his head away from me for the second time tonight. The brevity of our encounter does nothing to dampen my spirits; I have a feeling – some strange intuition – that this will not be the last I see of him.

Chapter Two

23rd December 2021

'Grandad, are you listening?' Sophie, my granddaughter, places a hand on my arm to focus my attention back to the depressing room we are sat in. Her eyes are full of concern for me and my drifting attention span.

'I'm sorry, Henry, we can't grant your request to take William home,' Dr Benn tells me. Her voice is supposed to sound empathetic, but all I hear is condescension. 'His condition is too fragile for him to be moved.'

There is no joy here in this brown and beige box of doom. The micro-Christmas tree on the desk bears no decorations, and the silver tinsel hung on the wall is limp and dull. It offends me, an ardent Christmas lover, to the highest degree.

'His stay here was supposed to be temporary. If it wasn't for that bloody pandemic, he would have been having care at home as we always intended. He shouldn't have to die here – we've suffered enough not being able to hold his hand or visit him without a glass panel between us.' I argue. 'Enough is enough!'

'Don't get upset, Dad,' says my son, Toby, on the other side of me. 'We all want Papa Will back, but the home has fantastic services, and we can be here round the clock with him.'

Toby and Sophie have never looked more alike than now, with their matching furrowed brows and pitying eyes. Dr Benn is doing her best approximation of compassion, but all of them are only serving to get on my nerves.

'This was his last wish before he was forced here – to die in the comfort of his own home with his loved ones. Why …' I can't talk. My chest tightens and I'm dizzy from the frustration of their nonsense.

'It's okay, Mr Brown. Take a few moments,' says Dr Benn, and I try to calm the pounding of blood in my ears. 'I understand this is a difficult time for you, but your home isn't equipped to handle palliative care, and, with the utmost respect, neither are you. This sort of thing takes a huge emotional toll on loved ones.'

'I was managing his care fine before he came into this funeral home!' I shout.

'They're just trying to help,' Sophie pleads with me, 'You're nearly 80, and Papa Will needs oxygen and a wheelchair to be moved anywhere. We all wish he could go home, but he's safer here.'

'Bollocks to you all!' I say, leaping out of my chair.

I ignore their calls after me and storm out, hiding in the toilet a few doors down. The cubicle is cold and sterile, just like the rest of this hell hole.

I will not leave my William here, if it's the last thing I do, I'll get him out.

*

When I feel calmer, I head to William's room instead of Dr Benn's office. Toby and Sophie are in the corridor with William's nurse and all three are in animated talks. There's something in the air; Sophie and Toby are fidgeting nervously, but they are smiling, so whatever it is, it can't be bad.

'Dad, thank God!' shouts Toby, rushing over to me. 'Where've you been?'

'Just composing myself,' I say, batting away the hand he's stretching out to help me walk. 'What's going on?'

'Something's happened,' Sophie answers, her words laden with emphasis.

I look to the nurse to explain. She's smiling too, but hers betrays some caution.

'Out with it, love,' I urge. 'I can take it.'

'William is experiencing what is known as terminal lucidity, or as we call it, "the Surge".' She pauses, and I can see she's weighing her next words carefully. 'William's more alert and livelier than he's been since his initial decline last year, and he can remember past events and memories–'

'He's back, Grandad,' Sophie interrupts.

'Not exactly,' the nurse says to her with reproach. She addresses me again, but much kindlier. 'He is the William you remember, but his diagnosis hasn't changed. He isn't getting better.'

'What does that mean?' I ask.

'Some patients experience a Surge right before they pass. It's a strange phenomenon and there's no definitive explanation for why or how it happens, but it does. It may last a few hours or a few days, but we can be certain that William will pass soon after it fades.'

Time stands still at these words. I'm acutely aware of every minute detail happening around me: the nurse reaching to steady me as I fall; Sophie's hands flying to her mouth in shock; Toby shouting my name, and the creeping black closing in around my vision.

It's funny, I think. We've known he's going to die for some time now, it shouldn't be a shock. It shouldn't strike me like lightning and stop my heart, but it does.

'Breathe for me, Henry.' The nurse's voice is an echo in my head. 'In, out, in, out.'

I focus on this mantra. In. Out. In. Out. It helps – the black slowly recedes, and time comes rushing back.

'He's not gone yet?' I wheeze.

'He's doing well,' the nurse confirms. 'For now.'

Two words again, laden with emphasis but their meaning much clearer this time. I stand to head for William's room and the others make to follow me.

'Can you give us some time alone?' I ask, trying to steady the tremble in my voice.

'Maybe you should take it easy for a minute, Dad,' Toby suggests.

'I'm fine, honestly!' They don't understand – it's not their fault, how could they? I've wasted so much time with William already, enough for several lives over, and I won't waste another second. 'Please, I just want to be with him while this miracle lasts.'

'Of course,' says the nurse, and she lures Toby and Sophie away with the promise of tea and biscuits.

When they are out of sight, I brace myself to enter William's room, scared that he might have already gone in the time my little episode took. I can see him through the windowpane. His appearance is much the same as it has been for the past few months; thin and frail, but … his eyes are no longer burdened with the confusion of not knowing who or where he is. He is back. I push the door and the creaking draws his attention.

'Henry, oh, Henry, my dear! Where have you been?' He trills at me, propped up by his pillows. His voice is shaky, but his Irish-come-New-Yorker lilt is much stronger than it has been for the past few months.

I'm by his bed now, and our hands find each other, like they always have. His grip is as firm as mine and I draw strength from it.

'How are you feeling?'

'Bloody marvellous! Except for this terminal elderly-ness.' He laughs and I join in. I haven't laughed for a long time, and it feels strange, unnatural even. 'They tell me I've gotten worse since the experimental stuff?'

The clinical trial he's referring to was over a year ago, and it sobers me as I try to navigate the delicacy of the situation. How do I tell him the end is so near?

'That's right,' I confirm, struggling to meet his gaze now.

Despite his declining health, William's hazel eyes have retained their vibrant colours: stripes of forest green amid flecks of warm amber, swimming in dark and cinnamon browns. I could take a perfect autumn walk in those eyes, and they are so bright right now that I can hardly believe they are destined to dim so soon.

'What's the sentence, then?' he asks, stoically.

'They say you could have a few days, at best.'

I can't bring myself to tell him the worst-case scenario, because saying it out loud would make it real to me, and I am nowhere near ready to process that yet.

'Oh.' He burrows down into his pillows. I can see the cogs turning in his mind and I know he's trying to think of a positive spin for me, the worrier in our relationship. 'We'll have to make this time count then, won't we?'

'What shall we do? I could order us in some games or films? A picnic in bed? Anything you want.'

'Henry Morgan-Brown! Have you lost your marbles?' William scolds. 'You should know I would never be content to die in this place. Me! A world-wide star and connoisseur of all things fine. I need to die in style, not surrounded by these asylum-white walls – which do nothing for my fair complexion, I'll add.'

I smile at his grandstanding.

'We're fighting a losing battle, dear. I told them you needed to be at home, but it fell on deaf ears.'

'Ah, home,' he sighs, wistfully. 'Yes, I would like that. But you know, I wish I could see some of our old haunts again. I hate to be morbid, but if I'm going to die, I'd rather go out on the streets I once ruled than in this godforsaken room.'

'What would you suggest?'

'Let's go on the run before I give up the ghost.' His eyes twinkle mischievously. 'It can be your Christmas present to me.'

'Oh, can it?' I chuckle. 'What if I've got you something better?'

William turns serious, and his grip tightens.

'Nothing could be better than one last adventure with you. And at Christmas too, could the stars have aligned any better for us?'

'I can't deny that,' I agree, clearing my throat to stop my tears welling up.

William claps with delight.

'Help me get dressed then, dear.'

'You want to go right now?' This shouldn't surprise me; William waits for no-one.

'No time like the present!'

He throws back the covers and shuffles his bare feet to the cold floor. We move as fast as we can, and before long, I have him in his wheelchair, wrapped snugly in his tartan blanket and with the portable oxygen bag, and its spare battery, hung on the back. No going back now.

'Best check the coast is clear.' William nods to the door.

I creep into the corridor to cast about – it's quiet, another boon for us soon-to-be fugitives. I grab the handles of the wheelchair and throw my weight behind it. I notice every squeak we make on the floor and every person we pass who doesn't give us a second look. Incredibly, we make it to the car park without interruption, but just as I've strapped William into the back seat, I hear a frantic voice calling me.

'Grandad! Grandad, stop!'

It's Sophie, rushing over to us with a phone pressed to her ear. I hear her calm whoever is on the other end before she reaches us.

'What do you think you're doing?'

'I'm taking my husband out for the day,' I pant, folding the wheelchair.

'Here, let me,' Sophie says, taking over. 'Dad's worried sick about you both.'

'He needn't be,' says William cheerily. 'We're quite all right.'

'You know you're not supposed to leave,' Sophie chides, closing the boot. 'It's not safe.'

'We're not going to wait around feeling morose,' William replies. 'We're going on an adventure. You could come with us, you know.'

'If you're with us, you could keep us safe.' I add slyly.

I know I'm putting her in a tight spot – leave us to go on our way and accept the risks or, come with us and draw the ire of those who would keep us here.

'Come on,' coaxes William. 'Sure, it'll be some good craic, and you'll not get this chance again with me. I'll be dead soon, don't you know.'

'Don't say that, Papa Will!' Sophie cries.

'Why not?' William cackles, 'It's the truth, isn't it?'

'What will it be, Soph?' I ask, walking round to the driver's side while she hops about from foot to foot.

'Okay, okay,' she concedes after some hesitation. 'But I'm driving, and I'm texting Dad wherever we go.'

'Fine by me,' I reply, offering the keys. 'Chauffeur away!'

Sophie rolls her eyes, but there's a smile turning up the corners of her mouth.

'Where to first?' she asks, once we are all strapped in.

'Soho?' William suggests.

'Hmm, no. How about the boats at Battersea Park?' I reply, and then–

'The Trocadero!' we shout in unison.

'No.' My mind is working double-time with a plan. 'If we're going to do this, we should start at the beginning.'

'Ah, yes!' says William, with a twinkle in his eyes. 'That magnificent place where it all began.'

I give Sophie the directions and settle in happily for the drive.

Chapter Three

Christmas Day – 1958

It's late at night when the tapping at my window starts. It takes me a few minutes to dislodge the haze of sleep and realise that someone is throwing stones at the panes. I check the small wooden clock on my bedstand. Eleven o'clock. There's only one person who would bother me this late at night, let alone on Christmas Day. I cross the room as quietly as I can, and inch the window up. When I stick my head out, a light mist of rain sticks to my cheeks.

'Finally! I've been stood here for ten minutes trying to wake you up.'

Illuminated by the headlights of her father's car is my best friend, Sophie. She's emulating Maureen O'Hara with a long fur coat and scarf wrapped around her hair to keep her pintucked curls in place. A shock of red on her lips compliments the Christmas season perfectly.

'Sophie! Are you barmy? What are you doing here at this time of night?' I laugh, watching her pose in the cold.

'I've come to kidnap you,' she calls, over the chugging of the motor.

'Is that so?' I tease, using the ledge outside my window to lean further out.

'Yes, and you've no choice in the matter. There's five of us already, and with you we're an even six, so hurry up.'

'All right. Let me get dressed,' I say, already halfway out the window to grab what I need.

I do not need to know where we're going – fun follows Sophie wherever she goes, and I am always glad to be included by her, despite my proclivity for caution. I successfully manoeuvre the creaks in our stairs and inch the front door open. The night is coldly refreshing, and I take a deep breath to savour the mischief in the air.

'Hurry up, Henry!' Sophie shouts, and I hop into the back of the car. It's a squeeze; Sophie's sister, Elizabeth, is sat up front on the knee of her boyfriend, George, and immediately to my left is their older brother, John. 'Henry, you know everyone but our cousin, William. William, do stop being a sourpuss and say hello.'

The boy next to John turns away from the window and both of us startle.

My ginger cherub has returned to me.

I cough to break the awkwardness. 'Nice to meet you,' I manage, with a nod. He returns the nod, but his next words are directed at Sophie and not me.

'I'm not being sour,' he states tersely.

'So, you're not at all jealous I won the coin toss for the coat, hmm?' Sophie laughs, ruffling the fur collar against her cheeks. Her tinkling laughter fills what little space is left in the car, infecting us all bar William.

'I wasn't jealous, I just knew it would have looked better on me with my sunglasses,' William retorts, and I marvel at the idea of a boy in a full-length fur coat and sunglasses in the dead of a winter's night. 'Anyway, I've moved on. I've not left the sticks to sit around in a car all night. Stop going on with yourself now, we've places to be.' He waves his hand at her, dismissing the topic from the air, and Sophie, still laughing, obliges his command.

I'm so intrigued by William that I find it hard to join in the conversation the others are having. I'm desperate to find out more about him – I can discern from his accent that he is from Ireland, but whereabouts is a mystery. He, meanwhile, is deliberate in his ignorance of me and, feeling the need to say something, I ask:

'Where are we going?'

'Westminster Abbey,' Sophie replies, 'On an expedition for hidden treasure – and whoever finds the best prize wins a bottle of vintage wine pilfered from Father's private collection.'

Of course, it's the Abbey, the one place Sophie knows I would never turn down. We make the journey from Chelsea in good time, though it's so dark and quiet I'm amazed an alarm hasn't been raised by our presence on the streets. The silence is even more pronounced when Sophie turns off the car and the chug-chug-chug of the engine dies down. We emerge into the cold, rubbing our arms and stamping our feet in protest at the night's chill. The Abbey looms over us, a magnificent example of architectural grandeur, and every exhale of our breath sends clouds of little ghosts flying up to it only to be swallowed by the darkness.

We dither for a few minutes, until I ask the obvious question.

'How are we going to get in?'

'Father knows the Surveyor of the Fabric,' says Sophie.

'They've been friends since their Oxford days,' John elaborates. 'We got the idea when old Bowers came for dinner at the restaurant a few weeks ago – Sophie dazzled him with her knowledge of gothic architecture, and he was putty in her hands when she requested a secret tour of the Abbey for her and some "likeminded friends".'

This comes as no surprise to me; Sophie could charm the most hostile snake out of its basket if she wished to see it dance.

'Once we're inside, we'll split into teams of two.' Sophie directs. 'I'll go with John and keep Bowers distracted, Elizabeth you with George, and Henry can partner with William.'

I force my face to remain impassive though I'm secretly thrilled by this pairing.

'We'll meet back here in exactly two hours, and whoever has the best treasure wins the wine,' Sophie continues gleefully, waving the prized dusty bottle for all to see.

As we approach the heavy brown of the Great West Door, the huge Christmas tree outside pulls my focus until I spot a figure waiting for us in the enclosure of the regal arch. He's much younger than I expected and bears no air of the upper-class refinement that I've come to expect when meeting an acquaintance of Sophie's family. As it turns out, he is not "Old Bowers", but the nightly watchman sent to greet us in his absence.

'Master Bowers sends 'is regrets that he's been indisposed of this evening,' says the watchman. 'I'm to tell you that you'll have no bother tonight, but you must only go on the lit path and you're to return to me within an hour so I can see you out. I'm to tell you that he expects your best behaviour.'

We all clamour to reassure him that we have no intent for mischief, but it's hard not to lose ourselves to excitement once we're alone in the Nave.

I love this building, everything about it, from its history of notable figures across art, science, and religion, to the construction of the building itself. The Nave is vast and crypt-like in the dead of night, and our footsteps echo around, bouncing from pillar to pillar and up to the vaulted ceiling. A path of large, lighted pillar candles has been set for us to follow and we walk it slowly until the watchman returns to his business. We congregate around the nativity scene while Sophie instructs us in our mission.

'All right, time to split up. Everyone meet back here in forty minutes so we can be sure to walk back out together. Here, take these.' Sophie hands out a heavy flashlight to each team. 'On your marks, get set … GO!'

'Come on, there's only one place we're going,' William tells me, briefly pulling my upper arm as he veers toward the North Transept.

'Do you even know your way around?' I ask.

'No, but I've read about Poet's Corner so often I feel I could make my way there,' he replies smartly.

'You'll want to go this way, then,' I say, redirecting him to the Southern Transept. We walk quickly, which is a great shame in my opinion, as we could meander through each part of the Abbey for hours and still not cover all its wonder. We slow down only when we reach Poet's Corner; our torch creeps into each dark crevice, casting gargantuan, gnarly shadows on the walls as the light passes over the various busts and carvings.

My cursed shyness threatens to stymie any productive conversation we might have, and desperate to break the silence I ask, 'If you and Sophie are cousins, how come I've never heard of you before? I've known Sophie my whole life.'

'There was an estrangement in the family,' William states, eyes firmly glued to our surroundings. 'Sophie and I only met the other day for the first time.'

He doesn't expand on this estrangement, nor what ended it. The sentence is a dead-end and I decide not to push him on it. Eager to keep the conversation flowing however, I offer up some of my own family history instead.

'I know what that's like, we had "an estrangement" in our family too.'

'Yeah?'

'Uh-huh. My dad comes from money. *Old* money. He went to boarding school with Sophie's dad and they were best friends growing up,' I explain. 'They both got into Oxford, and my dad met my mum there and fell in love with her. When he brought her home, his parents told him to make a choice — her or his inheritance. He chose my mum and they cut him off.'

'What was wrong with your mum, like?' William asks, confused.

'She's black.' My blunt statement makes William tear his eyes away from the inscription on the floor to look at me. 'And she was the help at the time, so it caused a huge scandal.'

'Jaysus,' says William, with a low whistle. 'That's rough.'

'They were both really young at the time; Mum had moved from the countryside and didn't know anyone. Dad had to drop out of university and most of his friends and family shunned him. Sophie's dad stuck by him though; he's a decent man.'

'Yeah,' William agrees. 'He paid for my family to come up for Christmas and he's paid for their travel back to Ireland.'

'You're staying with Sophie's family?' I ask hopefully, spotting a segue into bringing up the previous night. 'How come they weren't out carolling with you last night?'

'It's our family tradition. Every year, we go out round our village and, as they go back in a few days, we thought we'd do it one last time while we have the chance.'

William's voice cracks. I can't imagine how he must be feeling.

'Carry on with your tale,' he says stiffly.

He turns his back on me and shines the torchlight onto the bust of Jenny Lind. Before answering, I note the beautiful juxtaposition of William, the Irish songbird, admiring her, the Swedish Nightingale.

'Once Dad turned twenty-one,' I continue. 'He inherited a trust fund set up by his grandad. His parents contested it, and my parents were poor for a long time, but they had each other. Dad always says: "a man's riches lie in his heart, and mine is full of treasure".'

'Sounds awfully romantic.'

'I suppose … Mum always felt guilty for being the cause of his family grief and even more so after the war. Dad went to fight, and when he came back, his parents were dead. They were bitter to the end, but Dad would have been there for them if he could.'

'I know a bit about that sort of regret,' William says. 'My dad wouldn't say goodbye to me before I left. His last words were to tell me not to bother coming back home so long as he's alive. He thought I should stay and live my life the way *he* wanted. I refused to do that, so I guess I'm stuck here as long as they'll have me.'

William laughs weakly and I want to comfort him, but it's not the done thing.

Instead, I ask, 'What made you want to live in London?'

William grins and holds the torch under his chin, making a ghoulish mask of his face.

'To quote a poet, as would be most apt in these surroundings, "When house and land are gone and spent then learning is most excellent."' He sings these words with a flourish and an accompanying jig, then explains, 'I've no house anymore and no land to my name, but London may as well be the centre of the world compared to Enniskillen. In beauty, home will always win – no contest! But I plan on being famous one day and that's much easier to do here than there. I'm like a goldfish – I've outgrown my little bowl and need the wide waters of the ocean to flourish.'

'If last night was anything to go by, I'm sure you'll make it as a singer. You know your obscure poets too – Samuel Foote, I believe?' I say, impressed.

'Aye,' William confirms, shining the torch onto Chaucer's tomb. 'You know he was an outcast by the time of his death? Smeared for apparently being a raging homosexual!'

The way he delivers this salacious bit of gossip sets a heat rising through me which flushes my neck. The way he says the word "homosexual" isn't the same as the way everyone else says it. There's no disgust, or hushed tone – no implication of sin. I'm embarrassed, but I have no idea why. In any case, I'm glad his focus is on the decaying inscription in front of him and not on me.

'You know he's buried here?'

'I think I read that somewhere.' William spins to face me, blinding me with the light.

'Allegedly, he's buried in an unmarked grave in the West Cloister,' I say, one hand waving in the direction of the Cloister Gardens and the other shielding my eyes.

'Unmarked grave, eh? I've an idea as to how we win this thing,' says William, suddenly bringing us back to the purpose of our night. 'Here, hold this.'

He hands me the torch while he digs around in his pockets. The light is angled in a way that illuminates his black trousers and I notice they are tight – not in a way that suggests he's too big for them, but one that suggests he's had them tailored to fit like this. At least in style I can tell that he and Sophie are related.

'Aha!' He pulls out an object and places it flat on his palm, holding out his hand for me to see.

I shine the light and peer in closely. At the nexus of his criss-crossing heartlines lies a large, dirty coin, so blackened with age and corrosion it's near impossible to make out any markings that could tie it to a specific era or region.

I gently lift it, and as my fingertips graze William's soft skin, I realise how closely we are standing, and a different kind of heat rises through me. It's new and foreign, uncomfortable but exciting.

'What is it?' I ask, stepping back to hold it up under the light and put some distance between us.

'It's an heirloom, passed down through all the women in our family. Murphy lore states that when Queen Méabh of Connacht's lady-in-waiting was lost to a river, she herself rode out to slay the giant who had chased Lady Erne and her maidens to their watery deaths. After the deed was done, she gifted a silver coin from his treasure to each of the party who had rode with her and threw the rest of the horde into the waters for atonement of the giant's sins. The river was named Lough Erne, after the lady, and when light hits the water and makes it shimmer, it's said that you can see the women dancing under the surface in a palace built from their ghostly riches.'

William tells this myth so dramatically a chill goes through me.

'How come you have the coin if it's passed through the women?'

'I guess me Mam thought I was as close to a daughter as she'd ever get.' William laughs, and the spell is broken.

'Come on, we'd better get back to the others.'

'What'll we say if they come back and find out we've lied?'

'Well …' I shrug ruefully. 'We'll have drunk the wine by then.'

A wide smile breaks over William's face. It's so radiant, the corners of his mouth stretch high, showing his teeth – which I notice are crooked, but in a handsome way – and a deep dimple appears in his left cheek. As quickly as it comes, it's gone, replaced by a cool veneer of indifference. We head back to the group, but not before I make a silent promise to myself to make him smile like that again.

To be continued …

For those who want to finish the adventures of Henry and William, "The Last Christmas" is due for release in autumn 2022.

Biographies

Lawyer by day, writer by night, **Lucy Alexander** is a London-based author of romantic fiction. Her debut novel "Gingerbread" was shortlisted for the *Penguin Michael Joseph Christmas Love Story* competition and is due to be released in 2022.

When she's not in the office or writing, Lucy enjoys curling up with an Agatha Christie novel and a nice cup of tea, and escapes the city whenever she can to enjoy the south coast countryside where she grew up.

Lucy plans to take a year out from London life to focus on her writing - follow her progress on Instagram @lucyalexander_1

*

Michelle Harris spent twelve years teaching Secondary School English and Drama, before making the sensible decision to give it all up to write about unicorn poo on the internet, working as a social media manager for an online toy shop. She is now a freelance social media manager with a sideline in writing bespoke poetry, (she is a poet and she knows it). She lives in Greater London with her husband, two children, and a dog that thinks he's a human.

When her children were younger, Michelle briefly dipped a toe into the diverse waters of the mum-bloggerspere and wrote an opinion column for Mother Pukka, called "Angry Bird" (although she's actually pretty zen). Her writing was also included in "The Mother Book" from Selfish Mother, a collection of motherhood musings that was sold to raise funds for charity Mothers2Mothers. She is thrilled that her short story "The Ghost of Christmas Past" is included in 2021 Christmas Collective Anthology.

Michelle loves to write with humour and warmth about relatable situations, and describes herself as a "see-the-funny-side-of-lifer". When she grows up, she's going to be Judi Dench.

Twitter https://twitter.com/MichelleBHarris
Instagram https://www.instagram.com/michelle_b_harris/

*

Marianne Calver is a primary school teacher from Greater London. She was thrilled to be shortlisted for the *Penguin Michael Joseph Christmas Love Story* competition 2021. "Christmas for Two" is her short story debut.

Marianne lives in happy chaos with her husband, three children, their occasionally obedient dog and some fish. When not teaching or writing, Marianne is most likely to be found walking, researching her family history or making wonky costumes for her children that she could probably buy cheaper online. You can find Marianne on Instagram @mariannercalver

*

Joe Burkett lives in the idyllic west coast of Ireland with his husband. He is a doting uncle to his six nephews and nieces and enjoys spending time with his family. Any excuse for a party is Joe's motto. When he's not party planning, Joe loves nothing more than joining his friends for a gin, taking selfies of himself while out walking and cooking the perfect Sunday roast.

"August in December" is Joe's debut short story as part of the Christmas Collective Anthology. He was shortlisted for the *Penguin Michael Joseph Christmas Love Story* competition in 2021. Joe is the Creative Director of the "Joe Burkett Theatre Company". His childhood hobby formed the basis of his career and he adores training the next generation in all things theatre. With ambitions to continue his writing career and potentially collaborating with a fellow writer on a book series, Joe's dream is to turn his love of telling stories into the next stage of his career.

If you fancy checking out Joe's selfies or to hear the latest about his short stories and novels, you can follow him on IG @JoeWritesStories

*

Cici Maxwell is the chosen pen name for Amy Gaffney, and is taken from her two cats, Cici, a rather spoilt dame, and Max, who was a fluffy white bundle of madness until he went missing. He's hugely missed, especially his antics from the middle of the Christmas tree. Amy hails from Kildare and is a graduate of UCD's Creative Writing MA where she was Co-Editor in Chief of *The HCE Review* 2017-2018. A lover of all things Christmas, Amy was thrilled to discover she was shortlisted for the *Penguin Michael Joseph Christmas Love Story* competition in May 2021. She was also shortlisted for the *Dalkey Creates* Short Story Competition in 2020. Her poetry has been published in *Poetry Ireland Review* Issue 125, *Irish Times Hennessy New Irish Writing*, *Ropes* Unearthed 2019, Limerick Poetry Month, and in *Skylight 47*. In 2019 Amy's prose has been published online in *The HCE Review*, online at *Public House Magazine*, and *The Honest Ulsterman*. Amy's short story "Mother May I" was shortlisted for the *An Post Book of the Year* Award 2019 in the writing.ie Short Story of the Year category.

Follow her on Twitter: @gaffneyamy or Instagram @amy_gaffney24

*

Jake Godfrey is a writer hailing from Dorset. He has contributed articles to *The British Comedy Guide* and *Film Stories* magazine, with hopes of publishing his first novel in the near future.

*

Jenny Bromham is a writer, developmental editor and creative writing teacher currently living in Madrid with her husband and three daughters. Outside her work, she loves to write romance and children's fiction. She realises that on the surface this might be a strange mix, but these are both genres of hope and possibility with undercurrents of magic, wonder and fun – everything she likes to see in the stories she reads, as well as writes. Jenny was a winner of the *Montegrappa First Fiction* competition and shortlisted for the *Penguin Michael Joseph Christmas Love Story* competition. 'More than Mistletoe' is her first venture into the published world beyond her job. When she's not writing, Jenny loves reading, travel, wine and, of course, Christmas!

Follow her on Twitter for editorial reflections, writing updates and general bookish discourse @JennyBromham

*

As with the heroine in her soon-to-be-released debut novel "A Dream of Lazy Sundays", new chick-lit author, **Sarah Shard's** world shattered when her father passed away suddenly in 2015, triggering a sequence of events which turned her world upside down. Amid the chaos, she found solace in the magic of the written word, thus beginning the start of an unexpected new chapter. Away from her award-winning career in project management, Sarah now spends as much time as she can immersed in the fictitious villages she creates from the balcony of her home in Saddleworth, England.

Sarah is a lifelong fan of chick-lit and romantic comedies, and she hopes to bring moments of joy, frustration, laughter, surprise and love to her readers. She writes as she reads, creating the (almost) perfect book boyfriends she would love to fall in love with, but as in real life, love doesn't come easy. Her stories take you on the ups and downs in the search for that happy ending every reader hopes for. As well as her Christmas novel, Sarah is also working on a new series of books which she calls "chick-lit with a sprinkling of magic" set against the backdrop of the fictitious Cornish seaside village of Beacon Hope.

*

Martha May Little's appreciation of a good love story started early in life with 'Anne of Green Gables' and has shown no signs of abating since. She studied English Literature and Philosophy at University, and now lives in a small town outside Edinburgh with her husband and three children.

Martha believes there is a Hallmark-worthy love story in everyone and is currently developing her debut romance novel, "Living Gracefully". When she isn't writing or reading, she can be found walking her Labrador, Storm, cultivating her love of mid-morning naps or unwinding with a podcast or K-Drama.

Follow her on Twitter: @marthamaylittle

*

Bláithín O'Reilly Murphy is the author of "Distinctive Weddings: Tying the Knot without the Ropes" and "The Meaning of Purple Tulips". She retired from her award-winning wedding planning career in 2017 to start a family and is mum to two beautiful angel daughters in heaven and one personality-filled little dude!

She loves to write festive-filled romances that keep the readers on their toes featuring female characters who haven't yet realised their own strength. Her upcoming short story "Sealed with a Christmas Kiss" is the enticing prequel to her festive novel 'It Started with a Gift' which was shortlisted for the *Penguin Michael Joseph Christmas Novel* competition in 2021. She is obsessed with Hallmark Christmas Movies and Korean Dramas which she says gives her writing an emotional edge!

Bláithín is never far from a toasted scone or glass of Prosecco and she tries her best not to kill her plants in her spare time. She lives near the Irish coast with her darling husband, adorable son, and 3 cute fur-babies. Her great ambition for later life is to be the crazy cat lady living on the corner of your street that everyone secretly loves, and to own a bookstore, where everyone gathers for readings, and signings, and socialising; and hopefully buys a book or twenty. She can be found oversharing in her IG stories and trying to sound witty and relevant on Twitter as @WhatBlaDidNext

*

Donna Gowland is a writer and teacher who lives with her husband and two daughters by the seaside in Merseyside. When she isn't teaching, writing, or daydreaming she loves reading romances and walking her dog Darcy. Donna has written for *The Guardian, Seren Poetry Press* and *The Female Gaze* and is a proud member of the RNA New Writers' Scheme.

"Love Forever" is Donna's debut romance short story. The story was inspired by a newspaper article about a man who heard a song and it brought back the memory he lost in an earlier accident, bringing him back together with a former love.

Connect with Donna @DLGowlandWrites on Twitter

*

Debut author **S. L. Robinson** is a marketing graduate from the University of Liverpool. She lives in Liverpool with her son, and at the end of 2020, left her role as a contract law paralegal to pursue her dream of writing.

Sarah writes broadly across fiction genre, which enables her to procrastinate on many different works to the one she should be focusing on. She loves cooking, crocheting, DIY and contemplating existentialism. She also loves brightly coloured wigs.

For more news follow her on Twitter and Instagram: @slrtheauthoress.

Printed in Great Britain
by Amazon